"[Livia J. Washburn] has cooked up another fine mystery with plenty of suspects . . . a fun read . . . great characters with snappy dialogue, a prime location, a wonderful whodunit. Mix together and you have another fantastic cozy from Livia Washburn. Her books always leave me smiling and anxiously waiting for another trip to visit Phyllis and her friends."

—Escape with Dollycas into a Good Book

"This mystery is nicely crafted, with a believable ending. The camaraderie of the Fresh-Baked Mystery series' cast of retired schoolteachers who share a home is endearing. Phyllis is an intelligent and keen sleuth who can bake a mean funnel cake. Delicious recipes are included!"

—RT Book Reviews

"Washburn has a refreshing way with words and knows how to tell an exciting story."

—Midwest Book Review

"Delightful, [with a] realistic small-town vibe [and a] vibrant narrative . . . A Peach of a Murder runs the full range of emotions, so be prepared to laugh and cry with this one!"

—The Romance Readers Connection

"The whodunit is fun and the recipes [are] mouthwatering."

—The Best Reviews

Other Fresh-Baked Mysteries by Livia J. Washburn

A Peach of a Murder

Murder by the Slice

The Christmas Cookie Killer

Killer Crab Cakes

The Pumpkin Muffin Murder

The Gingerbread Bump-off

Wedding Cake Killer

The Fatal Funnel Cake

Trick or Deadly Treat

A Fresh-Baked Mystery

LIVIA J. WASHBURN

AN OBSIDIAN BOOK

OBSIDIAN
Published by the Penguin Group
Penguin Group (USA) LLC, 375 Hudson Street,
New York, New York 10014

USA | Canada | UK | Ireland | Australia | New Zealand | India | South Africa | China
penguin.com
A Penguin Random House Company

First published by Obsidian, an imprint of New American Library,
a division of Penguin Group (USA) LLC

First Printing, October 2014

LIBRARY OF CONGRESS CATALOGING-IN-PUBLICATION DATA:
Washburn, Livia J.
Trick or deadly treat: a fresh-baked mystery/Livia J. Washburn.
p. cm.—(Fresh-baked mystery)
ISBN 978-0-451-41669-8 (paperback)
1. Newsom, Phyllis (Fictitious character)—Fiction. 2. Baking—Fiction.
3. Murder—Investigation—Fiction. 4. Weatherford (Tex.)—Fiction.
5. Mystery fiction. I. Title.
PS3573.A787T75 2014
813'.54dc23   2014015766

Printed in the United States of America
1   3   5   7   9   10   8   6   4   2

Set in New Caledonia   •   Designed by Elke Sigal

Trick or Deadly Treat

*Dedicated to the memory of
my mother, Naomi Washburn.
She was a wonderful mom
and a great teacher.*

Chapter 1

*P*hyllis Newsom put her hands over her ears and said, "Oh, my goodness!"

"Yeah, they're kinda loud, aren't they?" Sam Fletcher said with a grin. "And enthusiastic, to boot."

They stood in a cement-floored runway between rows of metal cages filled with dogs of all shapes, sizes, breeds, and mixtures of breeds. The air inside the cinder-block building contained an assortment of smells, all of them pungent and none particularly pleasant, but Sam didn't seem to mind. In fact, he looked as happy as Phyllis had seen him in a while.

Maybe this wasn't such a bad idea after all, she thought.

When he had first told her that he wanted to get a dog, her immediate impulse had been to say no. A flat, nonnegotiable no. And since the big, old two-story house on a tree-shaded street in Weatherford, Texas, belonged to her and Sam only rented a room there, it was Phyllis's decision to make.

The problem was, Sam wasn't just a boarder, subject to his

landlady's rules and decisions. The four retired teachers who lived in the house—Phyllis, Sam, Carolyn Wilbarger, and Eve Turner—had become more like family over the years. They were best friends as well, and in Sam's case, Phyllis had to admit that the two of them were more than just friends. She couldn't just dismiss what he wanted out of hand.

Because of that, she found herself in this big, smelly, noisy room full of barking dogs.

The young woman who worked as a volunteer at the animal shelter wore a plastic name tag that read JULIE on her shirt. She smiled, waved a hand at the cages, and said, "Feel free to look around all you want, folks. I'm sure you'll find just the right dog for you."

"Thanks, Julie," Sam said. He went over to the closest cage, which held a German shepherd, and put his hand close to the bars so the dog could sniff it.

According to the paperwork in a clear plastic envelope attached to the cage, the dog's name was Daisy and she was three years old, no health problems, good with children. That wasn't really a consideration since no children lived in Phyllis's house. Her grandson, Bobby, visited sometimes, though, so actually it was important that whatever dog Sam picked was well behaved and safe to be around children, she thought.

"Howdy, Daisy," Sam said as he scratched the dog's muzzle. "How ya doin', girl?"

Phyllis smiled. The affection Sam felt for this dog, for all dogs, really, was obvious. He was a genuinely good man, and she was glad she had gotten to know him, even this late in their lives.

Daisy licked Sam's fingers. Phyllis could tell that he didn't want to move on to the next cage, but he had to take a look at the rest of the dogs. Phyllis stayed with him as he made his way slowly along the runway.

She saw beagles, schnauzers, Chihuahuas, and lots of mutts. Big dogs, small dogs, shorthairs, longhairs. Most were eager and friendly, as if they knew that the humans who came to see them held their fate in their hands. A few seemed sullen, and Phyllis wondered if they had been mistreated and no longer trusted anybody who went on two legs.

What was that famous line from *Animal Farm*? "Four legs good, two legs bad"? Something like that, she decided. Unfortunately, all too often that was true. Her own experiences over the past few years with the uglier side of life had taught her that.

Animals killed, certainly, but only humans were capable of murder.

Sam broke into her thoughts by looking at her, shaking his head, and saying, "Well, coming here turned out to be a bad mistake."

"How so?"

"I want to take all of 'em home with me. I don't reckon there's room for that, though."

"I have a pretty big backyard," Phyllis said, "but not that big."

Sam sighed and said, "All right. I reckon I'm gonna have to—"

He stopped as the metal door at the end of the runway, between the kennel area and the office, swung open and a male volunteer came through carrying a dog. The animal was wrapped in a blanket and whimpering in pain.

"Lonny, what happened?" Julie asked as she hurried toward the newcomer.

"Aw, somebody hit this poor fella out on the road. I saw it happen just now as I was coming in. Looks like maybe his front leg is busted."

"Do you think he belongs to somebody around here?"

Lonny shook his head and said, "I dunno. He doesn't have a collar and he's pretty skinny, so I've got a hunch he's a stray."

Sam walked up to the volunteers with Phyllis trailing behind him. He said, "That's a Dalmatian, isn't it?"

"Yeah," Lonny said. "Full grown, but not too old, I'd say."

"I always wanted a Dalmatian when I was a kid. Are you folks going to adopt him out?"

"Mister, he hasn't been processed in. You can have him right now if you want him. You're gonna have to give me your word that you'll take care of him, though. He needs medical attention."

"Where's the nearest vet?" Sam asked.

Lonny and Julie looked at each other, and Julie said, "That would be Dr. Baxter, about a mile back up the road toward town."

"Then that's where I'm takin' him right now," Sam said. "You can follow me if you want, to make sure that's what I do."

"I don't guess that's necessary," Lonny said. "You got a car outside?"

"My pickup," Sam told him.

"I'll put him in the back for you."

Sam shook his head. "I'll hold him. My friend here can drive."

Sam's decision to take the injured dog seemed awfully impulsive to Phyllis. She said, "Sam, are you sure you want to do this?"

He answered by reaching out and gently taking the blanket-wrapped Dalmatian out of Lonny's arms. Sam was tall and lanky, but he was also strong enough to hold the medium-sized dog.

"Be careful," Julie told him. "Injured dogs sometimes bite."

"This fella's not gonna bite me," Sam said with a shake of his head. "I can tell we're gonna get along just fine."

Phyllis hoped that was true. It seemed to her that Sam was taking on quite a bit here. He had always been one of the calmest, steadiest people she knew, not given to being rash or reckless, but evidently he could do things on the spur of the moment, too.

"Truck keys are in my pocket," he said to her. "Let's go."

She delved into the front pocket of his jeans, found the keys, and said, "All right." As they walked out of the shelter, she turned her head to say, "Thank you," to the two volunteers.

Sam's pickup was parked fairly close. Phyllis hurried ahead and unlocked and opened the passenger door.

"Can you get in without any help?" she asked.

"Yeah, I reckon we can manage." Carefully, Sam eased himself into the seat with the dog half lying across his lap and half cradled against his chest. It reached its head up and licked his jaw. Sam laughed and said, "And they were worried about you bitin' me. Hang on there, fella. We're gonna get you taken care of."

Phyllis closed the door and went around to get behind the wheel. She asked, "Do you want me to help get your seat belt fastened?"

"Naw. We won't bother with it. We're not going very far. Just don't get in any wrecks along the way."

"But it's against the law not to have your seat belt fastened."

"Yeah, but I'm a grown man. If anybody gets a ticket, it'll be me, not you."

Phyllis sighed and turned the key in the ignition. He was right, of course, and actually, it was unlikely they would get in an accident here on this side road on the outskirts of Weatherford. But it still bothered her to be breaking the law as she started driving toward the vet Julie had told them about.

Of course, if anybody wanted to get technical about it, she had been accused of breaking other laws in the past that were more serious than not fastening a seat belt. Things like obstruction of justice and tampering with evidence . . .

She found the place she was looking for without any trouble. A sign that read BAXTER VETERINARY CLINIC sat beside a driveway that turned off to the left. The driveway led through some trees to a paved parking area beside a brown brick building with a completely fenced-in area divided into runs behind it. A continuation of the driveway circled around to a large metal barn with its doors standing open. A pickup was parked next to the barn.

Another pickup and two cars were parked beside the building. Phyllis eased into an empty spot and stopped Sam's truck. She hurried around to open the passenger door for him, but he had it open by the time she got there.

Still with no apparent difficulty, he carried the dog toward the front door. Phyllis held it open for them, and they went into an office that smelled a little like the animal shelter but not nearly as strong.

A man with unruly dark hair and salt-and-pepper beard stubble stood behind a counter, talking to a woman who had a pet carrier on the floor at her feet. A cat inside the carrier meowed loudly and insistently.

"Two tablets every twelve hours," the man said as he put a plastic pill bottle on the counter. "That ought to take care of the infection in a few days, but keep giving her the pills until they're all gone."

"All right, Doctor," the woman said. "Thank you."

"Call us right away if she gets worse."

The woman nodded and said, "I will." She picked up the carrier and turned toward the door. When she saw Sam standing there holding the dog, she said, "Oh, my goodness. What happened?"

"Car hit him," Sam said. "Looks like a front leg may be busted."

"You've brought him to the right place," the woman said. "There's no better vet around here than Dr. Baxter."

The man smiled and said, "I appreciate the vote of confidence." To Sam he went on. "Bring him right on back here into surgery. I've got another patient waiting, but that's just for booster shots and this is an emergency."

He swung open a wooden gate to let Sam behind the counter. As he did, an attractive blond woman in her thirties came out of an office in the back. She looked a little impatient at having to wait for Sam to go by with the Dalmatian. When the way was clear, she said, "I'll see you at home tonight, Hank," and briskly left the vet clinic before Baxter had a chance to respond.

"Right back here," he told Sam as he opened another door.

Sam carried the dog into a big room with an operating table in the middle of it.

Phyllis stood back, watching as Sam carefully placed the injured dog on the table. As Baxter unwrapped the blanket, he said, "You'll have to excuse me if things get a little hectic around here. My assistant and my office manager are both out sick today, so I'm holding down the fort by myself."

"You should get your wife to help you," Phyllis said, thinking of the blond woman who had been leaving as they were coming back here.

Baxter shook his head and said, "Susan has patients of her own to see."

"She's a vet, too?" Sam asked.

"Nah. A people doctor." Baxter shrugged. "A real doctor, some might say."

"Yeah, people who don't know any better," Sam said.

Baxter lightly ran his fingers along the dog's left front leg, which even Phyllis could see looked a little funny. The dog whined but didn't struggle or try to bite.

"That's a good boy," Baxter told the Dalmatian. "I know that had to hurt." He looked up at Sam. "It's broken, all right. What I'd like to do is go in there and make sure it's reset properly, then put a pin in it to ensure that it stays that way. Then I'll cast it. After he wears the cast for a couple of weeks, he should be okay."

"Will you need to keep him tonight?"

Baxter nodded and said, "Yes, just to let the anesthetic wear off and to make sure there are no problems. He should be able to go home in the morning." He stroked the dog's flank and frowned slightly. "He's pretty skinny. He *is* your dog?"

"He is now," Sam said. "He was a stray that one of the volunteers down at the animal shelter found a little while ago. I claimed him before they ever processed him in."

"All right. We'll get him fixed up, and it'll be up to you to get him fattened up, Mr. . . . ?"

"Fletcher. Sam Fletcher. This is my friend Phyllis Newsom."

"Pleased to meet you both," Baxter said with a nod. "I'm Hank Baxter."

"This'll give me a chance to fix up a place for him to stay," Sam went on. "That way we'll have it ready for him when he comes home tomorrow."

"Sounds good, if that's what you want to do. I can work up an estimate for you—"

Sam waved that off. "It'll be all right. You go ahead and fix him up, like you said."

"Okay. Go on back out front and we'll do a little paperwork. I'll meet you there in a minute after I put . . . What is the dog's name, anyway? Does he have one?"

"Buck," Sam answered without hesitation. "That fella's name is Buck."

Chapter 2

As they were driving away from the vet clinic a little later, with Sam behind the wheel again, Phyllis asked, "What made you decide to call him Buck? You were very emphatic about it."

"Buck Jones, of course."

"Of course," Phyllis repeated, knowing Sam's great fondness for old Western movies. "He was the one who died in the nightclub fire, wasn't he?"

She had heard Sam talk about the incident before and was a little surprised that some of the details had stuck in her mind.

"Yep, the Cocoanut Grove fire in Boston. Ol' Buck made it out all right, but then he decided to go back in and see if he could rescue some of the folks who hadn't. He never came back out."

"It sounds like he was a hero in real life, not just on the screen."

"That's the way I see it," Sam said. "Anyway, Buck's just a good name for a dog."

"I think so, too."

After a few minutes, Sam said, "I gave some thought to callin' him El Diablo."

"Why in the world would you name a dog El Diablo?"

"Because when I was little—I told you I always wanted a Dalmatian when I was little, didn't I?"

"You did," Phyllis said.

"Anyway, when I was little I just called 'em spotted dogs, but my mama figured it'd be a good idea to teach me their real name. That would've been all well and good if I could've pronounced it, but I had a little trouble with it. Didn't really cause a problem, though, until one day when Mama had the WMU ladies from the church over to the house and I said somethin' about wantin' a dog. One of the ladies asked me what kind of dog I wanted and I answered as proud as you please, 'A damnation!'"

Phyllis burst out laughing.

"So that's why I thought El Diablo might be a good name, that bein' Spanish for the devil and all, but I went with Buck instead," Sam concluded as Phyllis sagged against the door and snorted a couple of times.

Sam added, "You might not want to lean on the door that way. I guess it'll probably be all right, though, since you got your seat belt on."

They went into the house through the door in the garage that led to the kitchen, where they found Carolyn Wilbarger standing and looking into the pantry with an intent frown on her face.

"Is something wrong?" Phyllis asked.

"What? Oh, no, nothing's wrong. I was just thinking about something." Carolyn turned from the pantry and went on. "Well, did you find a dog at the animal shelter?"

"In a manner of speakin'," Sam said.

"What does that mean?"

"I got a dog, and he came from the animal shelter, but I didn't actually adopt him from there."

"What did you do, steal him?" As soon as she'd asked the question, Carolyn's eyes widened. "Oh, good heavens, that's exactly the sort of thing you'd do, isn't it? Did you really steal a dog from the animal shelter?"

"Of course not," Phyllis said. She explained quickly about Buck.

When Phyllis was finished, Carolyn said, "Hmph. Well, it's nice of you to take care of a crippled dog, I suppose."

"He's not crippled," Sam said. "Well, right now he is, I reckon, but the vet said he ought to be fine once his leg heals up. I'm gonna make sure of it. In fact, I'm gonna go out on the back porch and see if I can finish up that doghouse I started."

Sam had been working on building a doghouse, off and on, for the past couple of weeks, ever since he had brought up the idea of getting a dog. Since he hadn't known what kind of dog he would wind up with or how big it would be, he had designed the house to be fairly large.

To Phyllis it looked almost big enough for a Shetland pony. When it was finished, Buck would fit in it with no trouble at all.

Sam went out the back door and left Phyllis and Carolyn

alone in the kitchen. Carolyn kept her voice fairly low as she asked, "Well? What do you think of this dog?"

"He seems nice enough," Phyllis said. "He's a Dalmatian."

"Like the ones in that movie. Sometimes they're pretty dogs." Carolyn added ominously, "But they're still dogs. Smelly, hairy dogs who do rude things on carpets."

"That's why Buck is going to live in the backyard."

"Uh-huh." Carolyn sounded like she didn't believe that for a second. "Until Sam asks you if he can stay inside, you mean."

"Oh, I don't think Buck would like that. He'd rather be outside, where he can run around once his leg is better. The yard is plenty big enough to give one dog room to romp."

"We'll see," Carolyn said. "In the meantime, I want to show you something." She picked up a magazine lying on the kitchen counter. "Look."

"Is that the new *Taste of Texas*?" Phyllis asked.

A *Taste of Texas* was one of her favorite magazines. She'd had a subscription to it for years. It was devoted to Texas cooking, and Phyllis always found several recipes in each issue that she wanted to try. Carolyn was also a fan, so every copy that came into the house wound up being read cover to cover multiple times.

"It is," Carolyn answered Phyllis's question, "and it's a special contest issue."

Phyllis's eyes widened, and she said, "I didn't know they had contests."

"It's the first annual."

Ever since the two of them had retired from teaching, Phyllis and Carolyn had indulged their passion for baking, and cooking in general, by entering contests. Recently, in fact, they had both competed at the State Fair of Texas. Sam had even gotten in on that by entering one of the competitions, and by no stretch of the imagination was he an avid cook.

Quite a rivalry had developed between Phyllis and Carolyn as each of them edged out the other for victories in various contests, but for the sake of their friendship—and peace in the house—they had tried to play that down in recent years.

"You can see they have three separate contests," Carolyn said as she showed Phyllis the magazine cover. "Breakfast, lunch, and dinner. I was thinking we could enter separate contests and increase our chances of both winning, like we did at the state fair."

"That's not a bad idea," Phyllis agreed. "Which one would you like to do?"

Carolyn shook her head and said, "Oh, no, it's your magazine. You should have first choice, and I'll pick from the other two."

"It's no more my magazine than it is yours," Phyllis protested. "If you want to get technical about it, it belongs to PylisMewcom, since that's the name on the address label."

"I don't care. You go ahead and pick, Phyllis."

"Well, if you're going to insist . . . I've been thinking about trying to come up with a white chili casserole recipe. That would make a good dinner entrée, don't you think?"

Phyllis could tell from the expression on her friend's face that she had made a good choice. Carolyn nodded and said, "That sounds delicious. I was leaning toward a casserole, too. A hearty breakfast casserole. I was just checking the pantry and thinking about possible ingredients when you and Sam came in."

"If there's anything I can do to help you . . ."

"Same here." Carolyn laid the magazine on the counter and opened it. "Let's take a look at the rules . . ."

After poring over the magazine with Carolyn for a while and thinking about the casserole she might bake, Phyllis took a break and went outside. She'd heard plenty of hammering going on in the backyard, along with the whining hum of a circular saw and a screw gun. The house had a large wooden back porch, and Sam was constructing the doghouse at one end of it.

When Sam noticed her, he stepped back from his work and grinned at her.

"What do you think?" he asked with a note of pride in his voice. "Reckon Buck will be happy in it?"

"I think any dog would be," Phyllis said.

Phyllis didn't know that much about doghouses. She was probably more familiar with the one that Snoopy slept on top of in the comics than anything else. Her family had had a dog for a while when she was growing up, but it had slept underneath her parents' farmhouse with its pier-and-beam foundation. The only pets she and her late husband, Kenny, had had while their son, Mike, was growing up were fish and birds.

But even so, she could tell that this doghouse was well put together, like all of Sam's carpentry projects, and looked like it would be comfortable. It was big and roomy, and Sam had tacked down a nice piece of thick carpet on its floor. Phyllis had some old blankets he could put in there for Buck to curl up in, too.

The doghouse roof had shingles on it, so if any rain blew in under the porch roof, it would stay dry inside. The roof extended out quite a bit in an overhang to protect the arched entrance.

Sam pointed and said, "I cut a window in the back and put one of those louvered covers on it, so it'll keep rain out but let air through. The trees block the north wind, but it'll catch any breeze from the west. That'll be nice in the spring and fall, and I can close it up during the winter."

Phyllis smiled and said, "I think Buck is a lucky dog. If we hadn't happened to be at the shelter when that man brought him in, who knows what might have happened to him."

"Shoot. I'm the one who's lucky to have found him," Sam said. "You can look in a dog's eyes and tell how smart he is, you know. He's a mighty smart fella. I'm sure of it."

"Maybe you can teach him some tricks."

Sam made a little face and shook his head. "I'm not much on tricks. I like a dog that'll walk with you and that you can talk to. You get a good enough dog, I swear sometimes it seems like they're talkin' back to you. That's the way it feels anyway." He hesitated for a moment, then went on, "After my wife passed on, I must've walked a thousand miles up and down those country roads out where we lived, just tryin' to make sense of it all. And the old dog that we had then was right with me every step of the way. Sometimes I think those walks with that old varmint were the only thing that kept me from goin' outta my head. He was always ready to go, always willin' to listen to whatever I had to say. Now, that's a good dog. Sure was hard when I lost him, too."

"It must have been," Phyllis said. She had to swallow before she could get the words out, and her eyes were moist.

"Oh, well," Sam said with a smile. "It wasn't long after that

I moved in here with you fine ladies, and things got better. Didn't really have time then to sit around and feel sorry for myself, because there was always somethin' goin' on."

"Too much going on, if you ask me. All those horrible murders . . ." She shuddered. "I never intended to spend my retirement catching killers!"

"You do seem to have a knack for it. That and bakin'." Sam slapped the top of the doghouse. "And now we're gonna have a dog, too. Can't hardly wait to show ol' Buck his new home."

Seeing how happy he was, Phyllis thought again that she was glad she had decided to go along with what he wanted. He had tiptoed around the subject for a while before he ever came right out with it, and to tell the truth, when he'd told her that he had an important question to ask her, she had been convinced it was going to be something else entirely.

She had believed he was going to ask her to marry him.

When he'd said instead that he wanted to get a dog, Phyllis hadn't known at first whether to be relieved or disappointed. It hadn't taken her long to figure out that she was relieved. That way she hadn't had to make a decision and give him an answer.

She loved Sam, but as far as she was concerned, things could go on the way they were for the time being. They were both happy, and there was no need to risk that.

"I think I might go call the vet clinic," Sam went on. "Doc Baxter gave me his card. I want to find out how Buck's doin' after his surgery."

"I'm sure if there was any problem the doctor would let you know," Phyllis said.

"Yeah, more than likely. But I think I'll call anyway."

He went into the house, leaving Phyllis on the porch. She stood there for a moment, looking at the doghouse, then walked over to it and rested a hand on the roof.

"Buck, you had better be nice to that man," she said quietly, even though the future occupant of the doghouse was several miles away. "If anybody deserves to have a good dog, it's Sam Fletcher."

Chapter 3

*S*am called the vet's office again the next morning, and after telling the woman who answered the phone who he was, he asked if Buck was ready to be picked up.

"I think so, but let me go and check," she said. After a couple of minutes, she came back to the phone and reported, "Yes. Dr. Baxter said you can come get him anytime you want."

"All right. I'll be there in a little while. Thanks."

He was already in the kitchen, so after he hung up the phone, he turned to the table where Phyllis, Carolyn, and Eve sat and said, "Good news. I can go get Buck anytime."

"Buck," Eve Turner repeated. "I like that name. It's so manly."

Carolyn opened her mouth to say something, but Sam saw Phyllis give her a quick look and Carolyn just cleared her throat and kept whatever she'd been about to say to herself.

Sam could guess that it would've been some comment

about how Eve liked anything she considered manly because Eve liked men so much.

That was true, or at least it had been. When Sam was first introduced to Eve several years earlier, she had practically purred. Her interest in him was blatantly obvious. She had been married a number of times in the past and was on the lookout for another husband, to the point that she was almost like a stereotypical character on a TV sitcom.

Sam had found out how wrong he was to jump to that conclusion when an unexpected tragedy had brought to light the truth about Eve's past. Since then she had been a changed person, still smart and friendly but no longer on the prowl, so to speak.

"Phyllis, do you mind goin' with me to pick him up?" Sam asked. "I could go by the store and buy a big carrier for him and put it in the back of the pickup, but I'll feel better if you can drive and I'll hold him, like we did when we took him to the vet."

"Of course," Phyllis said. "That would probably be safer, too. We can go as soon as I've finished cleaning up from breakfast."

Carolyn waved a hand and said, "Oh, we can do that. You two go on anytime you're ready."

"You're sure?"

"Of course," Eve said. "We'd be glad to."

"Well . . . all right." Phyllis gestured at the housedress she wore and said to Sam, "Let me go put on some jeans, and then I'll be ready."

As they drove away from the house a few minutes later, Sam was excited and eager to see how Buck was doing. He'd had dogs off and on his entire life, and he realized now that canine companionship was something he'd been missing in recent years. He had felt that lack without being able to pin down the cause of it until recently.

"Were Dr. Baxter's helpers back at work this morning?" Phyllis asked.

"I reckon so. It was a woman who answered the phone when I called."

"Maybe he talked his wife into giving him a hand after all."

"I don't think so," Sam said. "This lady, whoever she was, sounded younger. And considerably perkier, I'd have to say."

"Yes, Mrs. Baxter wasn't what anyone would call perky," Phyllis agreed. "If she's a doctor, I hope she has a better bedside manner with her patients than she displayed yesterday. Although I probably shouldn't say such a thing."

"You're just makin' an observation. And the same thought occurred to me."

As he drove through the streets of Weatherford, Sam noticed a number of pumpkins sitting on the porches and in the yards of some of the houses they passed. Here and there a few gaudily dressed scarecrows were on display, too. It reminded him that Halloween was only a week away.

The scarecrows also reminded him of the harvest festival a few years earlier, where Phyllis and Carolyn had almost literally tripped over a murder victim. He glanced over at Phyllis now and thought that nobody would ever guess a retired history teacher would turn out to be so good at catching folks who killed other folks.

"What?" Phyllis asked.

"Nothin'," Sam replied with a shake of his head. "I was just thinkin' about how Halloween is next week."

"I know. We probably ought to do something, but I'm not sure what."

The parking lot at the veterinary clinic was busier this morning, but several spaces were still open. Sam parked in one of them, and he and Phyllis went inside to find the waiting room half-full of people, dogs, and cats.

The cats were all in carriers, and so were some of the dogs, but several of the dogs were on leashes, sitting with their owners. Sam saw a dachshund, a couple of beagles, and a big fluffy white dog whose breed he couldn't identify. Some of the cats were meowing loudly and annoyingly.

A short, curvy redhead in her mid-twenties was behind the counter today. She had to go with the perky voice he had heard earlier, Sam thought. When she smiled at them and asked, "Can I help you?" that confirmed it.

"We're here to pick up Buck," Sam said.

"Oh, of course. You're Mr. Fletcher. Let me call back there and tell Tommy to bring him up."

The redhead picked up a phone and punched a button. A moment later, she said, "Tommy, could you bring Buck up? His mom and dad are here to get him."

Phyllis started to say, "Oh, we're not—" but then she stopped herself.

"I'm sorry," the redhead said with a smile. "We just see so many pets here, I guess we're used to thinking of them as people's babies."

"That's all right," Phyllis said. "It's perfectly understandable that you'd feel that way."

Sam had to wonder what she had been about to deny, though: that they were Buck's parents, or that they were a couple.

"Let me go ahead and get you his bill," the redhead went on.

She told Sam the amount, which included vaccinations, lab work, and heartworm preventative, and he gave her his credit card, then signed the slip and took the printout she gave him. It was a considerable amount, but Sam didn't hesitate.

A young man came up the hallway behind the counter. He was carrying Buck. Dr. Baxter trailed behind him.

"And we have some pills for Buck, too," the redhead added. She set a small paper bag with the top folded down on the counter. Phyllis picked up the pill bag and then took the receipt from Sam so he could carry Buck.

"He did just fine," Baxter said as Sam and Tommy transferred the Dalmatian between them. Buck's left front leg was completely wrapped up with dark blue elastic wrap, and he had a white plastic cone fastened around his neck to keep him from biting at the cast. "He may still be just a little groggy, but he'll be fine. Go ahead and give him his normal food and water, and you can start him on the antibiotic, the steroid, and the pain pill this evening. He already got them this morning. Be sure and give him the antibiotic and the steroid until they're all gone. After a couple of days, if he doesn't seem to be in any discomfort, you don't have to keep giving him the pain pills."

"Is it all right for him to walk on that cast?"

"Yes, although he may not want to at first because it'll seem awkward to him. But he'll get used to it. Dogs are pretty adaptable. That's why even the ones with only three legs can get around pretty good."

"What about the cone? How long does he have to wear that?"

"Oh, just until tomorrow, I think. Unless you see him biting and chewing at the cast. Some dogs do and some don't. But if he does, the cone needs to go back on."

"Got it," Sam said with a nod. "Thanks, Doc. When does he need to come back?"

"I want to see him again in a week just to check on him; then we'll x-ray the leg a month after that to see how it's healed before taking the cast off. Of course, if you have any problems, give us a call right away."

Sam nodded and turned toward the door. Phyllis told Baxter and the redhead, "Thanks again."

As they started to leave the office, Sam heard the redhead say, "Oh, by the way, Dr. Baxter, your wife called a few minutes ago. She said she wanted you to call her back."

"Did you tell her we have a full waiting room?" Baxter asked with a definite edge of annoyance in his voice.

"Yes, but she said—"

"Never mind, Holly. I'll take care of it."

Sam and Phyllis were out the door by now. Sam didn't hear anything else because Phyllis let the glass door close behind them.

Sam hefted Buck a little in his arms and rubbed the top of the dog's head as they started toward the pickup.

"How you doin', fella? That's a really sporty-lookin' deal you got on your leg."

He wondered why that snippet of overheard conversation had even registered on his brain as they left the clinic. He supposed being around all the trouble that Phyllis had gotten mixed up in over the past few years had trained him to pay attention to the things that were said and done around him.

You never knew when the least little thing might be the key to solving a murder.

And that was just about the craziest thing that had ever occurred to him, he told himself as he went on to Buck. "You're a mighty fine fella, aren't you, boy? Yes, sir. A mighty fine fella."

It seemed to him like Buck squirmed a little in happiness. Sam felt sort of like that himself.

"Did you see the sign in there?" Phyllis asked as she drove away from the clinic.

"Guess I didn't notice it," Sam said. "What sign was that?"

"About the Halloween party they're having there next week. It said there'll be free treats and prizes for the best costumes."

Sam scratched behind Buck's ears and frowned as he repeated, "Costumes? Like for the animals?"

"I suppose so."

He shook his head and said slowly, "I don't know. I'm not sure about dressin' up dogs and cats in Halloween costumes."

"You mean you don't think it's adorable?"

"Maybe with cats and little dogs. Put a big dog in a costume and to me he just looks sad, like it's offended his dignity or something. Of course, cats always look like they're offended, so it's hard to say with them."

"Well, I certainly don't think you ought to dress up Buck and take him to the party," Phyllis said. "I was wondering about those doggie treats, though. I read something a while back about people who bake their own dog treats, because the ones you buy in the store really aren't supposed to be very good for them."

"I wouldn't know about that. Most of the treats I've given dogs have been soup bones and such."

"Most bones aren't good for them. Neither is chocolate or onions or ham."

"You mean dogs are sort of like humans," Sam said. "Anything that really tastes good, they're not supposed to eat."

She laughed and said, "There are plenty of good things they can eat. I seem to remember I saw a recipe for sweet-potato-and-peanut-butter treats. That sounds good, doesn't it?"

"Sounds good enough I might want to try one myself," Sam said with a grin. "You thinkin' about bakin' some?"

"I'm thinking about it," Phyllis admitted. "It might be fun."

"Well, if you do, I know somebody who'd probably be glad to help you test 'em out."

She smiled at him and said, "Are you talking about Buck . . . or you?"

"I guess we'll have to wait and see how good they smell while they're cookin'."

They reached the house a few minutes later. This time Sam waited for Phyllis to come around and open the door after she parked the pickup in the garage before he climbed out with Buck in his arms. He was careful not to bang the leg with the cast on it against anything.

Carolyn and Eve had the door to the kitchen open before Phyllis and Sam got there. Eve said, "Oh, he's adorable! Such a handsome dog."

Carolyn was more restrained in her response. She nodded and said, "Yes, that's a Dalmatian, all right."

Phyllis went ahead to open the back door before Sam got there. He stepped out onto the porch, paused, and said, "I should've put in a temporary ramp to make it easier for him to get up and down the steps. I'll have to do that . . . as long as it's all right with you, Phyllis."

"Of course it is," she told him. She, Carolyn, and Eve had followed him onto the porch. "Do whatever you need to, Sam."

He went down the steps to the yard. Buck was starting to squirm a little, so Sam lowered him to the ground and said, "Here goes nothin'."

Buck put his nose to the ground and moved slowly across the yard, hobbling because of the cast on his leg, but overall he was able to get around without much trouble.

"Would you look at that?" Sam said with a big grin on his weathered face as Buck ranged back and forth across the yard. "He's explorin' all over—"

"Yes," Carolyn said when Sam abruptly fell silent. "He's going to do *that* all over, too."

Chapter 4

Building a temporary ramp for Buck turned out to be easy. There were only three steps down from the porch to the yard, so Sam took a four-foot-by-four-foot piece of plywood, screwed it to a frame made of two-by-twos, and set it down over the steps. It was heavy enough to stay in place without being fastened to the porch, and Buck was able to scamper up and down it without any trouble. Like Dr. Baxter had said, he was adaptable.

It was a beautiful autumn day, crisp and cool in the shade, warm in the sun. Sam sat on the porch in a plastic lawn chair and watched Buck as the Dalmatian explored every inch of the backyard and marked every tree and bush. After a while, Buck seemed to get tired. He sat down in the sunlight and tried to stretch out on his belly, but he couldn't do that because of the cast. He wound up lying on his side instead, with his head against the cone rather than the ground.

"I know you'd rather have that contraption off, Buck,"

Sam said, "but it's for your own good. It and the cast will both be gone, all in good time."

Buck's tail thumped against the ground as he wagged it at the sound of Sam's voice.

It wasn't long before man and dog were both asleep.

A while later, Phyllis opened the back door and started to step out on the porch, then stopped as she saw that Sam had dozed off. Out in the yard, Buck raised his head slightly and looked at her. Phyllis backed off and eased the door closed so as not to disturb either of them.

Carolyn came into the kitchen behind her and started to say, "How are they—"

She stopped when Phyllis quickly held a finger to her lips. Decades of teaching rowdy elementary school students had left Carolyn with a booming voice, and her time in retirement hadn't changed her normal tone that much.

"What's the matter?" she asked in a quieter voice. "Is the dog asleep?"

"They both are," Phyllis said. "It's adorable."

"I'm sure it is," Carolyn said, but she didn't make any attempt to look for herself. "Have you given any more thought to those contests for *A Taste of Texas*?"

"Actually, since Sam and I got back this morning with Buck, I've been thinking about dog treats."

Carolyn frowned and repeated, "Dog treats?"

Phyllis explained about the upcoming Halloween party at Dr. Baxter's veterinary clinic and said, "I remembered seeing a recipe for homemade dog treats a while back, so I thought I might bake some and take them over there for the party. I looked online and found several recipes I wouldn't mind trying."

"Are you sure your relationship with Sam isn't making you get a little carried away with this dog business?"

"I don't think it's getting carried away to bake something that pets would enjoy."

"You were going to come up with something for the magazine contest, though."

"I can do both," Phyllis insisted. "In fact, I've made a list of what I'll need for that white chili casserole I mentioned, and I can pick up everything the next time I go to the store." She paused. "Along with the ingredients for the doggie treats."

Carolyn shook her head and said, "I give up. Tell me about the dog biscuits."

"Well, they're made with peanut butter and sweet potatoes . . ."

Phyllis told her friend about the recipe, and she could see that Carolyn was getting interested in spite of herself. They talked about other things that could go into home-made dog treats, such as chicken, liver, or cheese, and eventually a gleam that Phyllis recognized appeared in Carolyn's eyes.

"You know," she said, "if we each made a different kind of treat, the dogs at the clinic could have a little variety."

"They could," Phyllis agreed. She had a pretty good idea what was coming next.

Carolyn confirmed that hunch by saying, "And we could see which one they seemed to like the best."

"So that would make it like a contest."

"Oh, I don't know that I'd go so far as to call it a contest. There wouldn't be any prizes or anything. It would just be for . . . informational purposes, I suppose you could say."

"Of course. And the dogs would get the main benefit out of it."

"Exactly. What do you think?"

Phyllis thought that Carolyn couldn't resist the idea of turning this into a competition. Maybe she missed their friendly rivalry. Sometimes Phyllis thought she did, too.

She didn't mention any of that, however. Instead she said, "I think it's a good idea. We'll each come up with our own recipe, and we'll let the dogs choose."

"All right." Carolyn got a calculating look on her face. "I'll have to do some thinking about this."

"I will, too," Phyllis said.

She wouldn't be surprised if Carolyn was disappointed in the way the unofficial "competition" worked out.

Not because Phyllis expected the dogs at the party to pick her sweet-potato-and-peanut-butter treats over whatever Carolyn prepared, though. She figured they would gobble the treats with equal enthusiasm.

They were dogs, after all.

How discriminating could they be?

For the next couple of days, Phyllis was busy thinking about the recipes she would use for both the dog treats and the casserole for the magazine contest. She and Carolyn made separate trips to the grocery store, and Carolyn had a secretive air about her regarding what ingredients she was going to use in her dog treats. Her old competitive nature was coming out again. Phyllis could tell.

But that was all right. Judging by Carolyn's enthusiasm, she had missed competing against her old friend.

To tell the truth, Phyllis had missed it a little, too.

While they were doing that, Sam spent a lot of time on the back porch with Buck, either reading a book or surfing the Web with his iPad. The weather continued to be gorgeous.

Buck seemed to have gotten used to his cast. Whenever Sam had the cone off, Buck didn't make any attempt to chew at the cast, so Sam finally just left the cone off all the time. He explained to Phyllis that he would continue to keep a close eye on Buck's behavior and would put the cone back on the Dalmatian if necessary.

Phyllis could tell that it was sort of hard for Sam to leave Buck outside as evening fell. Buck just went in his doghouse, curled up, and went to sleep, though, seemingly as comfortable and content as if he had lived there all his life.

One night the sound of frantic barking woke Phyllis not long after she had gone to bed. There were other dogs in the neighborhood, of course, but she could tell this racket came from Buck. He wasn't an incessant barker like some dogs, but he had barked enough since being there that she recognized the sound of it.

At first she just tried to ignore it, but Buck was persistent and sounded like something was really bothering him, so she decided she had better get up and check on him. By the time she got her robe on and stepped out into the hall, Sam was already out of his room and at the top of the stairs, about to start down them.

"You heard the ruckus, too," he said.

"It would be hard to miss," Phyllis said. The barking had spread to the other dogs in the neighborhood, so now there was a veritable chorus going on.

"I'm sorry he disturbed you. He sounds really worked up about something."

"Don't worry about me. Let's just go make sure he's all right."

They went downstairs together without turning on any lights. After living there for forty years, Phyllis was so familiar with her surroundings that she could get around all right in utter darkness if she had to. The house wasn't completely dark, though. The faint glow of a night-light came from the kitchen and guided them.

Sam reached for the knob of the back door to open it, but Phyllis stopped him by saying, "Shouldn't you see if you can tell if anybody's out there first?"

"Yeah, I reckon that would make sense." Sam leaned close to the door and pulled aside the curtain over the window in its upper half so that there was a narrow gap through which he could peer. He put his eye to it.

"Do you see anything?" Phyllis asked after a moment.

"Buck's standin' on the porch lookin' out into the yard," Sam reported. "I don't see anything— Oh, Lord! Buck, no!"

Sam twisted the dead bolt, grabbed the knob, and jerked the door open.

"Sam, what is it?" Phyllis cried.

"There's a skunk out there!" As he rushed out onto the porch, Sam went on. "Buck, come back here!"

Phyllis cringed as the pungent, unmistakable odor of skunk blew in through the open door.

"Blast it, Buck. Get away from the darned thing! You, skunk, shoo! Get away from here!"

"Sam, be careful," Phyllis called. "You don't want him to get you."

Sam muttered something. Phyllis couldn't exactly make out the words, but she was afraid he'd said something about how it might be too late for that.

From behind her, Carolyn said as she came into the kitchen and turned on the light, "What's all this commotion? Is that . . . Oh, good grief! That's terrible!"

It really was, but Phyllis knew the smell would fade. It already wasn't as strong as it had been a few moments earlier. There was a good breeze tonight, and it would carry away the scent.

Except where it had gotten on Buck and maybe Sam, too. Phyllis could see them in the light from the kitchen as Sam came up the ramp with Buck hobbling behind him, and as they approached, the smell grew stronger again.

"The, uh, skunk's gone," Sam announced through the screen door.

"You couldn't tell that by the smell," Carolyn said.

"It coulda been a lot worse. He just sorta hit Buck with a glancin' blow, not a full-fledged drenchin'. Even less of the stuff got on me. But we didn't get off scot-free, did we, old son?"

Buck whined and wagged his tail.

Phyllis started to laugh. Carolyn said, "I'm not sure what's funny about this. We may have to fumigate the whole house."

"It's just that I've never seen a couple of more hangdog expressions," Phyllis said.

"Hey, Buck ought to be proud," Sam said. "He defended

his territory. It's just that in this case, it might've been smarter if he'd stayed in his doghouse and let the skunk leave in its own good time." He reached down and scratched Buck's head. "But that's all right, boy. I'm proud of you anyway."

"You're both going to have to bathe in tomato juice," Carolyn said. "That's the only thing that will get rid of skunk smell." She waved a hand in front of her face. "And I'm not sure there's enough of it in the world to take care of this stench."

"Maybe there's something else that will work better," Phyllis said. "I'll have to look it up on the Internet."

"Well, what'll the two of us do in the meantime?" Sam asked.

"It's not very cold tonight. I think you'll be all right on the porch for a while."

Sam sighed and shook his head. "Banished," he said. "We may have to find out if there's room in that doghouse of yours for both of us, Buck."

Chapter 5

*S*ome quick research told Phyllis that a mixture of hydrogen peroxide, baking soda, and dishwashing detergent was supposed to be much more effective at removing skunk odor than the traditional tomato juice. Since she had all those ingredients on hand, she mixed up a batch in a spray bottle and took it out onto the back porch after donning a pair of rubber gloves.

"This ought to work," she told Sam. "You hold on to Buck, in case he doesn't like being sprayed."

Carolyn watched from the back door and voiced her skepticism by saying, "You should use tomato juice."

"That can be our fallback solution," Phyllis said as she began to spray the mixture on Buck's coat. She worked it in with her gloved hands.

Somewhat to her surprise, the stuff began to work almost immediately. When the skunk odor had dissipated quite a bit, Phyllis said, "We're supposed to hose him off now, but it's too cold out here for that. I think we're going to have to take him in and put him in the bathtub."

"Good Lord," Carolyn muttered under her breath. Phyllis ignored her.

"Are you sure you don't mind havin' a dog in the tub?" Sam asked.

"Well . . . I don't suppose it's what I would prefer under ideal circumstances, but I don't see that we have any choice."

"I sure appreciate this."

"Don't be silly," Phyllis said. "Buck is a part of the family now, isn't he?"

"It's mighty good of you to look at it like that."

Sam picked up the dog and carried him into the house. The downstairs bathroom didn't have a tub or a shower, so they had to take Buck upstairs. To protect the cast on his leg, Phyllis wrapped plastic around it and taped it in place; then they put Buck in the tub and used the handheld showerhead to wash off the deskunking solution.

"I'm sort of odiferous myself," Sam pointed out.

"You can wash your robe and pajamas with some peroxide and baking soda in the machine along with the regular detergent. That ought to take care of it."

"If you'll leave that spray bottle, I'll sluice myself off with the stuff once we get Buck taken care of," he said. "I don't know what's gonna get the smell out of the house, though."

"Vinegar," Phyllis said. "The same website where I got this recipe said to put out little bowls of vinegar and it would absorb the smell."

"Or cover it up, anyway."

"Well, I don't know about you, but I think I'd rather smell vinegar than skunk."

Sam laughed and nodded. "I guess that's what they call the lesser of two evils."

Buck didn't mind the bath, but he wasn't crazy about the hair dryer when Phyllis began to direct the warm air over him. Sam held on to him and tried to calm him down.

"You can't go back outside in that night air when you're damp," Sam said. "You might catch a chill."

"We need an actual dog bed that we can bring inside and put in the garage or the utility room when it's too cold for him to stay out," Phyllis suggested.

"That's a good idea. I should've thought of that before now. I've had plenty of dogs."

"Things are going pretty fast," Phyllis said. "There's a lot to keep up with."

"It's sort of like havin' a youngster again, isn't it?"

"Yes, it is," Phyllis said. Buck was the closest thing to a child that she and Sam would ever have, she thought. She frowned slightly to herself as she realized what an odd thought that was to cross her mind.

It took until well after midnight to get everything taken care of, but things finally settled down so that everyone could get some sleep. Phyllis hoped that no more skunks would come around, tonight or any other night.

But if they did, the backyard now had a fierce and de-voted—if somewhat reckless and impulsive—defender.

The vinegar worked to take the skunk odor out of the house, so that by the next day there was only a lingering scent of pole-cat that hung around the kitchen, Sam, and Buck. So even though Phyllis would have preferred that the nocturnal in-vader had stayed away to start with, at least she had learned something useful, she told herself.

Over breakfast that morning, Carolyn said, "You know, something occurred to me. The people at that vet clinic probably plan to hand out dog biscuits of their own at that Halloween party. You know, whatever kind they sell. It's an advertising gimmick. They might not appreciate us just show-ing up to hand out something that we made."

"That's a good point," Phyllis said with a frown. "Plus there's the matter of them not knowing what is in the treats. They might not trust us."

Sam said, "What do you mean? Like somebody might put poison in treats like that and give 'em out?"

"You should never underestimate the meanness in the world, Sam," Carolyn said. "I know you prefer to see the good in people, but unfortunately, that's in shorter supply than it used to be."

Eve said, "Yes, we've all heard stories about terrible things people have done on Halloween."

"Shoot. I always figured those were, what do you call 'em, urban legends," Sam said.

"Unfortunately, some of them were true," Phyllis said. "And Carolyn's got a good point. We can't just show up with doggie treats and expect Dr. Baxter and his staff to let us hand them out." She shrugged. "I guess we'll have to give up on the idea."

"Not at all," Carolyn responded instantly. "What it means is that you and I need to go out there and talk to this Dr. Bax-ter, Phyllis, so he'll know what sort of people we are and see that we don't mean any harm."

Phyllis thought about that for a moment and then nodded. "I don't suppose it would hurt," she said. "If Dr. Baxter refuses to go along with the idea, at least we tried."

"We'll go this morning," Carolyn said. Once she made up her mind, Phyllis knew, she didn't see any point in delaying what she intended to do.

Because of that, by ten o'clock the two of them were on their way to the veterinary clinic in Phyllis's car. When they got there, the place didn't appear to be nearly as busy as it had been the last time Phyllis was there. Only one car was in the parking lot.

They went inside and found the redheaded young woman behind the counter. Holly, that was her name, Phyllis recalled.

"Hello," she said. "My friend and I were wondering if we could talk to Dr. Baxter for a minute."

"Is this about a pet?"

"Well, not really. It's about the party you're having here next week." Phyllis pointed to the sign she had seen when she and Sam were there a few days before. "We were wondering if we could donate something for it."

"Well, I don't know. That would be up to Dr. Baxter. Did you see the barn when you drove up?"

"Around in the back?" Phyllis asked.

"That's right. He's back there checking out a goat. That's where he works with livestock."

"I didn't know you handled patients other than dogs and cats."

"Oh, yes," Holly said with a smile. "Goats, horses, cattle, pigs. Whatever you've got, Dr. Baxter will take a look at it if there's a problem. If he doesn't know what to do, he can send you to somebody who does."

"Well, we don't have any livestock, just a dog," Phyllis said.

Holly's face lit up with recognition. She said, "Sure, I remember you now. You're the mama of that Dalmatian with the broken leg, aren't you? Duke, right? No, wait. Buck, that was his name."

Phyllis smiled and nodded. "That's right," she said. "His name's Buck."

"How's he doing?"

"Very well, as far as I can tell. He gets around without much trouble, and he and Sam are getting along wonderfully."

"I'm glad to hear it." Holly pointed vaguely in the direction of the barn. "You and your friend can go on around there and talk to the doctor if you want."

"You're sure he won't mind?"

"No, I don't think so. You won't find a nicer guy than Hank."

"All right, thank you." Phyllis turned to Carolyn and added, "Let's go."

They were on their way out the door when Holly called behind them, "Have a good day, Mrs. Fletcher."

Phyllis let the door swing closed. As she did, she saw Carolyn looking over at her.

"What?" she said. "It's an honest enough mistake. I was here with Sam, and we never explained that we aren't married."

"It's none of my business," Carolyn said. "But the two of you *do* have a dog together now. Evidently that means something these days."

"We don't have a dog together," Phyllis said. "Buck is Sam's dog."

"Maybe . . . but it was you washing the skunk smell off of him last night." Carolyn paused. "Buck, that is. I don't really know how Sam managed. I'm not sure I want to know."

Phyllis rolled her eyes and said, "Get in the car."

"I'm just saying."

It would be easier to just go ahead and let Carolyn have the last word, Phyllis decided. They got in the car, and she followed the drive around from the parking lot to the big metal barn about fifty yards behind the clinic. The building's double doors were open, as they had been the last time Phyllis was there. She spotted Dr. Hank Baxter kneeling just inside the opening next to a wooly, short-legged goat.

Baxter glanced curiously in their direction as Phyllis stopped the car and she and Carolyn got out, but most of his attention was on the goat. His left hand stroked the animal's pelt to keep it calm, while his right held the end of a rectal thermometer he was using to check the goat's temperature.

"Hello, ladies," he said. "I'll be with you in . . . just one minute."

A moment later he withdrew the thermometer, looked at it, and nodded in satisfaction.

"Your temperature's back to normal, Festus," he told the goat. "Looks like we've got that little respiratory infection licked. I figured we did when I saw you got your appetite back this morning."

He straightened, set the thermometer aside on a little table, and opened the gate of a stall to herd the goat back inside. Then he closed the gate and turned to Phyllis and Carolyn with a smile.

"I appreciate your patience," he told them. "I didn't want to get distracted while I was doing that. I let go of a thermometer once when I was taking a goat's temperature, and it, uh, sort of slipped farther in than it should have."

"That's terrible," Carolyn said. "What did you do?"

"Well, I had to go in and get it, of course. Luckily, the problem didn't require surgery, just determination on my part and tolerance on the part of the goat."

Phyllis had to laugh. She said, "That's a very cute goat. Is it a baby?"

"Nope, full-grown. That's a Nigerian dwarf goat. They don't get very big. At least, the ones that are fit to be show goats don't. Now, what can I do for you ladies?"

"I'm Phyllis Newsom, and this is my friend Carolyn Wilbarger. I was here several days ago with my other friend Sam Fletcher and his dog Buck."

"Sure, Buck, with the broken leg," Baxter said, nodding. "How's he doing? No problems, I hope?"

"No, he's fine, other than a run-in with a skunk."

"Ooh. Sorry. That'll happen. Buck didn't get bit, did he? Skunks are notorious carriers of rabies."

"No. The skunk just sprayed him a little."

"I'm glad to hear it. No problem with the cast?"

"Not so far."

Baxter nodded. He looked like he was starting to get puzzled.

Phyllis went on. "The reason we're here is that I saw the sign in your clinic about the Halloween party next week."

"Yeah, that's something we do every year," Baxter said, smiling again. "I don't know how much the animals really appreciate it, but the owners and their families get a big kick out of it. We hold it late enough during the afternoon that kids can come after school. People love to take pictures of their pets dressed up in costumes and see all the other pets, too."

"And it's a good way to advertise the dog biscuits you give out, too, I suppose," Carolyn said.

"What?" Baxter shook his head and waved off that idea. "Nah. I don't care about that. It's just for people to have fun. You know, most of the time when people bring their pets to a vet clinic, it's because of a problem. Usually the animals have something wrong with them, sometimes something serious, and so they're scared and upset and their owners are, too, and those are the feelings they associate with the clinic. I want 'em to come on Halloween just to enjoy themselves and see that it's not so bad here, at least not all the time."

"That's an excellent idea," Phyllis said. "Carolyn and I were talking about homemade dog treats, and we got the idea we'd like to make some and bring them over for the party."

"Really?" Baxter seemed surprised by the idea. He thought it over for a moment with a look of concentration on his face before he began to nod. "Well, that sounds like something we might be able to do. What sort of ingredients were you thinking about putting in them? They'd have to be healthy."

"Of course. I was going to make some with sweet potato and peanut butter."

Baxter chuckled and said, "A couple of things that dogs really like. What about you, Ms. Wilbarger?"

Carolyn hesitated, and Phyllis knew that her competitive nature made her want to keep her recipe a secret. She couldn't very well do that, though, if they wanted Baxter to go along with the idea, so she said, "I was thinking of using pumpkin and oatmeal."

"That sounds like the dogs would really go for it, too," Baxter said.

"You don't mind, then?" Phyllis asked.

"No. If you ladies want to do that, go right ahead. Don't just bring the treats and drop them off, though. I expect you to stay and party with us."

"We'll be looking forward to it."

"Well, if that's all, I need to call the owners of this goat and tell them that ol' Festus is doing better and they can come pick him up."

Phyllis said, "Thank you, Dr. Baxter," and she and Carolyn started toward the car.

At that moment, an SUV drove around the vet clinic and headed for the barn. Baxter saw it coming and muttered, "Uh-oh."

"What's wrong?" Phyllis asked.

Before Baxter could answer, the SUV came to a stop and a burly man in a flannel shirt and a baseball cap got out. He looked angry and ready to plunge right into trouble . . . or start some himself.

Chapter 6

*B*axter moved forward to get between the newcomer and Phyllis and Carolyn. He didn't seem to be hurrying, but Phyllis noticed that it didn't take him long to cover the distance. He gave the man in the flannel shirt a curt nod and said, "Hello, Kyle. What can I do for you?"

"You know good and well what you can—" The man stopped short. He looked at Phyllis and Carolyn as if he had just noticed they were there. With a visible effort, he controlled his temper.

Baxter turned to Phyllis and went on. "Thanks for coming by, ladies. I'll see you next week. Buck's appointment is the day before Halloween, isn't it?"

"I think that's right," Phyllis said.

"Then I'll see you twice."

Clearly, Baxter wanted the two women to leave before he continued his conversation with this man, Kyle. Phyllis wasn't sure that was a good idea. Kyle might not be as likely to cause trouble if there were witnesses.

Of course, she might be overreacting, Phyllis reminded herself. Just because Kyle was annoyed about something didn't mean he was going to throw a punch at Baxter or anything like that. Anyway, even if he did, Baxter was a relatively young man who seemed to be very fit. Kyle was older, in his forties, with a considerable paunch. He was taller and heavier than Hank Baxter, though.

"Come on, Phyllis," Carolyn said. "Let's let these men get on with their business."

"All right," Phyllis said. She was still uneasy about leaving Baxter there alone with Kyle, but on the other hand, this was none of her affair. As she opened her car door, she added, "See you next week, Dr. Baxter."

The veterinarian lifted a hand in farewell as Phyllis and Carolyn got in the car. Phyllis turned the car around and drove away.

As she passed the SUV, she saw a sign on the vehicle's door that read WOODS'S GOLDEN RETRIEVERS, with a phone number and a website underneath it. Out of habit, she filed that information away in her brain.

"That man certainly seemed to be upset about something," Carolyn commented as they passed the clinic building and headed up the driveway to the street.

"Yes, and I'm not sure we should have left," Phyllis said.

"Dr. Baxter can take care of himself, I would think. Besides, it's the middle of the morning. Broad daylight. What could possibly . . . ? Oh. I forgot for a minute there who I was talking to."

"Don't start that," Phyllis said. "I go plenty of places and do plenty of things without anybody being murdered. Good grief."

Carolyn didn't say anything for a long moment. Then, "I don't know about you, but I think I'll be watching the news tonight anyway."

Despite what she had told Carolyn, despite what she wanted to believe herself, Phyllis had to admit that deep down she was relieved when there was nothing on the news that night about any sort of trouble at a veterinary clinic in Weatherford.

Just to be sure, though, the next day she called her son, Mike, who was a Parker County deputy sheriff, and asked him to check.

He promised to do so, but then asked, "What are you mixed up in now, Mom?"

"What do you mean?" Phyllis said. "I'm not mixed up in anything."

"Then why ask about possible trouble at some vet clinic?"

"It's the one where Sam took his new dog. I told you about that, remember?"

"Sure, but it doesn't explain why you thought something might have happened there," Mike said.

Phyllis hesitated, then said, "I was there yesterday, and there was a man who was upset with the doctor about something. I felt bad about leaving."

"Well, you shouldn't. The last thing you need to be doing is getting involved in a fistfight."

"I know, but I can't help being curious."

"Being curious has gotten you in trouble before," Mike pointed out.

"Yes, and it's gotten some people *out* of trouble who didn't deserve to be there, too," Phyllis responded.

He knew perfectly well what she meant. She had cleared the names of several people wrongly accused of murder, and the real killers in those cases were now behind bars because of her curiosity and determination.

Since Mike couldn't argue with what she had just said, he told her, "I'll see what I can find out. In the meantime, try to stay out of trouble."

"I'm your mother. Shouldn't I be saying that to you?"

"You'd think so. I'll call you back, Mom."

Mike hung up, and Phyllis said, "Hmph." He was probably right, but he could have been more polite about it.

With that taken care of, she went to her computer. Sam was in the backyard with Buck, Carolyn was in the kitchen, and Eve sat in one of the armchairs on the other side of the living room with her needlework basket in her lap. Eve had never been much of one for crafts, but she had taken it up more in recent months.

Phyllis remembered the website she had seen on the door of the angry man's pickup at the vet clinic the day before. She opened a new tab and entered it, and a moment later she was looking at the site for Woods's Golden Retrievers.

A large photo of a handsome golden retriever dominated the site's home page. According to the graphic under the photo, the dog's name was Texas Maximus, and he was an award-winning show dog who had brought home trophies from all over the country. He had even competed in the National Dog Show, the one that was on television every Thanksgiving after the parades. Phyllis figured she must have seen him, since they always watched the dog show. Well, she watched as much as she could while cooking. It had become a tradition in her house.

There were other pages with more pictures of the award-winning Texas Maximus, along with other dogs that had come from the breeding operation run by Kyle Woods. As soon as Phyllis saw a picture of Woods, she knew he was the same man who had driven up to the barn at Dr. Baxter's place while she and Carolyn were there.

He didn't look nearly as angry and threatening in these photos, of course. In fact, he wore a friendly smile on his face. The flannel shirt and baseball cap seemed to be his usual garb. He had them on in just about every picture. He was always with one of the dogs, either Texas Maximus or another golden retriever. Phyllis couldn't really tell them apart, but she supposed an aficionado of the breed could.

She clicked on Woods's bio and found that he had been in the dog-breeding business for fifteen years and was widely respected as a breeder of golden retrievers. Texas Maximus was the best dog he'd ever had, but a number of others had won awards as well.

Texas Maximus was also available for stud service, and when Phyllis checked out that page, she was surprised at the fees Woods charged. They weren't exactly astronomical, but they were higher than Phyllis would have expected. But to be honest, if someone had asked her what dog breeders charged for that particular service, she wouldn't have had any idea. But Woods's fees just seemed high. He had to be making a pretty penny off of Texas Maximus.

Of course, the dog probably wasn't complaining about being exploited.

There wasn't much about Woods's personal life on the website. Phyllis decided she had learned all she was going to, so she closed that tab and started to stand up from the computer.

She stopped and on a hunch did a quick Internet search for Woods, on both the Web and in the blogosphere. Sam had taught her about that. She was surprised by the sheer number of Webpages and blogs about dog breeding that the search turned up. It would take a long time to go through all of them, so she began clicking on the links at random.

It appeared that Woods was well respected as a breeder, but Phyllis got the impression from the blogs that he wasn't particularly well-liked. Some of the comments on various posts referred to him as arrogant and short-tempered. Phyllis could believe that, having seen the way he looked the day before when he'd gotten out of his pickup and confronted Hank Baxter.

On the other hand, she didn't find anything to indicate that he mistreated his dogs. That was one point in his favor, she supposed. There was nothing to make her think he was anything other than honest in his business dealings, too.

"Whatcha doin'?" Sam asked from behind her. Phyllis had been so caught up in her research that she hadn't heard him come in. He went on. "You're not thinkin' about gettin' a dog yourself, are you?"

"No, of course not," she said as she turned the monitor off. "I think one dog is plenty around here, don't you?"

"Well, I don't know," Sam said as he scratched his jaw. "Buck might enjoy havin' a playmate, and that backyard's probably big enough for two dogs. I reckon it'd be better to wait and see about that, though."

Phyllis stood up and nodded. She said, "I think so, too."

"So why were you lookin' at dog-breedin' websites?"

Sam was certainly being persistent today, she thought. And she didn't really have a good answer for him, either. No crime had been committed that she was aware of. And yet she had been checking out Kyle Woods as she would have done if he were a suspect in a murder she was investigating.

Was she becoming completely paranoid?

Well, no, that wasn't exactly the situation, she told herself. She didn't think Woods was out to get *her*. Woods didn't even know who she was. By now there was a very good chance that he had forgotten all about seeing her at the vet clinic.

Overly suspicious . . . that was a better description of how she was feeling right now.

Those thoughts flashed through her mind in a second. Sam was still waiting for an answer, so she said, "I was just curious, is all. I might be interested in getting another dog someday. But it was just idle speculation."

Without looking up from her needlework, Eve said, "You may have just opened a door there, dear."

"Nah, don't worry about it," Sam said. "Right now my hands are plenty full takin' care of Buck. It's been a while since I've had a dog. I'd sort of forgotten just how much work they can be, especially one who's got to have pills like he does." Sam smiled. "Lucky for me he's got a good appetite and gobbles down whatever I put in front of him. It's been pretty easy hidin' his pills in his food."

Phyllis eased toward the kitchen, glad that Sam's mind seemed to have moved on from finding her looking at dog-breeding websites. She didn't want him to think that she had become obsessed with crime!

When she went into the kitchen, Carolyn said, "There you are. I've been thinking about something."

Not the same things she had been thinking about, Phyllis would have been willing to bet.

"We're making treats for the dogs at that Halloween party," Carolyn went on, "but I'm sure the humans would like something, too. Why don't we bake some cookies and take them with us to the party?"

"You mean something we'd come up with together?" Phyllis asked.

"I suppose so. We don't want to overdo it."

Phyllis was glad to hear that. One informal competition between the two of them was enough. She nodded and said, "I think that sounds like a fine idea. What sort of cookies were you considering?"

For the next few minutes, they discussed the subject and wound up agreeing that they would bake a batch of coconut cream pie cookies, which sounded both delicious and intriguing to Phyllis. It was mostly Carolyn's idea, but that didn't bother her.

When the phone rang, Mike's number came up on the caller ID. Phyllis recognized it and said, "I've got it."

When she answered, Mike said, "I looked into that thing you asked me about, Mom. There were no reports of any trouble yesterday at any vet clinic, anywhere in Parker County. Does that put your mind at ease?"

"As a matter of fact, it does. Thank you, Mike." She paused. "What are you and Sarah doing for Halloween with Bobby?"

"Oh, the usual, I guess. Trick-or-treating in the neighborhood, maybe go to the fall festival at the church. And we'll come by your house, too. Bobby would be disappointed if his grandma didn't get to see him in his costume."

"What is it?"

Mike chuckled and said, "That would be telling. You'll see it next week."

"All right," Phyllis said with a smile. "The reason I asked, there's going to be a party at that vet clinic I was talking about."

"A Halloween party for animals?"

"And their owners. Carolyn and I are going, and I thought Bobby might like to see all the pets dressed up in their costumes."

"He probably would get a kick out of that," Mike said. "Where and when is it?"

Phyllis told him, and he promised to pass along the information to his wife, Sarah.

"I can't make any promises until I check with her, but we'll try to make it," he said. "So long, Mom."

Phyllis thanked him again for his help and said good-bye.

So that was it, she thought when she had hung up. There was absolutely no reason for her to be suspicious about anything.

Chapter 7

*T*he days went by quickly. Phyllis and Carolyn worked on their recipes for the contest in *A Taste of Texas*, for their doggie treats, and for the coconut cream pie cookies. Although they kept the contest recipes to themselves for the moment, the other recipes were no secret and Buck seemed to be perfectly happy to serve as a guinea pig for the different kinds of treats.

When he gobbled down both treats with equal enthusiasm, Carolyn said, "See? What did I tell you? Dogs just aren't very discriminating in their taste."

"Why are we doing this, then?" Phyllis wanted to know.

"For the dogs, of course. And who knows? They might prefer one over the other, and we know they'll have healthy treats."

Sam volunteered his services as a taster for the coconut cream pie cookies, and so did Mike and Bobby when they were over at Phyllis's house on Sunday afternoon. The cookies were a big hit and helped take their mind off the latest travails of the Dallas Cowboys as they watched that week's game on TV.

Monday dawned blustery, with a chilly wind and thick gray clouds scudding across the sky. That was typical autumn weather in Texas, too, replacing the glorious fall days they had been experiencing.

From the kitchen window, Phyllis could see Buck huddled in his doghouse. She said over her shoulder to Sam, who sat at the table sipping coffee, "You haven't bought a bed for Buck so we can bring him inside yet, have you?"

"Nope. Meant to this weekend, but I never got around to it."

"Well, I think you should today. He looks fine out there in his doghouse, but I'll bet he'd be more comfortable inside."

"Are you sure you're all right with that?"

"Well . . . I don't particularly want him on the furniture, but I don't see anything wrong with letting him stay in the utility room."

Phyllis knew Carolyn would poke fun at her when she found out about this, but at least she hadn't done as Carolyn had predicted. She hadn't waited for Sam to ask her if he could bring Buck in the house. She had made the offer on her own initiative.

"All right. I'll take care of it this morning," Sam said. "I'm supposed to take Buck back to the vet this afternoon for his follow-up on that busted leg."

"Do you want me to help you?"

"Sure, anytime. I'm always glad to have your company, Phyllis. You know that."

She smiled and said, "All right. You get the bed this morning, and we'll take him to see Dr. Baxter this afternoon."

"And tomorrow afternoon's the Halloween party. Gonna be a busy week."

Sam came back from the store with a large, comfortable-looking bed for Buck.

"It's made out of orthopedic foam," he explained as he placed the bed in the utility room, next to the dryer. That would be a nice warm place for Buck to curl up. "Figured with his busted leg he might appreciate the support. I know how much better a good mattress makes you feel."

Phyllis put down a water bowl, and Sam brought Buck in from the back porch. The Dalmatian looked warily at the new bed for a moment before he stepped up on it, turned around several times, and finally lay down and curled up. He sighed in what seemed to be contentment.

"There you go," Sam told him. "Just don't get the idea that you're a full-time house dog now, fella. You're still gonna be spendin' most of your time outside when the weather's nice."

Buck just looked at him as if to say, *We'll see about that.*

After lunch they got into Sam's pickup with Phyllis driving and Sam holding Buck in his lap, as they had done before. Buck wasn't hungover and groggy from the anesthetic this time, so he squirmed more than he had on the previous trip. He put his nose to the window and watched the landscape passing by with great interest.

A couple of cars were in the vet clinic parking lot, but the waiting room was empty when Phyllis and Sam went inside. Holly sat on a stool behind the counter, and as soon as Phyllis saw the redhead's face, she knew something was wrong.

It took her only a second to realize what that something was. Loud, angry voices came from behind a closed door off the hallway behind the counter. That was Dr. Baxter's office, Phyllis thought. She couldn't make out the words, but she could tell the voices belonged to a man and a woman. From their tone, it was obvious what was going on.

Only a married couple fought with that much passion and intensity.

Holly gave Phyllis and Sam a weak smile and said, "Hi, Mr. and Mrs. Fletcher. Why don't you take Buck into that exam room and I'll be with you in just a second?"

She pointed to the second door marked EXAM ROOM that opened off the waiting room.

Sam nodded and said, "That'll be fine." Phyllis opened the door for him, and he carried Buck into the exam room and set him on the metal table.

"Goodness," Phyllis said quietly as she closed the door. "That didn't sound pleasant."

Before Sam could say anything, the door on the other side of the room opened and Holly came in from the rear hallway. She put Buck's folder on the counter next to the sink and asked, "How's he doing?"

"Just great, as far as we can tell," Sam replied. "I haven't had to give him any pain pills in a few days, and he's been leavin' the cast alone."

"That's fine. Dr. Baxter will be with you in a few minutes."

She left them there, and when she was gone, Sam said, "I'm sorry about that Mrs. Fletcher business."

"Oh, don't worry about it," Phyllis said. "It's not the first time she's made that mistake. She's not the first one to do it, either."

"Maybe not, but I don't want you to be uncomfortable."

"Do I act like I'm uncomfortable?"

"Well, no, but . . ."

"I'm fine with things, Sam," Phyllis said. "If anybody else isn't, that's their problem, not ours."

"I reckon you're right about that."

Several minutes went by in relative silence. These rooms weren't very big, Phyllis thought. Anybody who was claustrophobic might start getting nervous pretty quickly in them. She was content, though, to just sit and wait with Sam and Buck.

Phyllis heard people talking through the walls, but these voices didn't sound angry, so she figured Dr. Baxter was in the exam room next door, dealing with whatever sort of patient was in there. More time passed. Sitting in a vet's exam room was a lot like sitting in a regular doctor's exam room, she thought. Even though everything was fine, after a while you couldn't help but start to feel a little nervous and uncomfortable.

Maybe she was a little claustrophobic after all. She hadn't liked being locked up in a jail cell, either, she recalled.

Whatever the cause, it was a real relief when the rear door opened and Dr. Baxter came into the room. He looked a little harried, but he put a smile on his face as he nodded to them.

"Hello, folks. Sorry you had to wait. We were dealing with a little, ah, emergency."

"That's all right," Sam said. "These things happen in doctors' offices."

Baxter said, "They do in this one, anyway." He grimaced slightly, as if he couldn't help it, and then gave a little shake of his head. "So, how's Buck doing?"

For the next few minutes, they discussed Buck's recovery.

Baxter checked his temperature, listened to his heart and respiration, and looked at his eyes and teeth.

"His appetite is good?"

"His appetite is fine," Sam said. "He seems like a perfectly healthy dog except for the broken leg."

"That's because he is," Baxter said. "His heart and lungs sound great. Another four weeks and we'll take X-rays to see about getting that cast off. The fracture and the incision should be healed by then, and he'll be set for a long, happy life, I hope."

"He will be if I have anything to say about it," Sam declared, and once again Phyllis was struck by the amount of feeling he had for this dog.

Baxter looked at Phyllis and asked, "Are you and your friend still coming tomorrow with the dog treats?"

"Yes, we are," she said. "With all you have going on around here, I'm surprised you remembered."

"Hey, it's a nice thing to do. I try to remember people who do nice things."

"We're bringing some coconut cream pie cookies for the adults. I mean the people. The humans." Phyllis laughed. "Goodness, I'm starting to think of pets as people's babies, too."

"It's hard not to. Animals are part of the family. At least, that's the way it ought to be." He didn't explain what he meant by that. "I'll see you tomorrow, I suppose, and I'd like to see Buck again in another week just to monitor him. There's no charge for this today, since it was just a follow-up."

Phyllis and Sam left the exam room through the front door. Baxter went out the back, but he circled around and came up behind the counter in the waiting room.

"Give Buck an appointment for next Monday or Tuesday, Holly," he told the redhead.

"Of course, Dr. Baxter," she said as she swiveled her stool to look at her computer monitor and reached for the mouse.

The glass front door of the clinic opened. The blond woman Phyllis had seen there before came in and said sharply, "One more thing, Hank."

Baxter looked angry, uncomfortable, and embarrassed, all at the same time. He said, "Good Lord, Susan, have you been sitting out there in your car all this time, stewing?"

"No. I started to go back to my office, but I decided I couldn't let you get away with it so I turned around."

"Get away with what, for God's sake?"

"Her," Susan Baxter said as she leveled a finger at Holly. "How dare you accuse me of anything when you have *her* right here in your office?"

"What?" Baxter rested both hands on the counter and leaned forward. He seemed to have forgotten that Phyllis and Sam were there. "Are you insane? There's nothing going on between Holly and me. She runs the office and helps out as an assistant. That's all."

Holly looked like she wanted to crawl under the counter and hide, but she swallowed hard and said, "It really is, Mrs. Baxter. I mean, Dr. Baxter."

Susan gave her an unpleasant smirk and said, "Well, of course you'd say that. But I know the truth."

"No, you really don't—" Holly began.

Baxter broke in with a bitter edge to his voice. "Don't waste your breath. She only believes what she wants to believe."

Susan snorted and said, "That's because I'm not a fool."

She turned, jerked the door open, and stalked out of the office, leaving an uncomfortable silence behind her.

"Well," Baxter said into that silence after a few heartbeats, "looks like I owe you another apology."

"Nope," Sam said. "None of our business. I'm sorry for your troubles, though."

Baxter shrugged and said, "These things happen, I guess. People can't get along all the time, even when they're married."

"Especially when they're married," Phyllis said. "But I'm sure your wife didn't really mean what she said."

"Oh, she meant it. But she's wrong. There's nothing going on here that shouldn't be."

"Of course not," Holly said quickly. "In fact, I'm dating Tommy. We're talking about getting married and going to veterinary school together."

"Which I think is a great idea," Baxter said, "although I'd hate to lose the two of you here at the clinic." He forced a smile back onto his face and went on. "I'll be out in the barn, Holly."

"All right, Doctor."

Baxter went down the hall and out a rear door. Sam cleared his throat and said to Holly, "You were about to make us an appointment for next week."

"Oh, of course, that's right." Holly checked her computer again and asked, "How about Monday at one o'clock?"

"Sounds good to me." Sam looked at Phyllis as if asking her if that was all right with her.

"You know me," she said. "My schedule is wide-open."

"All right. I've got you down." Holly picked up a pen and wrote the date and time on a card, which she slid across the counter to Phyllis. "I'm sorry you folks had to be subjected to that scene."

"Don't worry about it," Phyllis said. "I thought Mrs. Baxter was a doctor, too."

"Oh, she is. She's a surgeon."

"She doesn't seem to keep regular office hours. This is twice she's been here when you'd think she would be in her own office."

"She's a very good doctor. People are willing to wait for her, I guess."

Sam said, "I'm sorta glad she didn't become a vet, too. Not sure I'd want her takin' care of ol' Buck here."

"Yes, I have to admit I feel sorry for Hank sometimes," Holly said. "I shouldn't say that, but it's true." She took a deep breath and went on. "Oh, well. I'll see you tomorrow at the party, I guess."

"Is Mrs. Baxter coming?" Phyllis asked.

"I don't think so." Holly's tone made it clear she hoped that would be the case.

Phyllis and Sam both thanked Holly and left the office. As they were driving away, Sam said, "That redheaded gal may be datin' the other fella who works here, but I'd say she's got a little crush on the doc, too."

"When she's not thinking about it, she calls him Hank instead of Dr. Baxter," Phyllis said. "Of course, it could be that's just because it's an informal office."

"Yeah, maybe," Sam said, but he didn't sound convinced of it.

Phyllis wasn't, either. She had no real reason to think that Dr. Baxter was having an affair with Holly, and she hoped that wasn't the case. She felt an instinctive liking for Baxter. That would be diminished if she knew he was cheating on his wife . . . even a wife seemingly as unpleasant as Susan Baxter.

Luckily, it was none of her business, and she intended to keep it that way.

Chapter 8

The weather was still cool and cloudy the next day, but it wasn't supposed to rain and Phyllis was glad about that. Rain would spoil trick-or-treating for the kids, and even though that wasn't as big a deal these days as it had been when she was young, she knew the children still enjoyed it.

Also, rain would have interfered with the party at the vet clinic, so she hoped the forecast was right and the precipitation would stay away.

She and Carolyn already had the dog treats baked and bagged up, so they spent the morning making a big new batch of the coconut cream pie cookies, and since they had some leftover pumpkin, they made pumpkin oatmeal cookies, too. After lunch, once the cookies had cooled, they filled plastic containers with them, leaving a good-sized plate of them for there at the house.

"Are you and Buck going to the party with us?" Phyllis asked Sam. "I know you said you're not fond of animals in costumes. He would look very dashing as a pirate, or with a name like Buck, he would probably rather be a cowboy. A leather vest and a cowboy hat . . ."

"We'll come along, but I still don't want to make him wear a costume," he replied. "With the shock of the accident and having a new owner, I don't want to put him through anything else new. It won't hurt Buck to be around other animals, though. I'd like to see how well he gets along with 'em. If he doesn't, he needs to learn how to."

"I can't imagine him not getting along," Phyllis said. "He seems so friendly."

"Yeah, with us he is. But there's no tellin' how he might act with other animals. Only one way to find out."

"That's true. And I'm glad you're coming, anyway."

When it came time to load up and leave, Sam put a halter on Buck and clipped a leash to it. That way Buck could walk around at the clinic. Sam carried the Dalmatian in his lap while Phyllis drove the pickup, since that method had been working well. Carolyn followed in her car with the dog treats and the cookies.

The clinic's parking lot was nearly full when they got there, which was the most crowded Phyllis had seen it. A large canopy was set up on metal poles next to the building. A folding table had been carried out and placed underneath it. A couple of ice chests with bottled water and soft drinks in them sat on the table, along with open boxes of assorted dog treats.

More than a dozen boys and girls in an assortment of costumes ran around and played in the grassy area between the clinic building and the barn. A number of dogs dressed in Halloween outfits cavorted with them. As Phyllis got out of the pickup, she saw cheerleader dogs, Darth Vader dogs, pirate dogs, dinosaur dogs, gorilla dogs, and others she couldn't even identify.

There were a few cats, too, but their costumes consisted of little hats with earholes cut out of them. Judging by their expressions, the cats were already plotting revenge for this humiliation.

Several bales of hay were stacked up in a pyramid to provide a photo backdrop where parents could take pictures of their costumed children and pets. Several families were waiting their turn to do that.

Holly stood under the canopy, handing out drinks and talking to the visitors. Phyllis didn't see Dr. Baxter or Tommy, the other assistant.

She looked around for other familiar faces, thinking that Mike, Sarah, and Bobby might already be there, but she didn't see them. As Carolyn pulled up, Phyllis went over to her car to help her with the cookies and dog treats.

Sam set Buck on the ground and let him walk around. Some of the other dogs came up to him, and for a few moments there was a considerable amount of ritual sniffing going on. None of the dogs growled, though, so everything seemed to be friendly.

Phyllis carried the plastic bags full of dog treats while Carolyn brought the containers of cookies to the table. Holly saw them coming and greeted them with a friendly grin.

"Hi, Mrs. Fletcher," she said.

"Hello, Holly," Phyllis replied.

Carolyn said, "Are you ever going to set her straight about that?"

Holly's grin faltered a little. She said, "Set me straight about what?"

"It's nothing, really," Phyllis said. She wished that Carolyn hadn't brought up the subject, but since she had, it might be best just to go ahead and settle it. "Actually, I'm not Mrs. Fletcher. Sam and I aren't married. We're just friends. My name is Phyllis Newsom."

"Oh, dear, I'm sorry, Ms. Newsom! I just assumed since the two of you are always together . . ."

"I've just been helping him out with Buck, that's all."

"Well," Carolyn added, "I'd hardly say that's all. And the two of you are certainly more than just friends, too."

Holly held up her hands and said, "Hey, none of my business. I'm just sorry if I made anybody uncomfortable."

"Not at all," Phyllis assured her. To change the subject, she asked, "Where are Dr. Baxter and Tommy today? I thought they would be here."

"They're here," Holly said. She inclined her head toward the clinic building. "They're inside dealing with an emergency that came in a little while ago. Just because it's Halloween doesn't mean pets stop having problems. In fact, it's sort of a dangerous time of year for dogs and cats. There's so much they can get into that can hurt them. This dog got into a candy stash and ate a bunch of chocolate."

"Is he going to be all right?" Phyllis asked.

"I'm pretty sure he is. His folks got him here really quickly. But let's not dwell on bad stuff. What have you got there?"

"Cookies—coconut cream pie and pumpkin oatmeal for the humans," Phyllis said as she took the lids off the plastic containers and slid them underneath the containers on the table. She opened one of the bags. "And these are peanut-butter-and-sweet-potato doggie treats."

"Oh, how adorable!" Holly said with a big smile on her face again. "They're cut into shapes. Those are ducks, aren't they?"

Phyllis nodded and said, "Ducks, dogs, and bones."

"That's really cute."

Carolyn opened the other bag and said, "And these are pumpkin oatmeal cut out into little jack-o'-lanterns."

"I'm sure the dogs will love them. Would you ladies like something to drink?"

"I wouldn't mind a bottle of water," Phyllis said. Carolyn just shook her head.

After Holly had given her the water, Phyllis looked around for Sam and spotted him and Buck near the bales of hay. A group of children had gathered around them and were petting Buck, who seemed to be thoroughly enjoying the attention. Children were always attracted to Dalmatians, Phyllis thought. There was just something about those spotted dogs that appealed to youngsters.

A couple with a young daughter and a Chihuahua in matching ballerina costumes came up to the table. Holly offered them cookies, which they took with enthusiasm, and Carolyn broke a piece off one of her treats and offered it to the dog, who took it in her mouth, dropped it on the ground for a moment, and then ate it delicately.

Carolyn looked at Phyllis, who saw that old competitive gleam in her friend's eyes. She knew Carolyn would be disappointed if it wasn't a fair contest, so she broke a piece off one of her treats and offered it to the ballerina Chihuahua.

This time the little dog gobbled down the treat without any hesitation at all. Not a crumb touched the ground.

"She likes it!" the little girl said around a mouthful of coconut cream pie cookie.

"Of course she does," the girl's mother said. "Now, what do you tell the nice ladies?"

"Thank you!" the little girl said, practically squealing with joy. It was clear she was having a great time.

"You're very welcome," Phyllis told her.

"And so is your little dog," Carolyn added. She didn't sound quite so cheerful now that the Chihuahua had acted like it preferred Phyllis's treat to hers.

But the competition, such as it was, was young yet. Carolyn began breaking more pieces off the treat she held and offering them to the smaller costumed dogs and whole treats to the bigger dogs that passed by the table with their owners. A few of the cats took the treats, but most turned their noses up. Phyllis realized they should have made something different for the cats. She hadn't even thought about them.

After half an hour or so, Phyllis saw Mike's SUV pull into the parking lot. All the spaces were full, so Mike had to park on the grass next to the driveway. A few other visitors had already done that. The vehicle's doors opened, and Mike and Sarah got out. Mike wore his deputy's uniform.

One of the SUV's back doors opened and Bobby climbed out. He was dressed as Sherlock Holmes, in a long coat and a deerstalker hat. As he ran toward Phyllis, he called, "Grandma!"

Phyllis thought he was adorable, although she figured he was too young to really know anything about Sherlock Holmes. She knelt to gather him into a hug. He was too big now for her to sweep him up into her arms as she had done when he was a toddler.

Those days were long gone. He would be in school soon, and as Phyllis thought about that, she felt a pang inside at how fast he was growing and how time was racing by like a rocket. That was just part of growing older, she told herself, and it came to everyone, from Bobby with practically his whole life in front of him to her with the years of her life dwindling.

She put those thoughts out of her mind. This was no time for melancholy. She rested her hands on Bobby's shoulders, smiled at him, and said, "Sam and Buck are right over there. Do you want to go see them?"

He nodded eagerly.

"Well, here, take a cookie with you," she said as she handed one to him.

"And take a doggie treat for Buck," Carolyn added. She gave a piece from one of her treats to Bobby.

Phyllis let that go. Bobby hurried over to join Sam and Buck near the hay bales.

As Mike and Sarah came up to the table, Phyllis said, "You dressed him as a great detective for Halloween?"

"Hey, I thought it was appropriate," Mike said with a grin. "Considering who his grandmother is and all."

"Don't start," Phyllis warned him.

"I told him the same thing," Sarah said. She was a smart, pretty blonde, a perfect match for Mike, and Phyllis couldn't have asked for a better daughter-in-law. "You have to admit that he's adorable, though."

"Mike or Bobby?"

Sarah laughed and said, "Well, I was talking about Bobby, but Mike has his adorable moments, too, I suppose."

"Gee, thanks," he said. "Careful with all the flattery. You'll give me a swelled head."

"It's too late to worry about that."

"Have some cookies," Carolyn invited them.

Mike took one from the plastic container and said, "I knew you were bringing some of these today. I've been looking forward to them."

"Just don't eat so many that you ruin your appetite for supper," Sarah told him.

"Not much chance of that."

Phyllis felt the pleasurable warmth of having her family around her. At moments like this, she missed Kenny so fiercely it was like a physical thing, and she thought about what a shame it was he hadn't lived to see his grandson grow up. But Bobby had been born before he passed away, so he had known that he had a grandson, anyway, and he had seen for himself what a fine young man Mike had grown into. That was life, Phyllis thought, a potent mixture of blessings and loss.

A few minutes later, Dr. Baxter came out a side door from the clinic and headed for the table under the canopy. As he walked up to them, Phyllis said, "Hello, Doctor. Is that dog you were working on going to be all right?"

A tired but pleased smile curved Baxter's mouth. He nodded and said, "Yeah, he'll be fine. Thank goodness his owners got him here in time." He looked around the area between the clinic and the barn. "Looks like we've got a good turnout. Are these the famous doggie treats?"

"I'm not sure how famous they are," Phyllis said.

"But they've been pretty popular so far," Carolyn added.

"I'm sure they have been." Baxter picked up one of Phyllis's treats that was shaped like a duck and broke off the bill. Before she really realized what he was doing, he put the piece in his mouth and started chewing on it.

Clearly as startled as Phyllis was, Carolyn said, "That's a dog treat! The people cookies are over here."

Baxter swallowed and said, "Oh, I know that. But what's in this? Sweet potatoes, peanut butter, and oatmeal, right? Nothing harmful there." He chuckled. "Although if you were making them for human consumption, you'd probably want to add a little sugar. Still, they're not bad. I'll try one of those coconut cream pie cookies now."

He was reaching for the cookie when he stopped short and stiffened. Phyllis wondered what was wrong. She saw Baxter gazing up the driveway toward the road and turned to look in that direction herself.

Two Weatherford police cars had turned in and were coming toward the clinic.

Sam must have noticed them, too. He came over leading Buck and asked, "Were you supposed to get a permit for this shindig, Doc?"

"I don't know," Baxter said. "I didn't even think about that. But we've had Halloween parties like this before and never had any trouble."

Mike said, "I'll go talk to these guys and see what's up." He headed toward the police cars as they came to a stop.

"I sure hope there's not a problem," Baxter said as he shook his head. "I'd hate to have to cancel the party and tell all these folks to take their kids and pets and go home."

"Oh, I'm sure it's not that serious," Phyllis said. "The dogs are barking some, but it's not really what you'd call a disturbance."

"Some people will complain about anything, though," Carolyn put in. "They just can't stand to see other people having a good time."

Two uniformed officers got out of the first car and started talking to Mike. They were too far away for Phyllis to hear what was being said. She saw the glance that Mike cast toward her and the others at the table, though, and she could tell that he wasn't pleased with what he was hearing.

Then the uniformed driver got out of the second car and a man in a brown suit emerged from the passenger side. His stocky figure and graying red hair were familiar to Phyllis, and after a moment she remembered who he was.

His name was Warren Latimer, and he had been the detective in charge of a murder case in which the victim had been found lying right on Phyllis's front porch. The whole group, with Latimer in the lead, started toward the table.

The detective looked at Phyllis and gave a little start of surprise, so obviously he recognized her, too. He didn't break stride, though.

Phyllis caught Mike's eye. His face was grim now and he shook his head slightly. Phyllis wasn't sure what that meant, but it couldn't be anything good.

Most of the people at the party had noticed the police by now, and they started drifting toward the table to find out what was going on. As the crowd gathered, Latimer and the other officers came up to the group under the canopy.

"Dr. Henry Baxter?" Latimer said.

"That's right," Baxter replied. "What can I do for you?"

"Dr. Baxter, my name is Latimer. I'm a detective with the Weatherford Police Department. I have a warrant for your arrest."

Baxter's eyes widened. He said, "For having a Halloween party without a permit?"

"No, sir," Latimer said. "For the murder of Dr. Susan Baxter."

Chapter 9

For a couple of heartbeats that seemed longer, Baxter just stared at Latimer. Then he took a sudden step back as if somebody had punched him in the chest.

The three uniformed officers had spread out, Phyllis noticed now, as if positioning themselves to stop Baxter if he tried to make a run for it.

After that one step, though, Baxter didn't move. He continued to stare at the police detective in apparent disbelief as he said, "That's insane. Susan's not . . . She can't be . . ."

"You'll have to come with us, Doctor," Latimer said. "You have the right to remain silent." He went through the rest of the standard Miranda warning and concluded by asking, "Do you understand these rights as they've been explained to you, Doctor?"

"I . . . What? Do I . . . ?" Baxter's face was so haggard he seemed to have aged ten years just in the past few minutes. His head jerked in an obviously forced nod, and he said, "Yes. I . . . I understand. I just don't believe this is happening."

"It's happening, all right. Please put your hands behind your back."

Still looking stunned, Baxter complied with the order. One of the uniformed officers moved behind him and fastened his wrists together with a plastic restraint. Then he took hold of Baxter's upper arm and firmly but not roughly led him toward the first police car.

Holly spoke up and said to Latimer, "You're making a terrible mistake. Dr. Baxter wouldn't hurt anybody, not even his wife."

"Not even his wife, eh?" Latimer repeated. "Who are you, miss?"

She swallowed and said, "I'm Holly Cunningham. I work here at the vet clinic."

"What did you mean by that comment?"

"I . . . I don't know what you mean," Holly replied as she shook her head.

"You said Baxter wouldn't hurt anybody, not even his wife. That makes it sound like maybe you could understand if he wanted to hurt her."

"No! Of course not. That's not what I meant at all."

Latimer grunted. Phyllis could tell that he wasn't convinced by Holly's answer.

He turned to her and asked, "What are you doing here, Mrs. Newsom?"

Phyllis couldn't keep a slightly acerbic tone out of her voice as she answered, "In case you haven't noticed, Detective, there's a Halloween party going on here. At least there was, until you arrived."

Latimer looked around. His mouth twisted wryly as he said, "Dogs and cats in Halloween costumes." It was obvious he disapproved of the practice. He went on. "I guess you can go on with the party if you want to, but everybody has to stay out of the clinic building. I've got a search warrant for it and any other buildings on the property."

"But we have patients in there," Holly protested. "We have to get in there to take care of them. Tommy's in there right now."

"Who's Tommy?"

"Tommy Sanders. He works for Dr. Baxter, too."

By now the officer who had taken Baxter away had put him in the backseat of the police car and closed the door. He leaned against the front fender and crossed his arms over his chest.

Latimer said to the other two officers, "One of you get Sanders and bring him out here. The other can secure the scene until we carry out our search." He turned back to Holly. "This isn't a crime scene, as far as I know now. You probably won't have to stay out for all that long, just until we've finished going through the place. If it looks like we'll have to seal it off for a while, we'll make arrangements to have the animals in there transferred to another vet clinic. Nobody's going to hurt them."

"This is still just wrong," Holly insisted. "Hank didn't do anything."

Phyllis saw the little spark of interest in Latimer's eyes when Holly referred to Baxter by his first name. She knew what the detective had to be thinking. With a history of trouble in Baxter's marriage, the possibility of an affair with his pretty young assistant would give him even more of a motive for murdering his wife.

"We'll sort it all out," Latimer said. "In the meantime, why don't you stay right here, Ms. Cunningham? I'll be wanting to talk to you again later."

"Am I under arrest, too?"

"Of course not. But I can hold you as a material witness if I need to."

Holly shook her head and said, "I'm not going anywhere. I have to make sure our patients are taken care of."

"That's fine."

Latimer followed the two officers into the clinic.

Carolyn moved over beside Phyllis and said, "I don't believe it. I just don't believe it. It's a Halloween party with pets, for goodness' sake. And the police show up and arrest someone for murder." She gave Phyllis a meaningful look and added, "But I suppose it was inevitable."

"I had nothing to do with this," Phyllis said. "I just happened to be here. In fact, it was as much your idea as it was mine."

"That doesn't really change anything."

Phyllis didn't waste time arguing with her friend. Instead she turned to Mike and asked, "When you went over there to talk to those officers, did they tell you anything?"

"Just that they were here to serve an arrest warrant," Mike said. "They wouldn't even tell me who they were after. I told them I'd back 'em up if they needed any help. I'm glad the doctor had sense enough not to resist."

"Of course he didn't resist," Holly said. "He's not violent. He's one of the kindest, gentlest men you'll ever meet. If you'd ever seen him work with animals, you'd know that."

Phyllis liked Baxter, too. Even though she hadn't been

around him nearly as much as Holly had, she'd been able to tell from the way he was with Buck that he genuinely liked his patients and wanted the best for them.

But that didn't mean he was incapable of murder. She had seen for herself how good people were sometimes capable of doing things that seemed almost inconceivable.

The crowd buzzed with conversation. Some of them began to drift toward their vehicles, taking their costumed kids and pets with them. After seeing Baxter arrested and put in the back of the police car, it was obvious that the party wasn't going to continue. Curiosity held some of the people there, though. It wasn't even morbid, thought Phyllis. It was just human nature.

Tommy Sanders came out of the clinic building, escorted by one of the officers. He looked stunned and confused. When Holly saw him, she hurried over to him and put her arms around him, reminding Phyllis of how, the day before, Holly had mentioned that she and Tommy were dating. Evidently, that was true, but it didn't rule out the possibility of an affair between Holly and Baxter.

"Holly, those cops said I had to get out," Tommy told the redhead as he returned her embrace. "They said . . . It's crazy. I can't believe it. They said Dr. Baxter killed his wife. Where is he?"

She nodded toward the police cars parked on the grass next to the driveway.

"He's over there in one of those cars. They put some sort of handcuffs on him and put him in there." She looked up into the face of the tall, lanky Tommy. "Are all the animals all right?"

"Yeah, for right now. Are they gonna let us back in there?"

"They said they would. And if they change their minds, they said they'd see to it that the animals were all moved to another vet's."

"This is crazy," Tommy said again. "What happened to Mrs. Baxter?"

"I have no idea."

"Well . . . what are we going to do? Should we stay here?"

"That detective said for us to. I think he . . . he wants to question us."

"About Dr. Baxter?" Tommy shook his head. "I'm not gonna do anything to help them. I don't know what happened, but they've got the wrong guy."

"Whatever they ask, we have to tell them the truth," Holly said. "Otherwise we could get in trouble, too."

"Maybe so, but I don't like this. I don't like it at all."

Sam said, "The same goes for me, son. After the way Doc Baxter helped Buck, I don't think he'd do anything wrong." He looked over at Phyllis. "Don't you feel the same way?"

"I don't know enough to come to any sort of conclusion," she said. "But I'm sure the police will find out the truth."

"That's a sensible attitude," Mike said.

Phyllis felt a little flash of annoyance at that comment. Mike knew as well as anyone how good her instincts were when it came to situations like this. She hadn't been proven wrong yet.

But it was foolish to speculate when she didn't even know any details of the case. At this point, she had no reason to think that she would, either.

Carolyn sighed and put the lid back on the container of cookies as more and more people got in their cars and left.

"It was a nice party while it lasted," she said. She picked up a bag of dog treats in each hand and weighed them by feel. "I think your treats were more popular than mine, Phyllis. More of them seem to be gone, anyway."

"That doesn't matter," Phyllis said.

"No, of course not," Carolyn agreed.

That hadn't stopped her from trying to determine who had emerged as the victor in their informal competition, though.

"I guess Buck's the lucky one," Sam said. "He gets the leftovers. There's enough there to last him for a good long time."

"We might as well all go back to my house," Phyllis said. She smiled at Bobby in his Sherlock Holmes costume and added to Mike and Sarah, "Bring the great detective with you."

When they got to Phyllis's house, Sam expected her to have Mike call some of his contacts on the police force and try to find out the details of the case against Hank Baxter. The cops had to be pretty sure he had killed his wife, or else they wouldn't have arrested him to start with.

But the police were human and could make mistakes like anybody else, as Sam had seen with his own eyes. Carolyn and Eve had both been accused of murder in the past, and it was plain to see that neither of them was a killer. In those cases, and others, it was Phyllis's instincts, determination, and intelligence that had uncovered the real murderers.

She could do it again now and clear Hank Baxter's name.

The thing of it was, she didn't seem inclined to do so. She didn't ask Mike to check on anything for her. She just told Eve what had happened at the vet clinic and then started getting ready for the trick-or-treaters who would be coming to the door later that evening.

After putting Buck in the backyard for a while, Sam caught a moment alone in the kitchen with her and said, "Phyllis, we both know good and well that Doc Baxter didn't kill that wife of his, or anybody else."

"No, I don't think he did, either," Phyllis agreed. "He just doesn't seem like the sort of man to do that. But we don't really know him that well, Sam. We've only talked to him a few times, and then not for very long."

Sam scratched his jaw and said, "Yeah, I know, but you can tell a lot about a fella by the way he treats animals. Baxter's a healer, not a killer."

"The police will figure that out, I'm sure."

"The way they figured out all those other cases you got mixed up in? They didn't get it right in a single one of 'em."

She took a deep breath and said, "I know, but, Sam, I can't just keep on . . ."

"Catchin' killers?" he asked when her voice trailed off.

"Carolyn already makes fun of me for being a jinx. She said once that people were going to stop associating with me because murder always seems to show up wherever I am."

Sam checked the hall to make sure no one was going to overhear; then he said, "That's just Carolyn bein' tactless. You know good and well that's not the way it is. You've gone to the store and church and other places hundreds of times without anybody gettin' killed."

"Of course I have. But you can't deny there's something odd about the way things have happened over the past few years."

"I won't deny it," Sam said. "But this murder's already taken place. Stayin' out of it doesn't have anything to do with keepin' more of them from happenin'."

"I suppose not," she admitted. "But I saw the way Mike looked at me out there at the clinic. He was hoping I wouldn't wind up getting involved in this investigation. He worries about me, bless his heart."

"Of course he does." Sam sighed. "I guess you're right, Phyllis. You shouldn't wade into this one. Who knows? Maybe the cops will decide they made a mistake and let the doc go."

"I hope so," Phyllis said, "because I really do think he's innocent."

So did Sam. He was completely convinced of it. But if Phyllis didn't want to get mixed up in the case, he was willing to accept that and respect her decision.

Thing was, there was nothing stopping him from trying to catch the killer just because she didn't set out to do it.

Chapter 10

*T*he neighborhood where Phyllis's house was located was
one of the oldest parts of Weatherford, not far from the courthouse, and most of the residences along the tree-lined streets
had been built no later than the 1950s. Some were considerably older than that. At least on the surface, it was a haven of
sorts from modern life. Only the cars parked along the curbs
and the occasional satellite dish on a roof indicated that it was
the twenty-first century.

Because of that, the neighborhood was popular for old-
fashioned trick-or-treating on Halloween. For nearly two hours
that evening, a steady stream of costumed youngsters showed
up on Phyllis's front porch, their childish voices singing out,
"Trick or treat!" as the door swung open in response to their
knocks.

Sam and Buck had door duty for a while. The kids enjoyed having the Dalmatian greet them, although a few were
scared of dogs and hung back, in which case Sam led Buck

back into the living room and Phyllis or Carolyn dispensed the candy.

Mike took Bobby around the neighborhood fairly early; then the two of them and Sarah went back to their own neighborhood to finish off the evening.

Before they left, though, Sam took Mike aside for a moment and asked him, "What's gonna happen to Dr. Baxter now?"

"He'll be arraigned in the morning and the judge will set bail," Mike said. "You've been around several of these cases, Sam. You ought to know the drill by now."

Sam scrubbed a hand over his face wearily and said, "Yeah, you're right. The whole thing surprised me so much I guess I'm not thinkin' straight. He'll need a lawyer, won't he?"

"Yep. There are plenty of criminal defense attorneys around, though. You can't throw a stick around the courthouse without hitting somebody carrying a briefcase."

"Then the case will go to the grand jury and they'll decide whether or not to indict him?"

"That's it," Mike said. "The process is pretty cut-and-dried."

"Not to a fella goin' through it, I'll bet," Sam muttered.

"Well, no, probably not." Mike paused. "You think Baxter is innocent, don't you?"

"Yeah, but it's just a gut feelin'. I don't have a thing in the world other than that to go by."

"What about Mom?" Mike asked warily.

"You mean does she think he's innocent, too?"

"Yeah. That's exactly what I mean."

"She does," Sam said, "but you don't have to worry, Mike. She says she's gonna stay out of it."

"Uh-huh. I'll believe that when I see it."

Solemnly, Sam said, "I think she means it. She doesn't want to worry you anymore, and she's really tired of folks thinkin' that somehow she's a magnet for murder."

"I don't blame her for feeling that way." Mike hesitated again, then said, "The only problem is, she's always been right about these things. If she believes Baxter is innocent, there's a good chance he is, at least as far as I'm concerned. Warren Latimer is a good cop, but he thinks he's already got the killer he's after. He's not going to bust his hump looking into other possibilities."

"That's where your mama always took up the slack in those other cases." Sam didn't know whether he ought to tell Mike his intentions. Mike was an officer of the law. He wanted truth and justice, but it was also ingrained in him to believe that civilians ought to butt out of police work.

"Baxter just needs to get a good lawyer," Mike said. "If he really is innocent, there ought to be enough reasonable doubt to make sure he's not convicted."

Ought to be, Sam thought. But there was no guarantee of that.

By the next morning, he hadn't changed his mind. He didn't know how much good he could do, but he wasn't going to stand by and let a good man go down without at least trying to help.

The rain had finally moved in for the first day of November. It was just a chilly drizzle for the moment, the sort that could hang around for days at this time of year. Buck had spent the night in the utility room, and after Sam took him outside, gave him his breakfast on the porch, and let him do his business, he brought him back inside.

"All right if I leave Buck in the utility room?" Sam asked Phyllis. "I've got some errands to run this morning."

"Of course," she said. "He's good about going to the back door and barking if he needs to go out. Whoever had him before must have house-trained him."

"Yeah, before they abandoned him," Sam said. Buck had been on his own for a while before that car hit him. He wouldn't have been so skinny otherwise. He was starting to get some meat back on his bones now, though, with the good care he was getting.

Buck was curled up on his bed next to the dryer, sound asleep, when Sam left. Sam drove through the drizzle toward the vet clinic. He wore blue jeans and a denim jacket this morning, along with a lumberyard cap to keep the rain off his head.

Through being Phyllis's friend, he had met a few people in the police department and the district attorney's office, but he doubted if any of them really knew him from Adam. He couldn't just walk into the courthouse and start asking questions about the Baxter case. The vet clinic was a place for him to get his feet wet in this detecting business. After that he'd figure out what to do next.

A car was parked next to the building and a pickup was out by the barn, so somebody was there. Sam went into the office and found Holly behind the counter, talking on the phone.

"I don't really know," she told whomever she was talking to. "I have a list of other vets I can refer you to, though, until we get all this straightened out . . . Yes, I know you'd rather see Dr. Baxter. We all would . . . All right. Thank you. And I'm sorry."

She thumbed the phone off, gave Sam a harried smile, and said, "It's been like that all morning. I've been calling everybody who had appointments today and canceling them." She frowned. "You don't have an appointment, do you, Mr. Fletcher? I don't remember—"

"No, that's right, I don't," Sam said as Holly started to turn on her stool to check the computer. "Buck's home, doin' fine. I came to see how you folks are handlin' things and find out if you've heard anything about Dr. Baxter."

"That's really sweet of you. Tommy and I are holding down the fort the best we can. Like I said, I'm canceling the appointments and offering to refer people to other vets. That's what I'm doing with people who call for new appointments, too. I tell them we don't know when the doctor will be back in the office and that they need to . . . need to find somebody else . . ."

Tears gleamed in Holly's eyes as she had trouble going on.

"Sounds to me like you've got things under control as much as you can," Sam said. "What about the doc? Do you know if he's got a lawyer?"

Holly shook her head and said, "I don't know. They won't let Tommy or me talk to him. I don't think they're going to let anybody see him until after his arraignment this morning." She glanced at the clock on the wall. "Actually, that ought to be over by now, or pretty soon, anyway. Maybe we'll know something by lunch."

Sam pointed with a thumb and asked, "Tommy out in the barn?"

"Yes, he's tending to the patients we have out there. A couple of horses, some pigs, and a goat."

"You reckon it'd be all right if I went out there and talked to him?"

"I don't see why not."

Sam smiled and nodded. He could tell how upset Holly was, but he couldn't offer her much in the way of comfort at the moment.

The rain had tapered off to sprinkles while he was inside the clinic. As he drove around the building and headed toward the barn, he wondered if Holly's reaction was simply that of an employee sympathizing with a friend and employer, or something more. He still thought it was likely she had a bit of a crush on Baxter.

Maybe the real question was whether or not the doctor had returned that affection, if indeed he even knew about it.

Sam parked and went into the barn. Tommy was filling up water troughs in the stalls, using a hose. He lifted his other hand in greeting and said, "Hey, what's up, man? Something I can do for you?"

"I'm Sam Fletcher."

"Sure, I know you. Buck's daddy, right? He's a good dog."

"He sure is," Sam agreed. "I was just inside talkin' to Holly. Sounds like the two of you really got your hands full."

"Yeah, I suppose," Tommy said with a shrug. He twisted the cutoff on the end of the hose to stop the water flow. "We don't have much choice in the matter, though. Until Hank gets back, we need to keep things going. All the animals we have here still need attention. We'll take care of the ones we can, and the others will have to go to other vets, I guess." He started coiling the hose on a holder attached to the wall. "Buck gets his cast off in a few weeks, right? Maybe Hank will be back by then."

"You think so?"

"Well, sure. The cops will figure out who really killed his wife. Or at least they'll realize that Hank couldn't have."

"You sound pretty sure about that."

"Of course I'm sure," Tommy said. "Hank's a good guy. He wouldn't kill anybody. Not even a gold-plated—"

He stopped himself before he finished the sentence and shook his head.

"Not supposed to speak ill of the dead, I guess," Tommy went on. "But the way I see it, if Hank hadn't killed the other Dr. Baxter before now, with all the excuses she gave him, he was never going to."

"Hard to get along with, was she?"

"Well, you saw her a time or two, right? Those were some of her good days."

Sam grunted and said, "Hard to believe that."

"Well, believe it. She made that poor guy's life a living hell. It's a real shame, too, because from what I've heard, they were a good couple starting out. I didn't know Hank back then, of course, but he's talked some about it. She worked and put him through vet school. Then he took over making a living and she went to medical school. It wasn't until she became a doctor that things started to get worse between them."

"Why do you reckon that was?" Sam asked.

Tommy was like most people, Sam thought. Give him the opportunity to gossip, and he'd take it. The young man said, "You know how they say that some doctors get a god complex?"

"Yeah, I reckon I've heard that expression."

"Well, it hit Susan really hard. She's a surgeon, and they're supposed to be the worst about it. Everybody told her how wonderful she was, and she started to believe it." Tommy shrugged again. "And to be fair, from what I've heard, she was really good at her job. But she started to look down on Hank. To her he was just an animal doctor, and it was like she didn't think he was worthy of her anymore."

"That's crazy," Sam said. "I like animals more than I do a lot of people."

"Yeah, I know! Me too. And that's all Hank ever wanted to do—take care of animals, I mean. So it was hard on him when she kept throwing that junk in his face about not being good enough because he's only a vet. Man, if I was him I would've—"

Again Tommy stopped abruptly. A hollow laugh came from him. "That sounded bad, didn't it?" he asked.

"No. I know blowin' off steam when I hear it. I've got a hunch Mrs. Baxter got under the skin of a lot of folks."

"Yeah, like accusing Hank of fooling around with Holly. That's just crazy. He's nearly twice as old as she is. Anyway, she's got a boyfriend."

"You," Sam said.

"That's right. I don't know how Susan got all that crap in her head. Hank works too hard to be carrying on with any-body. The guy wouldn't have the time, even if he wanted to!"

"The other day it sounded like Hank was the one accusin' his wife of carryin' on."

"I don't know anything about that. I stay as far away from that crazy bi—"

Tommy fell silent as a car pulled up to the clinic and

stopped. A man and a woman got out and went inside, but from his angle, Sam couldn't tell anything else about them.

Evidently, Tommy recognized them, though, because he said, "I'd better get up there. Holly's liable to need some help."

"You know those folks?"

"I know them," Tommy said. His voice held a grim note. "The woman is Susan Baxter's sister. She's not quite as hard to get along with as Susan was, but I don't know of any reason she'd be here unless it was to cause trouble!"

Sam opened the door of his pickup and nodded toward the passenger door.

"Hop in and I'll give you a ride," he offered.

Whatever had brought Susan Baxter's sister to the vet clinic, Sam figured it might help his investigation to be on hand and find out.

Chapter 11

If Tommy thought it was odd that Sam went into the clinic with him, he didn't say anything about it. The man and woman who had arrived a couple of minutes earlier stood in front of the counter, with Holly on the other side looking defensive.

"I don't want to have to get the law involved in this, but I will if I have to," the woman was saying. "I have a right to go in there and look at whatever I want to. This clinic is going to belong to me."

"I don't know how you figure that, Mrs. Carlyle," Holly said. She glanced at Tommy like she was pleading for help.

"What's going on here?" he asked.

"You stay out of it," the woman told him. "The first thing I'm going to do when I'm running things around here is fire the two of you. Whoever buys the clinic will want to hire a new staff anyway."

Sam took an instant dislike to the woman. She was in her

thirties, he judged, and actually quite attractive, with a sleek figure in jeans, a sweater, and a long coat. Thick dark brown hair fell to her shoulders and onto her back. A few drops of rain had been caught in the strands and still sparkled in the light from the overhead fluorescents.

Her companion was tall and also stylish in an expensive suit, and handsome enough in a bland way, Sam supposed, except for the large bald spot on the back of his head. He needed some of that hair-growing goop.

Holly said, "Mrs. Carlyle wants to go into Dr. Baxter's office and go through the records on his computer. I told her I couldn't allow her to do that."

"Of course not. Not without Hank's permission," Tommy said. "This is still his place."

"A murderer can't profit from his crime," Mrs. Carlyle said. "That means he can't inherit Susan's half of this business. As her sister, I will. His pathetic attempt at a frame-up isn't going to work, and once he's convicted and sent to prison where he belongs, I'm going to court to take the other half away from him."

"Why would you do that?" Holly asked. "You don't want it."

"Of course I don't. Like I said, I'll sell it as soon as I can." The woman looked over at Sam and frowned in puzzlement. "Who's the redneck?"

"Sam Fletcher, ma'am," Sam introduced himself with as polite a nod as he could muster. "I'm one of Dr. Baxter's friends."

That claim stretched things a mite, but Sam didn't care. He was grateful enough for the way Baxter had taken care of Buck that he considered them friends even though they didn't

know each other well. Holly and Tommy didn't contradict
him, either.

"*Dr.* Baxter," Mrs. Carlyle said. "There was only one real
doctor in that family, and she's dead." Her face started to crum-
ple, and tears ran down her cheeks. "My sister is dead."

The balding man took her in his arms and patted her back.
"It's all right, dear," he told her. "There's no need for you to
upset yourself. Why don't you go back out to the car? I'll handle
this."

Sam noticed that the woman stiffened when the man put
his arms around her, as if she wanted to pull away from him.
She didn't, though. Instead she took a silk handkerchief from
the pocket of her coat and dabbed it at her eyes. After a moment she nodded and stepped back.

"All right," she said. "But you tell them, Jack. You tell them
we'll get a court order if we have to."

"Of course, Meredith," he assured her.

Meredith Carlyle glared at Holly and Tommy and threw a
hostile glance toward Sam for good measure before she turned
and walked out, the heels of her boots clacking against the
floor tiles.

Once the glass door had swung closed behind her, the
man said, "You'll have to excuse my wife. Susan was her only
sibling, and with both their parents dead . . ." He shrugged.
"They were really all each other had left as far as family goes."
A curt, humorless laugh came from him. "Well, other than
husbands, of course."

Tommy said, "Look, we're not trying to cause trouble here,
Mr. Carlyle. We just want to do the right thing. But you have
to understand. Mrs. Carlyle can't just barge in here and take

over. It hasn't even been twenty-four hours since Hank was arrested."

"You mean it hasn't even been twenty-four hours since Susan was murdered," Jack Carlyle said.

"Yeah, but Hank hasn't been convicted of killing her. He hasn't even been indicted yet. The cops could decide they made a mistake and release him."

"Oh, I don't think that's going to happen. Who else had any reason to want Susan dead?" Carlyle shook his head. "Let's face it. We all know how troubled their marriage was. When somebody is murdered, aren't the odds astronomical that the killer will turn out to be their spouse?"

Sam said, "That's not always the case, though."

Carlyle frowned at him and said, "Who are you again? I don't remember Hank ever mentioning you."

Holly said, "Mr. Fletcher brought his dog Buck here with a broken leg."

"Oh. So you're not really a friend, then. You're just a customer." Carlyle turned back to Holly. "Listen, young lady, you know Meredith is serious about this. She doesn't joke around. I'm sure we'll be going straight from here to our lawyer's office to get him working on that court order to turn over Hank's records." He spread his hands. "And hey, we're not trying to do anything shady here. Meredith just wants to know what sort of financial footing the clinic is on, so she'll be able to determine a good price when she goes to sell it."

"Hank is getting out of jail," Tommy said through clenched teeth. "He's coming back to run this place just like he always has."

Carlyle shook his head and said, "Oh, I seriously doubt that."

Tommy took a deep breath. His hands tightened into fists. "I think you need to leave now," he said.

"Tommy . . ." Holly said warningly.

Carlyle laughed and said, "Do you really think it would make things better to take a swing at me, kid? Then you'll be arrested, too. That's all you'll accomplish. It won't change a thing."

"It might make me feel better."

"Until they slammed the cell door on you. Then you'd be asking yourself what the heck you were thinking." Carlyle started toward the door. Over his shoulder he added, "Don't be stupid. Try to make the best of this. Maybe I can talk Meredith into keeping you on for a while. Not permanently, of course, but hey . . . you do what you can do."

With that, he stepped out into the drizzle.

"What a jerk," Tommy muttered.

Sam nodded. He watched through the glass door as Carlyle got into the car with his wife and drove off.

"They both are," Holly said. "I swear, if that woman gets her hands on this clinic, she won't have to fire me. I'll quit."

"And I'll be right with you," Tommy said. He sighed and turned to Sam. "Was there anything we could do for you, Mr. Fletcher?"

"No, I won't take up any more of your time," Sam said.

Holly asked, "Do you want me to make an appointment for you with another vet?"

Sam shook his head. "Nope. I'm gonna assume that Dr. Baxter will be back," he said. "If he's not, we'll deal with it then."

"Better not wait too long," Tommy cautioned. "You might

have trouble getting Buck in somewhere else. Give it until the end of the week, maybe."

"I'll do that," Sam said with a nod. He reached for the door. "Thanks again."

"Anytime," Tommy said.

As Sam drove away, he thought that he hadn't really learned anything new. He was no closer to proving Hank Baxter's innocence than he had been when he started.

This business of being a detective wasn't as easy as Phyllis made it look.

Once Sam had left on his mysterious errands, Phyllis went into the living room and sat down at the computer. Carolyn stuck her head into the room and said, "Don't forget about the recipes for that contest in *A Taste of Texas*."

"Don't worry. I haven't," Phyllis said. "In fact, I thought I might make the white chili casserole for supper tonight. It ought to be really good on a cold, gloomy day like this."

"All right. And we can have my breakfast casserole tomorrow morning."

Phyllis smiled and nodded. She said, "I'm looking forward to it."

Carolyn left her to what she was doing.

What *was* she doing? Phyllis asked herself. She had all but told Sam that she wasn't going to get involved in Hank Baxter's case. And yet what was she about to do?

She was about to search the Internet for news about Dr. Susan Baxter's murder.

If she really wanted to follow through on her decision, she

would turn the monitor off and stand up from the computer right now, she told herself. But she didn't, and a couple of minutes later she was reading a story about the case on the website of the local newspaper.

The facts were pretty skimpy. The day before, the body of Dr. Susan Baxter had been found in her office when her receptionist returned from lunch. It appeared that she had been killed by a blow to the head, although the official cause of death had not yet been determined. Later in the day, the police had taken into custody Dr. Henry Baxter, a local veterinarian and husband of the victim, and he had been charged with her murder.

That was it, just a dry recitation of those few details. It was the sort of story you would glance at in the paper and then promptly forget, unless you happened to be acquainted with the people involved. Spouses getting into an argument and one killing the other wasn't really news. Phyllis supposed the fact that both people in this case were doctors gave it enough so-called glamour to justify the story's placement on the front page of the paper.

She checked the website of the Fort Worth and Dallas papers. Susan Baxter's murder was mentioned in the Fort Worth paper, but it wasn't on the front page, not by a long shot. The Dallas paper didn't have anything about the story in its pages.

So if things ran their normal course, Susan Baxter was dead and her husband's life would be ruined, and the general public wouldn't care. It was just another tragedy in a seemingly endless series of tragedies that filled the world from the streets of Weatherford to the halls of the world's capitals, Phyllis thought.

She gave a little shake of her head and told herself not to be so blasted gloomy. That was a little difficult to do on a day like this, but she could at least make the effort.

Buck distracted her by going to the back door and whining. Phyllis turned off the monitor and went into the kitchen to let him out.

Given the rainy weather, his cast was wrapped in plastic again. When Phyllis opened the back door, he started to go out, then stopped, looked at the rain dripping from the eaves, and turned his head to look up at her.

"I can't help it if it's raining," she told him. "Just don't waste any time getting your business done, and when you come back up on the porch, I'll dry you off."

While Buck was outside, she got one of the old towels she had used to dry him after the skunk incident. Even though she had washed it with baking soda and peroxide added to the machine, she thought a very faint odor of skunk still clung to the towel. It was probably just her imagination, she knew, but even so, she didn't want to put it back with the other towels for regular use. As far as she was concerned, it was Buck's towel now.

He was waiting for her when she came out onto the porch. She sat down in the rocking chair where Sam usually sat and began drying the Dalmatian. Buck cooperated by sitting peacefully next to her feet. While she was doing this, it was almost like he was her dog instead of Sam's.

Not that she would ever try to steal him away from Sam. Those two made a good team. She wouldn't want to come between them. She rubbed Buck's ears and said, "You and Sam are buddies, aren't you, Buck? Yes, you are."

The back door opened and Sam stepped out onto the porch.

Phyllis glanced up at him and said, "Well, speak of the devil."

"Devil?" Sam repeated. "What'd I do?"

"Oh, I was just talking to Buck about you."

"Really? What were you sayin'?"

"Oh, you'll have to ask Buck about that. Did you get everything done you needed to?"

"I don't know. Not really, I don't think."

"Is it anything I can help you with?" Phyllis asked.

He shook his head and said, "Not right now, but thanks."

"Well, if you change your mind, just let me know." She started to get up. "Here, you can have your chair—"

"You're fine right where you are," Sam told her. He leaned against one of the porch posts. The roof had enough of an overhang that the rain didn't fall on him. There was no wind, so the light drops were coming straight down. Buck sat between them.

The three of them stayed there on the porch for a while, watching the rain in companionable silence.

Chapter 12

That afternoon, while Phyllis was working on her casserole recipe, Sam went up to his room and called Mike on his cell phone. Not surprisingly, he had to leave a message, but Mike called him back about a half hour later, while Sam was watching an episode of *Gunsmoke*.

"Hey, Sam, what's up?"

"I was just wonderin' if you'd heard any more about the Baxter murder case," Sam said.

The slight hesitation on the other end of the line made him think that Mike was probably frowning. After a moment Mike said, "Why are you asking about that? I thought my mother was going to steer clear of this one. Good grief. Has she got you doing legwork for her again? Already?"

"Nope, not at all. She doesn't even know I called you. I'm just askin' because I like the guy, and I'm worried about what's gonna happen to him."

"Oh." Mike sounded relieved. "Well, I don't really know

any more than I did yesterday evening. I assume Dr. Baxter was arraigned this morning and bail was set."

"You don't know how much it'd be or whether he was able to pay it, though."

"Not a clue," Mike agreed. He paused again. "I could call a friend of mine at the courthouse . . ."

"I'd sure be curious to know," Sam said.

"I'm not sure I like the way this is going. Are you thinking about doing something crazy, Sam?"

Sam laughed and said, "Who, me? You ever know me to be anything but steady, dependable Sam?"

"Well, no, but you've been around my mother for several years now. And I know you've helped her poke around in criminal cases before. You can get in trouble doing that."

"I know. I know. I just want to find out how the doc's doin', that's all."

With skepticism obvious in his voice, Mike said, "I'm still not sure my mother didn't put you up to this, but what the hey, I'll find out what I can and call you back, okay?"

"I appreciate it," Sam said. He said good-bye and went back to watching Festus squabble with Doc, but he had trouble keeping his mind on the TV show. Normally, those two had him smiling and laughing, but today he wore a slight frown as he tried to keep his thoughts from wandering.

When his cell phone buzzed a half hour later, he answered it immediately. Mike said, "Hi, Sam. I found out a little about the Baxter case, if you still want to know."

"Yeah, I do," Sam said.

"Dr. Baxter was arraigned this morning and the judge set bail at a million dollars."

Sam let out a low whistle. "That's a lot of money. Do you know if he was able to pay it and get out of jail?"

"A bail bondsman did. Baxter's out. I don't know, of course, but I suspect he put up his veterinary practice as collateral. It's probably not worth a million bucks by itself, but maybe he has some other property he was able to throw in."

"So he made bail and was released."

"That's what my friend at the courthouse said. Jimmy D'Angelo showed up and handled the arraignment, and then Baxter left with him."

"Who's this fella D'Angelo?" Sam asked.

"Defense attorney. He represented the defendants in several trials where I had to testify, but nothing anywhere near as major as a murder case. That's all I really know about him, though."

Sam nodded even though Mike couldn't see him over the phone. He was glad that Hank Baxter had a lawyer, although he didn't have any idea how competent Jimmy D'Angelo was.

"So now the case goes to the grand jury."

"Right," Mike said, "but that won't be for a few weeks."

"In the meantime the cops'll be investigatin' the case some more?"

Mike hesitated before answering. "They'll be looking for evidence to bolster their case. There must be some already, or Sullivan wouldn't have signed off on the arrest warrant. He'll want more, though."

"What if Sullivan's not reelected?"

District Attorney Timothy Sullivan was running for reelection, and the vote would be in less than a week. Sam intended to cast his ballot against the DA, who'd had Phyllis locked up for tampering with evidence and obstruction of justice in a previous case.

Sam supposed that technically Phyllis *had* tampered with evidence, but she hadn't obstructed justice in the slightest. In fact, if it hadn't been for her efforts, a cunning killer would have gotten away with murder. Phyllis had been responsible for justice being done.

"I'm afraid that won't really make any difference," Mike replied to Sam's question. "Baxter's case is already in the system, and it'll proceed no matter who the DA is. I don't think Sullivan has any personal ax to grind against Baxter. He's just doing his job, and that's what the next guy'll do." Mike grunted. "Anyway, I think it's pretty much a foregone conclusion that Sullivan will win the election."

"Yeah, politics is one of the few professions where bein' a weasel seems to give you an advantage." Sam sighed. "All right, Mike. Thanks. I didn't really want to ask this favor of you, but I didn't know what else to do."

"Sam, are you *sure* my mom's not gonna get mixed up in this?"

"All I know is what she tells me, and she said she wasn't."

"All right," Mike said. "I hope she doesn't change her mind."

"Yeah," Sam said, but the word sounded a little hollow in his ears. He was starting to come to the conclusion that as far as detective work was concerned, he was in over his head.

Later that afternoon, Sam told Phyllis, "I've got to go out again."

"Well, you're as busy as can be lately," she said.

"Not really. Just tryin' to get some things done."

"Well, go ahead," she told him with a wave of her hand as she stood at the kitchen counter with some mixing bowls in front of her. "I'll keep an eye on Buck."

Sam glanced out the window into the backyard.

"Rain's stopped," he commented. "Looks like the sun's tryin' to come out. I can put him out before I go if you want."

"No, that's all right." She looked down to where the Dalmatian was lying in a corner of the kitchen. "Is that fine with you, Buck?"

The dog's tail thumped against the floor as he wagged it.

Sam chuckled and said, "All right. I appreciate it."

He got in his pickup and drove the few blocks to downtown. He had looked up Jimmy D'Angelo on his laptop and found that the defense attorney's office was in a building just off the square, which came as no surprise because the courthouse was in easy walking distance from there.

Sam found a parking place and walked across the square. A brisk north wind blew, but it was a dry wind now that the rain was over. Big patches of blue sky showed through the clouds overhead as they broke up. It would be cold tonight, Sam knew, but Buck would be snug in his bed next to the dryer.

Sam found Jimmy D'Angelo's office. The defense attorney was part of a firm called Harvick, Webber, and Crane. D'Angelo was an associate. Maybe a partner. Sam didn't really know how that worked. The carpet was thick in the office, though, and the furnishings were expensive. The atmosphere was hushed. From the looks of it, the firm was quite successful.

A woman with ash-blond hair was behind a reception desk. She smiled at Sam and asked, "May I help you, sir?"

Sam had left his lumberyard cap at home since it wasn't raining anymore, so he didn't have to take it off as he returned the woman's smile and said, "Yes, ma'am. I was hopin' I could talk to Mr. D'Angelo for a minute."

"Do you have an appointment?"

Sam was expecting that question, so he was ready with an answer. "No, ma'am, but it's about one of his cases, and I think he'll want to talk to me."

"Which case?"

Sam didn't particularly want to blurt out that information, but as he glanced around the waiting room, he saw that it was empty, so he figured it would be all right.

"The Baxter case," he said. "Dr. Hank Baxter."

The woman got to her feet and said, "If you'll excuse me for just a minute. Please, have a seat." As she started to turn away, she paused and added, "If you wouldn't mind telling me your name . . ."

"It's Fletcher. Sam Fletcher."

"I'll be right back, Mr. Fletcher."

She went through a door in the wall behind her desk. Sam caught a glimpse of a wide corridor with darkly paneled walls before she closed the door. He went over to a brown leather armchair with thick upholstery. Probably not too many blue-jeans-clad butts had sat on it in the past, he thought. Or maybe they had. Rednecks sometimes needed lawyers, too, after all.

A few minutes went by. Sam tried not to fidget, but it wasn't easy. Then the door opened and the woman reap-peared.

"If you'll come right this way, please," she said.

Sam followed her through the door into the fancy corridor. Now he could see that portraits of a bunch of rich-looking men and women hung on the walls between the doors that opened on either side. Probably members of the firm, he thought. At the far end of the hall were massive oak double doors. He figured that on the other side of them was either a conference room or the private office of Harvick, Webber, or Crane, whoever was the head honcho around here.

None of the doors had nameplates or anything like that on them. The woman knew who was behind which door. She opened one of them on the left and stood aside for Sam to go in. As he did, a man stood up from behind the big desk that dominated the room.

"Mr. Fletcher," the man said. "Please come in." He extended his hand. "I'm Jimmy D'Angelo."

Sam knew as soon as the fella opened his mouth that he wasn't from around here. D'Angelo was short and stocky, with thick dark hair and a square, slightly florid face. His voice betrayed his northeastern origins, although Sam couldn't pin it down any more precisely than that.

He shook hands with D'Angelo, who then waved him into a chair that was every bit the equal of the one out in the waiting room. Maybe even better. The attorney said, "Margaret tells me that this visit is about the Baxter case. What can I do for you, Mr. Fletcher?"

"Well, Hank—Dr. Baxter—is a friend of mine," Sam began, "and I want to make sure he's got all the help he needs."

"So you're checking me out. Is that it?"

"I wouldn't go so far as to say that—"

"No, it's all right," D'Angelo said as he waved a pudgy hand. "I like the way you're looking out for the doctor because he's a pal. People don't look out for each other enough these days; you know what I mean? I see proof of that all the time in my job."

"I'm sure you do," Sam said with a nod.

D'Angelo leaned back and laced his hands together over his belly. He wore a large ring on each hand. He was well-fed, well-dressed, the epitome of success. Sam saw several framed diplomas on the wall. One of them was from Harvard.

"I like to think I'm a good lawyer," D'Angelo went on. "I'll represent Dr. Baxter the very best I can, Mr. Fletcher."

"If there's anything I can do to help . . ."

"You mean like money? I'll be honest with you; you don't look like a particularly wealthy man."

Sam tried not to take offense at that. He said, "I reckon I'm what they call comfortable—"

"Here's the thing, though," D'Angelo cut in. "I've been in Texas long enough to know that sometimes the richest guys don't dress like it at all. So I've learned not to judge people by the way they look."

"That's pretty smart," Sam said.

"Anyway, money's not an issue. Dr. Baxter is able to afford my retainer, and we'll work out all the details later. Right now I'm more interested in the case."

"You want to see justice done, too, then."

D'Angelo unlaced his hands and spread his fingers. "I didn't say anything about justice. I want to win."

Again Sam had to control his temper. He said, "A man's life isn't a game."

"Of course not. But surviving in a high-pressure law firm is. I haven't handled any murder cases since I came to Texas.

Winning this one would give me some street cred around here."

"Then you don't think Hank Baxter is innocent," Sam said.

"He tells me he is, and that's all I really need to know in order to mount a legitimate defense. Do you know anything that will help me do that, Mr. Fletcher?"

Sam put his hands on the arms of the chair and scraped it back a little. As he started to stand up, he said, "No, and I think I've wasted enough of your time. Sorry. I should go now—"

D'Angelo sat forward and used both hands to wave him back into the chair. "Please, Mr. Fletcher, sit down. I think we got off on the wrong foot here. Please, sit."

Reluctantly, and only to be polite, Sam lowered himself into the plush chair again.

"Listen, it doesn't matter whether or not I believe Dr. Baxter is innocent. My job is to defend him to the best of my abilities and secure the best possible verdict for him. Since you're his friend, would you be all right with letting me use you as a sounding board?"

"Well, I suppose so," Sam said with a frown. He had hoped to get some more information about the case from D'Angelo, and it sounded like the attorney was about to share that very thing, although Sam hadn't really done anything to prompt it.

"I'll tell you what I know about the case against the doctor, and you tell me how it squares up with what you know about him, okay?"

Sam nodded and said, "Okay."

"Early yesterday afternoon, Dr. Baxter—Dr. Henry Baxter—ah, for simplicity's sake, let's just call him Hank, since there are two Dr. Baxters in this case. Yesterday afternoon, Hank was seen going into his wife Susan's office over by the hospital. Susan's staff had already left for lunch, so she was there by herself. About forty-five minutes later, her receptionist comes back to the office. The door's locked, but she has a key so she lets herself in. She sees that the door to Susan Baxter's private office is open, so she glances in and finds Susan lying in front of the desk, dead from a blow to the head."

Sam winced. D'Angelo's words called up a mental image of Hank Baxter striking his wife in the head and killing her, and Sam didn't like it.

"The receptionist nearly loses it but holds herself together enough to call 911. It only takes a few minutes for the cops and the paramedics to get there. The receptionist has run back outside because she's afraid the killer may still be in the building. That's a pretty smart thing to do. But the cops go through the place and find that it's empty except for the body. They also find the drug cabinet smashed open and rifled."

"Well, there you go," Sam said. "Some addict broke in to steal drugs, thinkin' that the office would be empty for lunch. Susan Baxter caught him at it, and he killed her."

"Yeah, but the police say that's just a frame job, that the killer tried to make it look like robbery, mostly because they found a really fresh fingerprint on the cabinet, and it belongs to Hank Baxter. Not only that, they located a witness who saw Hank going into his wife's office and then leaving a short time later."

Sam shook his head and said, "Hank was her husband, and a doctor, to boot. Why would there be anything incriminating about his fingerprints bein' on that cabinet?"

"As a matter of fact, he has an explanation for why the print was there," D'Angelo said. "He claims he went by there to pick up samples of some meds because he wanted to try them in his practice."

"Human medicine?" Sam asked with a frown.

"You'd be surprised how many drugs that we think of as medications for humans are also used in veterinary practice, and not just antibiotics like amoxicillin," D'Angelo said. "At least, I was surprised when Hank explained it to me. They call it prescribing off-list."

"But the police don't believe him."

"Of course not. She was alone in the office when he got there. She was alone when he left. Nobody saw her again until the receptionist found her body. There was a history of violent disagreements between the two of them . . ." D'Angelo's beefy shoulders rose and fell in a shrug. "As far as the police are concerned, that was plenty for an arrest warrant."

"What about the murder weapon?" Sam asked.

"Nobody's turned it up yet. At least, nobody's admitting it. That detective, Latimer, is a cagey one. He'll keep his cards close to his vest as much as he can."

Sam found himself liking Jimmy D'Angelo more than he had at first. The lawyer seemed to be a plainspoken sort, which Sam appreciated.

"So Hank doesn't have an alibi," he mused.

"Not really," D'Angelo agreed. "He got back to the vet clinic shortly after his wife's body was discovered, so he can't argue that he didn't have time to kill her. He did."

Sam thought about where the vet clinic was located and how far it was to the medical district along Santa Fe Drive, where Susan Baxter's office was. The geography and the timing didn't favor Hank Baxter, or at least didn't rule him out.

D'Angelo went on. "The official theory is that the Drs. Baxter argued again, and this time Hank blew his top, grabbed something, and hit his wife hard enough to kill her. At this point the evidence is all circumstantial . . . but guys have been convicted on circumstantial evidence before." He leaned forward and clasped his hands on the desk. "So what about it, Sam? I can call you Sam, right?"

"Sure. What are you askin' me? Do I think Hank's capable of doin' that?"

"Exactly."

Sam tilted his head to the side for a second, then shook it slowly. "I don't think so. But I can't prove it. I, uh, haven't really known him that long."

D'Angelo frowned and asked, "Just how long have you known Hank Baxter?"

"Almost a week and a half." Sam added, "But you can tell a lot about a man by how he treats animals, and Hank fixed up my dog's busted leg. He's a good man. I know it."

D'Angelo drew in a deep breath and blew it out in a sound of anger and frustration. "I thought you were a potential character witness, Mr. Fletcher. That's the only reason I discussed the case so openly. But I'd look like a fool if I put you on the stand." He pressed his palms on the desk. "I think we're done here."

Sam got to his feet and nodded. "Sorry if I caused any trouble," he said.

"No trouble. Just keep everything I told you to yourself, all right?"

"Sure."

D'Angelo cocked his head and said, "Not that it really matters, I guess. The whole story will come out soon enough anyway. Sullivan's a grandstander. Likes to try his cases in the press when he thinks he can get away with it. The cops may be sitting on the details now, but in a day or two the DA will have a press conference and spill everything. He's too much in love with the sound of his own voice not to."

"For what it's worth," Sam said, "I agree with you about that."

D'Angelo grinned. He said, "Not really a big fan of our illustrious district attorney, are you?"

Sam thought about Phyllis sitting behind bars in a jail cell and shook his head. "Nope," he said. "Not a big fan at all."

Chapter 13

His visit to Jimmy D'Angelo's office had been a waste of time, Sam thought as he drove away from the square. He had learned some details of the case that he hadn't known before, but as D'Angelo had pointed out, it was likely that those details would become common knowledge in a few days anyway.

Even with an arrest already made, surely the police would check out any other evidence in the case, like the other fingerprints found in Susan Baxter's office. If they came up with a print belonging to a known burglar, or some druggie who had broken into doctors' offices before to steal drugs, that ought to be enough to convince them that their theory about Hank was wrong. At the very least, it would create reasonable doubt.

But what if the cops were right and the drug theft was an attempt to cover up someone else's involvement in Susan Baxter's murder?

Who else had a reason for wanting Susan dead?

That was an interesting question, Sam thought. He wasn't

quite sure how to go about answering it, but it was something to consider.

When he got back to the house, Phyllis was busy with her casserole, so Sam let Buck out into the backyard and sat on the porch for a while and watched the Dalmatian. Buck started to dig a hole, and Sam called to him, "Hey, there, Buck. Don't do that! You'll get your paws all muddy. Phyllis probably doesn't want holes in her backyard, either. Come here."

Buck came up on the porch. Sam picked up a piece of thick rope they had been using as a tug-of-war toy. Buck clamped his jaw on it and started pulling. He growled, although it wasn't a serious one.

Phyllis came onto the porch, sat down in the other rocking chair, and said, "Well, my casserole is in the oven. I hope it turns out all right."

Sam chuckled and said, "Since when did you ever cook anything that didn't turn out all right?"

"Oh, I've had my share of culinary fiascos," she told him.

"Not since I've been livin' here."

"Yes, well, I cooked for many, many years before you moved in."

"I reckon that's true."

After a moment of silence, Phyllis said, "You seem pretty distracted today, Sam. What have you been up to?" Quickly, she added, "Of course, you don't have to tell me if you don't want to. What you do is your own business."

"No, that's all right," Sam said. "I'm sort of in over my head on something. This business about Hank Baxter has got me bumfuzzled. I know you said you didn't want anything to do with it—"

"That doesn't mean you can't talk to me about whatever's bothering you. I'm always willing to listen to whatever you have to say."

Sam knew he could trust Phyllis more than just about anybody else in the world. Jimmy D'Angelo had asked him not to say anything about what they had discussed, but then the lawyer had added that it probably wouldn't matter anyway. Phyllis might not want to investigate the Baxter case, but surely she wouldn't mind talking about it.

"I went out to Hank Baxter's vet clinic this morning, and then I went to see his lawyer this afternoon."

"How did you find out who his lawyer is?"

"Well . . . I called Mike and he found out for me."

That rueful admission brought a chuckle from Phyllis. She said, "I know exactly how you're feeling, Sam. I've been there. You want to prove that your friend is innocent."

"You saw the way he took care of Buck. Do you think a man like that could commit murder?"

"I'd like to think that he couldn't," Phyllis said, "but it's hard to be certain about these things." She paused. "What did you find out?"

"Well, for one thing, Susan Baxter has a sister, and she's not much more friendly than Susan was. Not that I like to speak ill of the dead . . ."

"But it's a fact," Phyllis said. "Susan wasn't very friendly with her husband, at least from what we saw of her."

"The sister's name is Meredith Carlyle," Sam went on. "She was out at the clinic readin' the riot act to Holly and Tommy and tellin' them how things are gonna be. She plans on goin' to court and tryin' to take over complete control of the clinic so she can sell it."

"Could that be a motive for murder?" Phyllis asked.

Sam drew in a breath and said, "You know, I never even thought about that. That tells you I'm not really cut out for this sort of thing. But it seems to me like a mighty flimsy excuse for killin' somebody, especially your own sister. Sure, the vet clinic might be worth something, especially if you also throw in the sister's practice, but Ms. Carlyle and her husband looked like they're pretty well-to-do already. I just don't see it."

"That's what you're trying to do, though, isn't it?" Phyllis asked. "Find out who else might have a motive for wanting Susan Baxter dead?"

"Yeah," Sam admitted. "That thought sure crossed my mind."

"What about Dr. Baxter's lawyer? Did he tell you anything?"

"Yeah, I sort of made it sound like Hank and I are old friends, so he told me some of the details the cops haven't made public yet." Sam went over everything D'Angelo had told him about the case, then concluded by saying, "He had in mind puttin' me on the stand as a character witness for Hank, but when he found out we haven't really known each other that long, he changed his mind. He was a mite peeved with me, too."

"You may be too honest and honorable to be a detective, Sam," she said. "Sometimes you have to fool people to get them to talk to you."

"Yeah, I know."

"You're on the right track, though. From what you told me, it doesn't sound like there's any evidence to prove that Hank Baxter didn't kill his wife. So the only way to clear his name and keep him from being convicted is to find out who else had a motive and see if there's any evidence pointing to them."

"Yeah, that made sense to me, too, but I don't know who else might fit that description."

"What about Kyle Woods?"

Sam frowned and said, "Who?"

"Remember when Carolyn and I went out to the clinic last week to talk to Dr. Baxter about bringing the doggie treats to the Halloween party?"

"Yeah, I suppose so."

"Well, while we were there, a man drove up to see Dr. Baxter, and he seemed angry about something. His name was Kyle Woods. He breeds prizewinning golden retrievers."

Sam snapped his fingers as a memory came back to him. "That dog-breedin' website you were lookin' at," he said. "That was for this fella Woods's outfit, wasn't it?"

"That's right."

"But even if Woods had some sort of grudge, it was against Hank, not Susan Baxter."

"And Hank was arrested for murder, wasn't he? That sounds like pretty good payback for a grudge."

"Wait a minute," Sam said. "You're sayin' maybe Woods was mad enough at Hank that he killed Susan to get back at him?"

"If he followed Hank to Susan's office, and if he knew about all the trouble between the two of them, he might think that if he killed Susan, the police would automatically suspect Hank. In fact," Phyllis said, "I'd be very curious about the identity of that witness they found who placed Hank on the scene around the time Susan was killed."

Sam realized that his heart was beating faster. Phyllis was right. The theory she had just laid out about Kyle Woods made sense. It was incomplete—they didn't know why Woods had been angry with Hank Baxter that day last week—and they had no proof of anything, but nothing they knew invalidated it, either.

"Maybe I can find out," Sam said. "I think I need to find out more about Kyle Woods, too."

"Not a bad idea. It's where I'd start, anyway."

"I appreciate the help, Phyllis." Sam frowned again. "Say, you were checkin' up on Woods last week, before Susan was murdered. Why were you doin' that? Were you really thinkin' about gettin' a dog from him someday?"

She smiled and shook her head. "No. The thing of it is, I can't really tell you why I went to the trouble of looking up his website. I'd seen the name of his company on his truck, and I was curious, that's all. Like I told you, he seemed angry with Dr. Baxter, and I just wondered what it was all about."

"Sounds to me like you were gettin' ready in case something happened."

"You mean in case there was some sort of trouble?"

"Like a murder," Sam said.

"Oh, don't be—you think I go around looking for potential murderers?"

"You know the Boy Scout motto: Be prepared. And the way things have been goin' the past few years, shoot, nobody would blame you for thinkin' that way."

"Well, that's not what I had in mind at all," Phyllis declared, and she sounded certain about it.

But judging by the look on her face, Sam thought, she might be asking herself just how sure of that she was.

· · ·

It was late enough in the afternoon that Sam said he wasn't going to try to do any more investigating. He needed to mull everything over, he told Phyllis before he went upstairs to his room.

Phyllis went into the kitchen and found Carolyn there. Carolyn drew in a deep breath and said, "That casserole smells wonderful. Like an award winner, if you ask me."

"We can hope so," Phyllis said.

"What's in it again?"

"Chicken, onions, navy beans, corn, and seasonings, with a spicy cheddar cornbread top," Phyllis said. "What are you going to put in your breakfast casserole?"

"I'm leaning toward making it more of a quiche, with bacon in the crust, and spinach, onion, and artichoke in the filler."

"Oh, my," Phyllis said. "That sounds tasty."

"I think we both have an excellent chance," Carolyn said as Phyllis opened the oven door a little to check on her casserole. Satisfied that it was cooking fine and didn't need any attention at the moment, she eased the door shut.

"I did a little fine-tuning on the recipe," she said. "I'd better go make a note of that on the file before I forget."

On the computer in the living room, she called up the file and made her revisions on it. Eve was watching one of those judge shows where people argued with one another over small-claims cases, and Carolyn joined her on the sofa. Phyllis mentally tuned out the sound of the TV, and when she was finished changing the casserole recipe, she acted on impulse and did a search on the name *Meredith Carlyle*.

She wasn't sure of the spelling of either name, but her first guess proved to be right. The first link in the list took her to a story in the society section of the newspaper that included a picture of Meredith Carlyle and her sister, noted surgeon Dr. Susan Baxter, along with their respective spouses, insurance executive Jack Carlyle and local veterinarian Dr. Henry Baxter. The story was several years old, and either the Baxters had been getting along better then or else they were good at putting up a front, because they were all smiles in their fancy getups, as were the Carlyles.

The gathering was a fund-raiser for the local animal shelter. Phyllis wondered if Hank Baxter had had something to do with that. It seemed likely.

The search led her to other stories about Jack Carlyle and his business interests, which seemed quite successful as Sam had said, but not much about Meredith. Phyllis moved on to stories about Susan Baxter. She had been a well-regarded general surgeon. Phyllis didn't understand all the medical references in the stories she read, but she knew enough to realize that Susan had garnered a sterling reputation at a relatively young age.

Doctors like that were often recruited to practice at bigger hospitals. Phyllis wondered if that could have been part of the cause for the trouble between Susan and Hank. Maybe she'd had a chance to move up to a position that offered more money and prestige, and Hank didn't want her to take it because he didn't want to leave his veterinary practice in Weatherford.

She wasn't supposed to be looking for reasons for Hank Baxter to have killed his wife, Phyllis reminded herself. In fact, she wasn't supposed to be investigating this case at all.

But old habits were hard to break, and besides, it was important to Sam. Anyway, she thought, she was just doing a little background research online. It wasn't like she was going out and questioning suspects as she had done in the past.

Sam was, though. She hoped he would be careful. All it took to spook a killer was a feeling that someone was closing in on him, and then he was liable to strike out in an attempt to protect his deadly secret. Phyllis had seen it happen before. On several occasions, she and Sam had both found themselves in danger because of her investigations.

Maybe it wouldn't count as breaking her promise to Mike if she just gave Sam a discreet hand . . . strictly in the interest of finding out the truth as quickly as possible, of course.

To do that meant finding out who else had a reason for wanting Susan Baxter dead, or who hated Hank enough to kill Susan in order to frame him for the murder. That was all they had to find out.

Yes, Phyllis thought wryly. That was all.

Meredith Carlyle might be a good place to start. She ought to know whether or not her sister had had any enemies . . .

"Phyllis," Carolyn said, "what about your casserole?"

Phyllis's head jerked up. The casserole! She had gotten so involved in her research into the case and her own thoughts that she had forgotten all about it. She didn't smell anything burning, but she muttered, "Oh, good grief!" and jumped up from the computer anyway, turning off the monitor as she did so. She hurried toward the kitchen.

Murder could certainly wreak havoc with cooking!

Chapter 14

*L*uckily, the casserole wasn't burned when Phyllis took it out of the oven. It had cooked a little longer than she had intended, though, and she wasn't sure how that would affect it. They would find out at supper.

She was glad Carolyn had said something. If she had left the casserole in the oven for much longer, it would have been ruined for sure.

Carolyn followed her into the kitchen and said, "You seemed distracted by whatever you were looking at on the computer."

"I know. It was nothing important, though."

"Are you sure you weren't looking things up that might have something to do with that woman being murdered?"

When Phyllis looked at her, Carolyn went on. "All right. I'm a snoop. You didn't close the window, you just turned off the monitor. So I took a look. Eve told me not to, by the way, so don't blame her."

"Isn't that sort of an invasion of privacy?" Phyllis asked coolly.

Carolyn didn't answer that question directly. Instead she said, "I don't understand why you're so reluctant to look into this murder."

"I promised Mike—"

"Mike's been worried about you right from the start," Carolyn pointed out. "That never stopped you before."

"I didn't always have a choice," Phyllis said. "You were in trouble, or Eve was, or somebody had the audacity to commit murder right on my doorstep. I couldn't turn my back on those cases."

"But this time you barely know the man who was arrested. You never said anything to the victim. You've never even set foot in the place where the murder happened. Maybe by now it's just a habit. Or else you have a reputation to live up to. You *are* the crime-solving granny."

"Please!" Phyllis said. "That's just about the last thing I want to be known as. You know I don't like all the notoriety. I'm just worried about Sam. It's important to him, so . . ."

Her voice trailed off.

"It's important to Sam, so it's important to you," Carolyn said. "I don't see anything wrong with admitting that."

"I suppose not," Phyllis said.

"You're afraid that he's going to try to find out who killed Susan Baxter, and that he'll get in over his head."

Sam had used those exact words in describing how he felt. Carolyn was a bit more canny than Phyllis might have given her credit for. She said, "Maybe you should be trying to hunt down the murderer."

Carolyn waved a hand and said, "Pshaw! I have no interest in finding out who killed that woman. I'll leave that up to you and Sam."

"I feel bad about going behind Mike's back . . ."

"He's your son. If he doesn't like what you're doing, then it's his problem, not yours."

"I suppose."

Carolyn stepped past her to look at the casserole where it sat on top of the stove. She said, "Now that we've dealt with that, let's concentrate on the important things. Was the casserole all right?"

Sam thought the white chili casserole was delicious. Phyllis apologized for it being a little overcooked, but he said, "You couldn't tell it by me. That's mighty good eatin'. In fact, I think I'll have another helpin'."

He could tell she was pleased by his approval. As for Sam, the good meal and the pleasant company made him feel better after what had been a frustrating day.

That was what home was all about, he thought as he looked around at Phyllis, Carolyn, and Eve. No matter what the world threw at you, as long as you could sit down at the table with folks you cared about who cared about you, things would be all right in the end.

And if they weren't all right, as that line from a movie had it, well, then, it wasn't really the end yet.

After supper the ladies went into the living room to watch some movie on DVD that had Meryl Streep in it. Sam had absolutely nothing against Meryl Streep, but he had learned that the movies she made usually weren't really his sort of picture. So he opened his laptop and looked up Kyle Woods instead.

After brooding for the rest of the afternoon, thinking that he had no business trying to solve a murder, supper had revitalized him. Maybe he couldn't figure out who had killed Susan Baxter, but it wouldn't hurt anything to try.

Woods's dog-breeding operation was located on the Peaster Highway, northwest of Weatherford. Sam hadn't been out that way in a while, but he thought he remembered seeing the place before. He studied the website until he thought he had it figured out what he was going to do, then spent the rest of the evening reading a Western novel.

He got up the next morning, fed Buck, and then had breakfast with Phyllis, Carolyn, and Eve. Carolyn had gotten up early to prepare and bake her hearty breakfast casserole, and Sam thought it was as good as the white chili casserole he'd had the night before. Sam's glance darted from Phyllis to Carolyn and back again, and then he said cautiously, "Are you two ladies enterin' the recipes for these casseroles in a contest or something?"

"That's right, but don't worry; we're not competing against each other," Phyllis replied with a smile.

"They're for a magazine contest, but we'll be entering them in two separate categories," Carolyn added by way of explanation.

"Oh," Sam said. "Well, I reckon they both stand a mighty good chance of winnin', then."

"Which one did you like the best?" Carolyn asked.

Phyllis laughed and said, "Goodness, don't put him on the spot like that! You don't have to answer, Sam."

"Anyway, we all know what his answer would be," Carolyn said.

"Don't be so sure about that," Sam said. "I call 'em as I see 'em. And in this case . . . well, I like 'em pretty much both the same. I'll be rootin' for the two of you to win."

Eve smiled and said, "You're always the diplomat, aren't you, dear?"

"I live in a house with three ladies," Sam said with a chuckle. "And I didn't just fall off a turnip truck, neither." He reached for his coffee cup, drained the rest of the strong, black brew, and went on. "I got to get dressed and get goin'."

"What are you up to today?" Phyllis asked.

"Oh, you know, this 'n' that. Come on, Buck. It's warmer today. You can stay out in the backyard."

"If he acts like he needs to come in, I'll let him in," Phyllis promised.

The air was still cool, but the day was sunny and pleasant as Sam drove out of town and headed toward the small town of Peaster, a farming community that these days wasn't much more than a wide place in the road.

About twenty minutes later, he spotted what he was looking for on the left side of the two-lane highway. A large sign that read WOODS'S GOLDEN RETRIEVERS sat in the yard in front of a nice-looking brick house. A metal barn much like the one at Hank Baxter's vet clinic, only smaller, was off to one side. Filling up the property behind the house was an extensive collection of wired enclosures, each with a doghouse in it. Those enclosed runs terminated at a long shedlike building with electrical wires running to it from a pole next to the house. Sam supposed the shed was heated so the dogs could get in there during the winter when it was too cold for them to stay in their doghouses. Woods probably kept their feed in there, as well.

A pickup with Woods's name on the door was parked on a concrete driveway in front of a two-car garage at one end of the house. Sam pulled in behind it and stopped. The yard needed mowing, he thought, even though it was autumn. The grass looked like it hadn't been touched since midsummer.

Next to the garage but still attached, on the side away from the rest of the house, was what appeared to be an office. The upper half of the door was glass, and it had the company's name lettered on it as well. That was where Sam went, and when he took hold of the doorknob, it turned.

Inside was a nicely furnished office, confirming his guess. A row of filing cabinets stood along one wall. A large window looked out on the dog runs behind the house. There was also a big-screen TV, a comfortable-looking sofa, and a handsome desk with a computer tucked into a corner workstation. The man behind the desk wore a baseball cap and an open flannel shirt over a T-shirt. He didn't smile as he gave Sam a rather curt nod and said, "Hello. What can I do for you?"

Sam had never met Kyle Woods before, but he had seen the man's picture on the website and knew this was him. He held out his hand and said, "Sam Fletcher."

The man stood up with a little reluctance and shook hands.

"Kyle Woods," he said. "Looking for a dog, or do you have a bitch you need serviced?"

That was the first time anybody had ever asked him that particular question, Sam thought. It just went to show that no matter how old you got, you could still have new experiences.

"I was thinkin' about gettin' a dog," he said, "and I was told you have some of the best ones around these parts."

Woods seemed to warm up a little at that praise. He said, "Who told you that?"

"Vet down in Weatherford." Sam pointed in that direction with a thumb. "Hank Baxter."

The slightly friendlier expression on Woods's face vanished at the mention of Hank's name. With a frown, he said, "I find that hard to believe. Baxter and I aren't on the best of terms these days." Suspicion flared in the dog breeder's eyes. "Besides, isn't he in jail? I thought I heard something about him killing his wife."

"Really?" Sam tried to make himself look and sound surprised. "I hadn't heard about that. This was two or three months ago he told me about your dogs. I just haven't had a chance to do anything about it until now."

That was a shot in the dark, but it seemed to work. Woods grunted and said, "Well, that explains it, I guess. Baxter and I used to have an arrangement. He took care of all my dogs. Then . . . Well, never mind about that. It's not important. One thing that hasn't changed: If you're looking for a golden retriever, I have some of the best you'll ever find. People come from all over the country to do business with me."

"I can believe it, from the looks of those fellas out there," Sam said as he waved a hand toward the window and the enclosures beyond the glass. A number of dogs were visible in their runs. "Mighty fine-lookin' animals."

"Why don't we go take an even better look, Mr. . . . Fletcher, was it?"

"That's right," Sam said.

Woods went to the door, opened it, and motioned for Sam to go outside first.

They followed a concrete walk around the end of the building. It led to a door into the shed. As the dogs noticed the two men, several of them stood up and began to bark and wag their tails.

Even though Sam had fudged the truth a considerable amount during his visit, what he had said to Woods about them being good-looking dogs was the truth. Big, energetic, with thick golden coats, they were fine examples of their breed, at least to Sam's untrained eye. He didn't know all the intricacies that went into being an award-winning show dog. When they watched the National Dog Show on TV at Phyllis's house every Thanksgiving, he never had any idea which dogs would win. The judges always seemed to see things that were beyond him.

As they went into the concrete-floored shed, Woods said, "You *are* interested in a show dog, right, Mr. Fletcher? Not a pet for the grandkids?"

"Does it make a difference?" Sam asked.

Woods laughed. It wasn't a particularly pleasant sound. He said, "It makes a big difference. Several thousand dollars, in fact. Dog shows are big business. Cutthroat business." His voice had an arrogant sneer to it, as if he were trying to impress Sam. "I've been offered more than a hundred thousand dollars for my top dog, Texas Maximus."

Sam let out a low whistle. He was honestly impressed. He had seen things on the website about Texas Maximus but wouldn't have guessed that the dog was worth that much money.

"I turned down those offers," Woods went on. "He's worth more than that to me."

"He wins that much in prize money?"

Woods shook his head and said, "No. He doesn't compete anymore. He's worth it in breeding fees every year. A couple of times that much, in fact. Why sell him and get the money once when I can keep on doubling it every year for several more years?"

"Well, that makes sense," Sam agreed.

"You didn't tell me. Are you looking for a pet?"

"What if I was?"

Woods waved a hand expansively and said, "I've always got a few culls, perfectly healthy dogs with style flaws that are bad enough to keep them from competing."

Some of the dogs had come into the shed, which had a walkway closed off by wire from the runs. Sam looked through the wire at the dogs, who were still wagging their tails and clamoring for attention, and said, "None of these dogs look like what I'd call culls."

"Actually, they're not. I keep those in some pens on the other side of the creek that runs through the back of my property. These are all show dogs. But, no offense, a civilian like you probably wouldn't be able to tell that just by looking. I'm talking about things like an irregularity in bone structure, misaligned teeth, eyes a little too close together, things like that. They're still good dogs for pets. You just can't show 'em."

"Well . . . maybe I wouldn't mind takin' a look. I was thinkin' about gettin' a dog that'd be a good pet but maybe puttin' him in some shows, too. Sounds like that's out of my price range, though."

"Sure," Woods said, sounding like he had lost all interest in this conversation. "When we go back outside, there's a trail that runs toward the back of the property. Just follow it. It's about a quarter of a mile back to the other kennels. You see any you particularly like, just let me know. I'll be in the office."

Sam knew he'd been dismissed. When they left the shed, Woods went one way and Sam went the other. He had no interest in getting another dog, of course. He was well pleased with Buck. But he wanted to keep up the pose so he wouldn't make Woods suspicious, and besides, he was curious.

It took him a few minutes to reach the other kennels Woods had mentioned. They were on the other side of a little creek, which Sam crossed on a wooden footbridge. The dogs saw him coming and barked frantically. These enclosures were much more bare-bones, Sam noted. Several dogs were in each one. That was probably good, because they could crowd into the doghouses for warmth during the winter. Their coats were thicker, shaggier, and they didn't appear to have been groomed in a long time, if ever.

The dogs didn't seem to have been mistreated, Sam thought. They had water, and it was relatively clean. There were food bowls in each pen, along with a few toys. But there was just something shabby about the setup that told Sam their owner didn't really care about them.

Maybe it was the way they flocked to the fences, obviously starved for affection. He moved along the front of the enclosures, reaching his fingers through the openings in the wire and scratching as many floppy golden ears as he could as the dogs stood up on the fence to greet him. He could have stayed out there all day petting them, he thought, and it wouldn't have been enough to satisfy them.

He hated to leave, but he hadn't really found out what he'd come there to learn. He said, "So long, fellas," and turned to leave. He had to grit his teeth and force himself to keep walking as they barked behind him as if they were trying to call him back.

He walked back around to the office and let himself in. Woods was on the phone with somebody. The man held up a finger in the now-universal symbol for asking a visitor to wait. He didn't look happy.

"Hey, I'm sorry you're upset, but a deal's a deal," Woods said into the phone. "I held up my part of the bargain in good faith. You know Texas Maximus's reputation. The problem's with your bitch, whether you want to hear that or not." He paused, then said, "No refunds. You know that. Not even a partial one. I'm not in business for my health, you know."

Sam heard the sound of the other person hanging up emphatically, even violently. Woods took the phone away from his ear, glared at it for a second, and then muttered an obscenity.

"Sorry about that," he said to Sam as he put the cordless phone back on its base. "You find a dog down there that you like?"

"Found too many," Sam said with a smile. "I like 'em all. I'm gonna have to bring the missus back with me and let her have a look at 'em. Maybe the grandkids."

"Yeah, fine." Woods picked up a card from the desk and held it out to him. "Maybe you better call first next time. I'm not always here. This is a one-man operation."

"Your family doesn't help you out?"

"I'm divorced," Woods said. "Kids are grown and gone."

Sam slipped the card in his shirt pocket and said, "I'll be back." He started to turn away, then stopped and added, "It's none of my business, but you sounded earlier like you had some sort of fallin' out with Hank Baxter. I always thought he seemed like a nice fella."

"You're right. It's none of your business. Baxter's too stiff-necked. Too stubborn for his own good. I got tired of trying to make him understand how I do things, so I fired him as my vet. Hell, there are plenty of other animal doctors out there."

"Yeah, I suppose so. I'll be seein' you, Mr. Woods."

Woods just grunted and turned to his computer, obviously uninterested in anything else Sam had to say.

That was one unfriendly fella, Sam thought as he drove back toward town. Judging by that phone call Sam had overheard the end of, Woods had at least one unsatisfied customer, too. Sam still didn't know exactly what had caused the rift between Woods and Hank Baxter, other than the fact that Baxter didn't care for the way the dog breeder conducted his business.

It was a long way from that to killing a woman and framing her husband for the murder, and just because Woods was a jerk didn't mean he was capable of such a thing.

If it turned out that Woods had killed Susan Baxter, though, Sam wasn't going to be unhappy about it. Maybe those dogs—those culls, as Woods had called them—would wind up with somebody who appreciated and loved them.

That wasn't the way a detective ought to be thinking, he told himself. Somebody looking for a killer had to keep an open mind and not rule out anybody because they were likable or focus completely on one suspect because they were unpleasant. The only things that mattered were the facts and the inescapable conclusion they led to. So far he was a little short on facts, Sam thought.

But he was just getting started.

Chapter 15

$\mathcal{P}$hyllis had told Sam she would keep an eye on Buck, so she spent the morning digging deeper into Susan Baxter's life on the computer. Susan had been in her early forties, a little older than Phyllis had thought from the couple of times she had seen the woman briefly. She had been practicing in Weatherford for eight years.

Phyllis recalled what Sam had told her about Susan working to put her husband through veterinary school before she had gone to medical school herself. Because of that, Susan had been a few years older than some new doctors by the time she got her career going.

She hadn't wasted any time establishing herself as a top surgeon, however. Phyllis found a number of references to her in online medical journals, as well as several papers Susan Baxter had published in those journals. All the medical mumbo jumbo in those papers didn't mean anything to Phyllis, but it certainly looked impressive. Susan's ideas had to have some merit to them, since those journals were peer-reviewed.

Of course, how smart a person was didn't always have any sort of relation to what kind of person they were. From what Phyllis had seen of Susan Baxter, the woman was angry and bitter and not pleasant to be around at all. But maybe she had good reason to be that way.

Phyllis wasn't exactly a computer expert, but she knew enough to be able to locate arrest records. Some searching told her that both Hank and Susan Baxter had been arrested a couple of times each for charges related to domestic disturbances during the past six months. In each case, those charges had been dropped.

The fact that the police had been called to the Baxter residence that many times was worrisome. Even though those charges had been dropped, if the prosecutor managed to get them in at the trial, they would be damaging to Hank Baxter's defense. And to be honest, Phyllis thought, the history of trouble between the spouses really did make it more likely that Hank had killed his wife. Phyllis knew Sam wouldn't want to hear that.

She heard a noise and realized it was Buck scratching at the back door. She let him in, and without being told, he went straight to his bed in the utility room. He really was a pretty smart dog, Phyllis thought.

Sam came in a while later. Buck heard the garage door go up and was waiting at the kitchen door for him. A little tail wagging, hand licking, ear scratching later, Sam came into the living room.

"Where are Carolyn and Eve?" he asked.

"They've gone to the craft store," Phyllis said. "Eve needs some new projects."

"Never thought I'd see her bein' quite so crafty. I guess everybody's got to settle down a mite sooner or later, even spitfires like her. With all that traffic down on South Main, they're liable to be gone most of the day."

"I know. It's terrible." Phyllis shook her head. "Certainly not the way it was when we were younger. But there's no going back to the past, is there?"

"Even if there was, we probably wouldn't want to," Sam said. "Then we'd have to relive all the bad things as well as the good. I wouldn't want that. Reckon memories are enough."

"Yes, I think you're right," Phyllis said. "What have you been up to?"

"Well, that's one reason I asked where Carolyn and Eve were," Sam said as he sat down in one of the armchairs. "I went out to see Kyle Woods."

"The dog breeder?"

"Yep. The fella you saw arguin' with Hank Baxter last week."

Unable to stop herself, Phyllis leaned forward in her chair and looked intently at Sam. "Did you find out anything from him?" she asked.

"Well, mostly that I don't like him much."

"That seems to be pretty common."

"But he told me that Hank Baxter used to be his vet and took care of all his dogs. Then a few months ago they had some sort of fallin' out between 'em. Woods implied it was because Baxter didn't like the way he does business."

"He seems to be very successful at breeding golden retrievers," Phyllis said.

"Yeah, he's successful, all right. If you don't believe it, just ask him. He'll tell you all about it."

"A little full of himself, is he?"

Sam nodded and said, "Yeah, that was my impression. But I also got the impression that maybe he's not quite as successful as he lets on. While I was there, he argued with somebody else on the phone, somebody who wanted their money back because of a problem with . . . well, with the stud service."

Phyllis managed not to laugh, but she couldn't help smiling as she asked, "Sam, are you blushing?"

"Can't help it. I'm just the old-fashioned sort, I guess. Not real comfortable talkin' about such things with a lady."

"It's all right," Phyllis told him. "I'm not embarrassed, and there's no reason for you to be. Did his award-winning show dog Texas Maximus have trouble performing?"

"Good grief," Sam muttered. "No, that wasn't it. I think the fella just wasn't happy with the pups his dog had. Evidently, they don't have to have much wrong with them to be worthless as show dogs. Those judges must be really picky."

"I imagine. I've never really understood all the fine points of it, myself."

"Me, neither. Anyway, I told Woods that I was lookin' for a dog and that Hank Baxter told me to check with him, and that was when Woods acted surprised and told me he and Baxter weren't workin' together anymore. I was able to cover that by claimin' Baxter said something to me several months ago and I was just gettin' around to doin' something about it."

"That was smart," Phyllis said. "Using procrastination as an excuse nearly always works. People don't have any trouble believing it because people put things off all the time."

"Yep." Sam went on to describe the rest of his visit, including the so-called culls. He sighed and said, "That part of what I told Woods was true. I really did want to take all of 'em with me. But I suppose your backyard would be pretty crowded with twenty-five dogs in it."

"Not to mention, the city wouldn't let us have that many," Phyllis pointed out. "I'm sorry you had to leave them there, though. I hope they all find good homes."

"It was after that I asked Woods point-blank what caused the trouble between him and Baxter," Sam said. "He dodged the question, though."

Phyllis turned back to the computer and said, "Let's see if Woods has been in trouble with the law recently."

A few minutes of searching told her that Kyle Woods had not been arrested in Parker County during the past two years. However, acting on a hunch, Phyllis checked a database that contained civil lawsuit filings, and she found something.

"Look here," she told Sam as she pointed at the screen. "Woods has been sued three times for fraud. There's no disposition listed for any of the suits, which means they were either withdrawn or settled."

Sam leaned down from his considerable height to look over her shoulder. "You think those lawsuits had something to do with his dog-breedin' business?" he asked.

"I don't see what else they could have been about, although I suppose anything's possible. Not likely, though."

"So Woods has got angry customers and he's had lawsuits filed against him. It stands to reason that whatever he's up to, that's the reason Hank Baxter didn't want to be involved with him anymore."

"That makes sense to me, too," Phyllis agreed with a nod.

"So if Baxter had proof that Woods was up to something illegal . . ." Sam's voice trailed off as he shook his head. "No, that doesn't make sense the way I was goin'. Woods wouldn't kill Susan Baxter in order to scare Hank Baxter into keepin' his mouth shut. I think that'd just make Hank more likely to spill whatever it is he knows."

"But Hank isn't in a good position to testify against Woods now, is he? His credibility is ruined as long as he's under suspicion of murder. If he's convicted and sent to prison, he'll be even less credible."

"Why not just kill Baxter?" Sam asked. "That would shut him up for sure."

"Maybe Woods thought it would be easier to kill Susan and frame Hank for the murder."

Sam frowned as he thought about that. He nodded slowly and said, "Woods is a good-sized fella, but he's out of shape. He might figure it that way, all right."

"Still, that seems awfully extreme, murdering a woman you basically have nothing against just to discredit a man who might cause legal problems for you."

"Murder's pretty extreme no matter what the reason," Sam said.

"Yes, that's true, of course. And maybe it wasn't just that Hank represented a potential threat to Woods anymore. Remember, Woods came to see Hank last week. Maybe Hank asked him to come to the clinic and threatened to expose whatever it is he's been doing."

"Which we don't know for sure is anything," Sam pointed out. "Maybe the trouble Woods has been havin' with some of his customers comes from honest disagreements."

"That's a possibility, of course," Phyllis said with a nod. "But so is the other scenario, the one where Woods is doing something illegal, or at least shady enough that he didn't want Hank Baxter telling anybody about it."

Sam started to pace back and forth. He said, "We got to start keepin' a closer eye on Woods. If he's up to something, he's bound to slip up sooner or later." He stopped his pacing and turned to look at Phyllis. "I mean I'll have to keep a closer eye on him. You're supposed to be stayin' out of this, remember?"

Phyllis smiled and said, "I think we both might as well admit that that isn't going to happen, despite what I intended."

"Good intentions, road to hell, et cetera, et cetera," Sam said with a wave of his hand. "I still don't want you gettin' mixed up with Woods. I don't trust that fella. If he thinks somebody's messin' in his business, there's no tellin' what he might do."

"Which is exactly why he's a suspect in Susan Baxter's murder. But I understand what you mean, Sam. You do the legwork on Woods."

"What are you goin' to do?"

"Susan is bound to have had other enemies," Phyllis said. "The key to finding them is to learn more about her. I have a few ideas . . ."

Susan Baxter's practice was located in a complex of medical offices across Santa Fe Drive from the hospital. Phyllis parked her Lincoln in front of the building, and as she did, she saw a wreath hanging on one of the doors. Not surprisingly, that turned out to be the door to Susan's office.

At least there was no crime scene tape, which Phyllis took to mean that the crime scene and forensics investigators were through there and had collected all the evidence they were going to.

She thought that the office might be closed because of Susan's death, but the funeral wasn't until the next day so there was a chance someone might be there. Phyllis had looked up the information about the service on the funeral home's website before she drove over there.

When she tried the door, it was unlocked. She went inside and found herself in a nicely furnished waiting room with a counter and receptionist's window to her left.

It was also an empty waiting room at the moment.

"Can I help you?"

The voice came from behind the counter. The young woman who sat at the receptionist's desk was about twenty-five, Phyllis estimated, with long, light brown hair. Her nose had been broken at some time in the past, and that had left it with a tiny, almost unnoticeable bump that didn't distract from her wholesome prettiness. The red, slightly swollen eyes that showed she had been crying did a little bit, though.

"I'm sorry," Phyllis said automatically. She would have done that anyway if she'd encountered someone who was upset, but now she had another reason for wanting to present a sympathetic ear. "Is something wrong?"

"There's been a . . . a death," the young woman said.

"Oh, goodness!" Phyllis said. She had never thought of herself as much of an actor, but the past few years had revealed unsuspected talents in that area. She always felt a little guilty when she had to lie to people, but she told herself it was for a good cause. She went on. "One of Dr. Baxter's patients?"

"No, it's . . . Dr. Baxter."

Phyllis looked shocked. It wasn't that much of a stretch. It really was shocking that a woman had been beaten to death right here in this very office. Not in this waiting room, of course, but only a few feet away.

"That's terrible," she said. "I stopped by to make an appointment to see her."

"Do you have a medical problem?" the young woman asked. "I can refer you to someone . . ."

"I need to have some gallstones removed," Phyllis said. She had decided on that because she'd actually had such an operation several years earlier and thought she could bluff her way through a conversation about the procedure. "Dr. Baxter was one of the surgeons my doctor suggested, so I thought I would talk it over with her before I made up my mind."

That wasn't exactly the way these things usually worked, Phyllis knew, but it wasn't so unreasonable or far-fetched as to be suspicious. At least she hoped it wasn't.

The receptionist didn't seem to think twice about Phyllis's explanation. She said, "I'm sorry, but you understand . . ."

"Of course," Phyllis said. "I'll talk to my regular doctor again and get his advice on how to proceed. I'm really sorry to hear about Dr. Baxter. Was it a sudden illness, or had she been sick for a while?"

The receptionist's eyes widened. She said, "You don't know?"

Phyllis just put a puzzled look on her face and shook her head.

The receptionist leaned forward and said in a hushed voice, "She was murdered!"

Before Phyllis could do more than start to look shocked, another woman's voice said, "Raylene!"

There was a counter beside the receptionist's desk on the other side of the window, the way things were set up in most doctors' offices, so that patients could conclude their visit, pay anything they owed, schedule a follow-up appointment, or whatever before coming back out into the waiting room. While Phyllis and the receptionist were talking, another woman had come up to that counter from somewhere deeper in the office.

She was a brunette in her thirties, very attractive and well dressed. Instantly, the woman struck Phyllis as familiar, and after a moment she realized why. She had seen pictures of the brunette while searching the Web for information about Susan Baxter. She was Meredith Carlyle, Susan's sister.

Sam had told Phyllis about the unpleasant conversation between Meredith and the two young employees at Hank Baxter's clinic. Meredith lived up to that reputation as she snapped, "My sister didn't pay you to sit around and gossip, Raylene, and I'm certainly not going to, either."

It sounded like Meredith Carlyle thought she was in charge here at her late sister's office, just like she was trying to take over at the vet clinic.

Raylene caught her lower lip between her teeth for a second, then nodded. "Yes, ma'am," she said without looking up. "I'm sorry."

Meredith jerked her head toward Phyllis and asked, "Who's this?"

"Just a prospective patient, ma'am. I've already told her

she'll have to find another doctor to perform her gallstone surgery."

Meredith opened the door between the waiting room and the corridor that led back into the rest of the office. She came out into the waiting room and with obviously grudging politeness said to Phyllis, "I'm sorry, but we've had a tragedy here. The office is actually closed. We're just here trying to clean up some of the business affairs . . ."

"I understand," Phyllis said. "I'm sorry I intruded."

"No, that's perfectly all right. You didn't know . . . You really *didn't* know?"

"About what happened to poor Dr. Baxter?" Phyllis caught herself just before she used the phrase *your sister.* Meredith hadn't introduced herself, so the person Phyllis was pretending to be shouldn't have had any idea that she was Susan's sister.

"That's right. I don't see how you could have missed it. It's been all over the newspaper and the TV."

"Well, that explains it. I don't read the newspaper anymore, and the only TV stations I watch are those that show reruns of all my favorite shows from forty or fifty years ago."

Phyllis actually did watch those stations most of the time. Some people might argue the notion, but TV had been better back then as far as she was concerned. But she wasn't really anywhere near as clueless about current events as she was making herself out to be.

Meredith went on. "Well, I'm afraid we can't help you, but good luck with your medical situation."

"Thank you, dear," Phyllis said with a smile. "I suppose I should be going now." She started to turn toward the door but paused to look through the receptionist's window again. "And thank you, too. Raylene, was it? My, that's a pretty name. Is it an old family name? How is it spelled?"

"It's, uh, R-A-Y-L-E-N-E," the young woman said. She cast a nervous glance in Meredith's direction, as if she was worried that her former boss's sister might get mad at her again. But she added in answer to Phyllis's question, "It was my grandmother's name."

"Well, it's beautiful, and so are you."

Meredith said with a growing edge of impatience in her voice, "If there's nothing else we can do for you . . ."

"No, that's all," Phyllis said. "Good-bye."

Let them think she was just a dotty old woman with gallstones, she told herself as she left the office.

If either of them had anything to hide, sooner or later they would find out differently.

Chapter 16

After supper that evening, Phyllis told Sam about her visit to Dr. Susan Baxter's office. Their quiet-voiced conversation took place on the back porch while Buck poked around the yard in the last of the day's fading light.

"So I didn't really learn much, I'm afraid," Phyllis said. "But I did get a look at Meredith Carlyle. She was exactly like you described her, Sam."

"I was worried I might've been a little too hard on her," Sam said. "She just lost her sister, after all. That might've made her act, well . . ."

"Bitchier than she really is?" Phyllis shook her head. "I think most of the time stress just brings out the way we really are to start with. The filters people put in place in civilized society are down and their real selves come out. That's why people under duress are capable of great cruelty . . . or great courage."

"Spoken like a history teacher," Sam said with a smile.

"History teaches us a lot."

"So does basketball, mainly that if you want to succeed, you got to hustle."

"So what's our next move?" Phyllis asked.

Sam looked surprised. He said, "Shoot, I don't know. You were always the one who figured out what we needed to do next."

"But this is your investigation. I'm just helping, remember?"

Sam frowned in thought for a long moment, then said, "I want to find out more about whatever it was that made Hank Baxter stop bein' Kyle Woods's vet. If there's any chance Woods killed Susan, it's got to come back to that."

"I agree," Phyllis said with a nod. "But how are you going to find out? You said you already asked Woods, and he wouldn't tell you anything."

"There's at least one other person who knows," Sam said.

"Hank Baxter himself."

"Yeah." Sam sighed. "I may have to come clean with the doc and tell him what we're doin'. I don't know how he'll react."

"If he's innocent, I'd think that he would be very grateful someone believes him and wants to help him."

"Yeah. The worst he can do is tell me to butt out, too."

"Those two young people who work at the clinic might know something about it," Phyllis mused.

"Tommy and Holly? Yeah, they might. I hadn't forgotten about 'em. That's why I said there was at least one other person who could tell me what happened. Could be more. As a matter of fact, it might be smart to approach them first. They're friendly enough, and they know me by now. If I ask Baxter first and he doesn't want to tell me, he might order Tommy and Holly not to talk to me, too."

"That makes sense."

"I'll go back out there in the morning," Sam said.

"What about Susan Baxter's funeral?" Phyllis asked. "It's tomorrow afternoon."

Sam scratched at his jaw, looked doubtful, and said, "We can't very well go to that, can we? We weren't exactly friends of the family."

"The notice about the service didn't say that it was private. If there are enough people there, it's possible no one would notice us."

"You really think we'd find out anything useful at a funeral?"

"You never know until you try," Phyllis said.

After breakfast the next morning, Sam drove out to the vet clinic. He was going to have to come clean with Baxter's two young assistants and admit that he was investigating Susan Baxter's murder. He didn't have any idea how they would react to that, but otherwise he was at a dead end.

As he approached the driveway that led to the clinic, he saw another pickup pull out from it and turn in the other direction. Sam slowed as he saw the writing on the other vehicle's door and recognized it.

That was Kyle Woods leaving the clinic.

Another vehicle was coming up the driveway from the clinic toward the road. This was a car with a man behind the wheel. Sam eased his pickup to the side of the road as if he were stopping at one of the houses along there. He stopped and waited as the car slowed down for the driver to look both ways along the road before pulling out.

Sam recognized the man behind the wheel. He was Tommy Sanders, Hank Baxter's assistant.

Tommy turned in the other direction as well and fell in behind Kyle Woods's pickup. That could be perfectly innocent, Sam told himself. Just because they had left the clinic one right after the other and were going in the same direction didn't mean Tommy was following Woods.

But it didn't mean he wasn't, and as far as Sam could see, there was only one way to find out.

Questioning Tommy and Holly could wait. Right now he wanted to find out where Tommy was going.

He knew he was acting purely on gut instinct as he pulled out from the side of the road where he had stopped the pickup. He had read enough Western novels and watched enough Western movies to know that sometimes a man had to play a hunch.

Tommy was about a quarter of a mile ahead of him. Sam sped up a little to narrow the gap without getting too close. He thought it was highly doubtful that Tommy would recognize his pickup, but if Sam was right behind him, the young man might glance in his rearview mirror, see his face, and realize who he was. The trick was to hang back but still stay close enough that he wouldn't lose sight of Tommy's car.

By the time Tommy reached US 180, also known as Fort Worth Highway and formerly US 80, the main east-west artery through town and that part of the country before the interstate came through, Sam was a couple of hundred yards behind him. Sam worried that the red light at the highway would let Tommy through the intersection but catch him. His foot got a little heavier on the gas. He couldn't speed too much, though, or he'd risk being stopped by a Weatherford police car. That would be the end of his attempt at trailing the young veterinary assistant.

Sam made it through the light on yellow. He had seen Tommy turn left onto the highway and head toward the court-house square. Sam felt relieved when he spotted Tommy's car up ahead. A couple of vehicles were in between them now, which ought to make it even easier to trail the young man. Sam couldn't be sure, but he thought he even saw Kyle Woods's pickup farther ahead.

When the little informal procession reached the square, Sam still had two vehicles, a car and an SUV, between him and Tommy. He saw Woods's pickup make a right onto Farm to Market Road 51 and head north. Tommy did likewise, and so did Sam.

The road to Peaster turned off this road. Sam had to fall back again as they reached the northern edge of town and traffic began to thin out, but he felt certain now that Woods was on his way back to his house and Tommy was following him for some reason. Tommy wasn't trying to trail Woods without being spotted, though. In fact, his car was right be-hind the dog breeder's pickup.

Sure enough, they both turned onto the Peaster Highway. Sam did, too. When they reached Woods's house, Woods turned in at the driveway and pulled around beside the shed next to the dog runs. Tommy parked in the driveway in front of the office and got out of his car.

That was all Sam saw before he drove on past. He didn't think he could get away with pulling in behind them. No tall tale he could spin would keep Woods from being suspicious of him showing up again.

A quarter of a mile farther on, Sam came to an unpaved county road. He swung into it, backed up, and turned around to drive toward Weatherford again. By the time he passed Woods's place, Tommy's car was empty and there was no sign of the young man. He and Woods were probably in the shed or inside the office, Sam thought.

This was pretty interesting. Hank Baxter had stopped being Kyle Woods's vet, but clearly some connection still existed between Tommy and Woods.

Sam didn't slow down. He drove on past and headed for town. He didn't think Woods or Tommy would tell him what was going on if he asked them straight out.

But there might be another way to find out what he wanted to know.

When Sam got back to the vet clinic, only one car was parked in the lot. He figured it belonged to Holly, and when he went in, he found her behind the counter, confirming his guess.

"Howdy," he said with a smile, trying to be as avuncular as possible, although considering the gap in their ages, grandfatherly might be a more apt description, he thought.

"Mr. Fletcher," she said. "You don't have Buck with you, do you? His appointment isn't for a few days yet."

"No. I just came by to see how you folks are doin'. Has Dr. Baxter come back to work yet?"

"No, he hasn't." Holly lowered her voice. "His wife's funeral is today."

"Is he goin'?" That seemed to Sam like a legitimate question to ask under the circumstances.

"He says he is. He says that Susan—the other Dr. Baxter—was his wife, and even though they were having trouble, he still loved her."

"That lady who was here the other day . . . Susan Baxter's sister, was she? . . . I don't think she'll be very happy if he shows up at the funeral."

"No, she won't," Holly agreed. "But Dr. Baxter said that Meredith Carlyle wasn't going to keep him away." She shook her head worriedly. "I'm afraid there's going to be more trouble."

"Well, we can hope not," Sam said. "How are things goin' here at the clinic?"

"Nearly everybody has picked up their pets and taken them somewhere else. At this rate, the practice may have to shut down soon."

"That'd be a real shame. I haven't known you folks for long, but I can tell that all of you really care about animals." Sam looked around. "Where's Tommy today? Out at the barn?"

"No, he's . . . running an errand. That's the one bright spot, I guess. One of our old customers came by and wanted to talk to Tommy about a job."

"You mean this fella wants to work here? Or he wants to hire Tommy?"

"He wants to hire Tommy. When I said that was a bright spot, I might have been stretching the truth a little. I'm not sure it's a good idea. But if Dr. Baxter can't keep the clinic going, Tommy's going to need another job, especially if he's going to try to attend vet school. With the economy the way it is these days, a person can't be too picky, I guess."

"You said this was a customer of the doc's talkin' about hirin' him? Not another vet?"

"No," Holly said. "A dog breeder. A very successful one. He's had a number of champions."

Sam nodded and made himself look impressed. He said, "Well, that might be a pretty good deal, I guess. Tommy would be helpin' him with his business?"

"That's right. There are all sorts of medications and supplements to keep track of, and some of the dogs have to have injections and things like that."

"Show dogs, eh?" Sam chuckled. "They're not on the juice, are they?"

"Pardon me?" Holly said with a puzzled frown.

"You know, like baseball players on steroids. They don't do things like that with show dogs, do they?"

Holly's face tightened up. She said, "I don't know anything about that."

Sam's pulse kicked into a higher gear. He wondered if he had accidentally stumbled into the thing that had caused the dispute between Hank Baxter and Kyle Woods. Were there doping rules in dog show competitions? Sam had no idea, but he was willing to bet that some time on the computer would allow him to find out. If that was true, could a doping scandal have ruined Woods's lucrative business? Was there enough at stake to provide a motive for murder?

Sam knew he was going to have to look into this. But for the moment he grinned and waved a hand and said, "Shoot, I was just jokin'. Didn't mean nothin' by it."

"Oh." Holly seemed to relax a little, but she went on. "If there's nothing I can do to help you, Mr. Fletcher . . ."

She had been remarkably forthcoming, although her candor wasn't really a surprise to Sam. She was a friendly young woman, and she liked to talk. He had known that already, or he wouldn't have come here to see if he could find out anything through some apparently casual conversation.

"No, I'll be back Friday with Buck," he said. "I sure hope Dr. Baxter is workin' again by then."

"I wouldn't count on it. This has been a terrible ordeal for him. It was bad enough to have his wife die, but for her to have been murdered and then have the police arrest him for killing her . . . If anything like that ever happened to me, I'd want to just curl up into a ball and hide out from the world. I wouldn't care about work."

"I might not, either," Sam said. "If the doc's not here, could Tommy check Buck?"

"Well, sure, he could. He's done things like that plenty of times before, but Dr. Baxter was always here to make sure everything was all right."

Sam didn't want to lose his excuse for coming out here to the clinic, but he had to think of Buck's welfare, too, he reminded himself. He said, "Under the circumstances, maybe it'd be better if I made an appointment with another vet."

"I think that would be a good idea, for Buck's sake. I can call one of the other clinics we've been sending patients to and make the appointment for you, if you'd like."

"Will it be with somebody who's good?"

"Of course. Just because Buck's not going to be our patient anymore doesn't mean we don't want him to receive the best of care."

"All right, then," he said with a nod. "Go ahead and do that, if you don't mind."

Holly reached for the phone and asked, "Would you rather it be Friday morning or afternoon?"

"Either one," Sam said. "My schedule's wide-open."

It took Holly a couple of minutes to make the appointment. She repeated, "Two o'clock?" to the person on the other end of the phone connection and raised her eyebrows at Sam. He nodded to indicate the time was all right with him.

They settled on that. Holly hung up and wrote down all the information on a card that she handed to Sam.

"They'll take good care of you and Buck there," she said. "I'll miss seeing him, though. He's such a cutie."

"Oh, we'll be back," Sam said confidently. "Once things have settled down, Doc Baxter will be Buck's vet from now on."

"I hope you're right," Holly said, but she sounded rather doubtful. She looked sad, and it was easy to understand why. She was faced with possibly losing her job, and as she had said, with the economy in the shape it was in, jobs weren't easy to come by.

Of course, Hank Baxter had an even worse fate possibly facing him: prison.

Sam said good-bye and turned to leave the office. His head was full of thoughts, mostly about Tommy and Kyle Woods. If the dog breeder was mixed up in something illegal or at least unethical and needed somebody to help him now that Baxter was out of the picture, Tommy was in a particularly vulnerable position. Sam wondered how he might be able to talk with the young man again.

He was so absorbed in those musings that while he was aware of another vehicle pulling into the parking lot, he didn't really pay much attention to it. He was reaching for the handle of the pickup's driver's-side door when the doors of the car opened and a familiar voice said, "Well, there's your good old friend now."

Sam looked across the pickup's hood and felt a shock of recognition go through him as he saw Jimmy D'Angelo standing there. The lawyer had just gotten out from behind the wheel of the car.

Hank Baxter stood on the other side of the car wearing a dark suit. He frowned and asked, "What are you talking about, Jimmy?"

"This guy," D'Angelo said as he pointed a finger at Sam. "He showed up at the office the other day asking questions and acting like you and him were lifelong pals. But as it turned out, he was lying."

"He sure as hell was." Baxter came around the front of the car. Angry lines formed on his face as he rounded the pickup, slapped a hand on the hood, and demanded, "Just what are you up to, Fletcher?"

Chapter 17

$\mathcal{S}$am supposed he couldn't blame Baxter for being suspicious and upset. After everything that had happened, Baxter had to feel like the whole world had turned against him.

But at the same time, Sam didn't like being confronted like that. He said coldly, "Take it easy, Doc. You don't have so many friends right now that you can afford to lose one."

"You're not my friend," Baxter snapped. "You're just a man who brought his dog here."

"And you did a good job of takin' care of that dog," Sam said. His tone eased a little as he went on. "That makes you a friend, as far as I'm concerned. A friend to Buck and a friend to me."

D'Angelo said, "You still haven't answered the question. You're up to something, Fletcher, and we all know it. You'd better come clean. If you're trying to sabotage my client's defense—"

"Good Lord," Sam said. "You fellas are way off base. I'm

tryin' to help your client. I'm tryin' to find out who really killed Susan Baxter."

Hank Baxter's eyes widened in surprise. He said, "Who asked you to do that?"

"Nobody. I just figure you're innocent, that's all. I don't want to think that somebody who cares for dogs as much as you do could be a murderer."

"Hitler had dogs," D'Angelo said.

A harsh, humorless laugh came from Baxter. He said, "You're not helping, Jimmy." He narrowed his eyes again as he looked at Sam. "You really think I'm innocent."

"Yeah, I do."

"Well, I appreciate that, I guess. Nearly everybody I see these days looks at me like they're scared I'm about to go berserk and start slaughtering people."

"If they'd seen the way you took care of Buck, they'd know better."

Baxter grunted and said, "That's good to hear. I'm not sure about this business of you investigating the case, though. Won't that get you in trouble with the law?"

"I'm not messin' with evidence or witnesses; just lookin' around and askin' a few questions. I'm not pretendin' to be a cop or anything like that."

D'Angelo asked, "Is Mrs. Newsom helping you?"

Sam said, "Yeah, a little—" He stopped short and frowned at the lawyer. "How'd you know about Phyllis?"

D'Angelo chuckled and said, "I have a confession of my own to make. When you came to my office the other day, before my secretary let you in to see me, I looked up your name online. That led me right to your connection with Phyllis

Newsom and your involvement in the cases she's solved. That's why I talked to you. That story you made up didn't fool me for a second."

Sam's frown deepened as he said, "Then all that stuff you told me about the case . . ."

"I was hoping you'd pass it along to Mrs. Newsom and that she'd be intrigued enough to take a hand in this. I'm not proud. If it helps my client, I'll take help from anybody, even a crime-busting little old lady."

"Wait just a minute," Baxter said. He looked completely confused by now. "What little old lady? What's going on here?"

"You remember the lady who was with me when I first brought Buck in? The one who brought those treats for the Halloween party with her friend Carolyn?"

"Of course," Baxter said. "Mrs. Newsom. I know who you're talking about." He looked back and forth between Sam and D'Angelo. "What I don't understand is this business about crimebusting."

"Phyllis has solved a few murders in the past," Sam admitted.

"Close to a dozen, in fact," D'Angelo said. "I've done more extensive research since you came to my office, Fletcher. It wasn't long ago she trapped that killer at the state fair in Dallas."

Sam shrugged. Phyllis's exploits as a detective had been written up in the newspapers, so they were a matter of public record.

"You thought this woman could help you win my case?" Baxter asked.

"I thought it was worth a shot. What do you say, Fletcher? Do the two of you want to work for me as consultants?"

"Me and Phyllis, you mean?"

"That's right."

"That'd make us like . . . private detectives?"

"Well, I wouldn't go that far," D'Angelo replied. "Like I said, you'd be consultants. That would give the two of you a little legal standing."

That was something they'd never had, Sam thought. They had always been strictly amateurs in their investigations. He didn't know how Phyllis would feel about making it even quasi-official.

"I'll have to talk to Phyllis about it," he said.

"Of course. In the meantime, why don't the three of us sit down and have a talk."

"About what?" Baxter asked.

"I want to fill Mr. Fletcher in on everything we know about the case. That'll help him make an informed decision."

"How do we know we can trust him?" Baxter glanced at Sam. "I don't mean for that to sound offensive, but really, I barely know you. I'm still not completely sure why you're so determined to help me."

"Because it's the right thing to do," Sam said without hesitation.

Baxter thought about it for a moment, then shrugged. "All right," he said. "Let's go into my office and sit down and talk."

D'Angelo asked Sam, "How about it, Mr. Fletcher?"

Sam had already decided that he needed to put his cards on the table with Baxter. He hadn't figured that he would get a chance to do it this soon, but it made no sense to turn down the opportunity. He answered D'Angelo's question by saying, "I think I'd like that."

Baxter glanced at his watch as they started for the clinic

door. He said, "I need to keep track of the time. Susan . . ." He had to stop and take a breath. "Susan's funeral is this afternoon."

Sam thought the emotional catch in Baxter's voice was more evidence that the veterinarian hadn't murdered his wife. Baxter seemed genuinely upset about Susan's death. Of course, it was possible he was acting. Sam had seen cold-blooded killers do that before.

In the end, though, they hadn't been good enough actors to fool Phyllis.

She should be here for this, he told himself. After all, it was her detective skills D'Angelo wanted to enlist in Baxter's defense, not his. But if he asked them to wait while he called her and got her over here, Baxter might change his mind about cooperating. With all the turmoil going on in his brain and heart, it was hard to predict what he might do.

Sam decided he would just have to remember everything that was said and repeat it back to Phyllis later on, as close to verbatim as he could. Actually, he had gotten pretty good at that over the past few years as he assisted her in her investigations.

As the three men entered the clinic, Holly looked surprised and stood up from the stool behind the counter.

"Mr. Fletcher," she said, "I thought you were leaving."

"I was," Sam said, "but then I ran into the doc here."

Baxter said, "I really don't care for being called Doc. Why don't you just make it Hank?"

"All right," Sam said with a nod.

"We'll be in my office, Holly," Baxter went on. "I don't want to be disturbed unless it's an emergency."

Holly still looked confused, but she nodded and said, "Of course, Doctor."

Baxter led them behind the counter and through the door into his office. It wasn't big, and its furnishings were plain and functional. Sam liked that. Baxter wasn't interested in putting on a show, only in taking care of animals.

There were two chairs in front of the desk, one behind it. Baxter went behind the desk and waved Sam and D'Angelo into the other chairs. He said, "There are some soft drinks in the refrigerator in the lab . . ."

"I'm fine," D'Angelo said.

"Me too," Sam said.

Baxter spread his hands and said, "Where do you want me to start?"

"Go over what you told the police," D'Angelo suggested.

"Again?" Baxter made a face. "I've told it so many times, and it never does any good."

"One more time won't hurt," the lawyer said.

Baxter sighed and nodded. "All right. The day that Susan was . . . killed . . . I went by her office to pick up some drug samples I knew she had. I wanted to see if they might help a patient of mine, a dog with liver disease."

"Is it all right for me to ask questions?" Sam said.

"Yeah, I suppose. Go ahead."

"Your wife was a surgeon. Why would she have these liver pills?"

"It's true that most of what she had in the office were pain meds," Baxter said. "But those pharmaceutical reps carry just about everything in those sample cases they roll around with them, and they hand out a variety of pills and capsules. In fact,

I'd heard Susan complain about one of them sticking her with samples of this drug. That's how I knew she had them."

Sam nodded. Baxter's explanation made sense. It was either true . . . or else he had put quite a bit of thought into it.

"Mr. D'Angelo told me about how you sometimes use human drugs on animals," Sam said.

"That's right. So I grabbed some lunch and then swung by Susan's office to see if she would let me have those samples. She was fine with that." Baxter's mouth twisted a little and his voice held a bitter edge as he went on. "They were still in my truck when the cops searched it later. But that didn't seem to make any difference. They said I just took them with me after I killed her to make my story more plausible, in case my attempt to frame some make-believe burglar failed."

"Yeah, that sounds like something the cops would say, all right," Sam agreed.

"Like I said, Susan didn't mind letting me take the samples. But since I was there anyway, she didn't waste the opportunity to belittle me about treating animals instead of people." Baxter's hands clenched into fists on the desk. "For God's sake, you'd think she would have realized it's a lot easier to treat a patient who can tell you what's wrong! With animals it's half guesswork."

"Take it easy, Hank," D'Angelo advised quietly. "You've got to learn to be able to talk about this stuff without flying off the handle. You lose your temper in front of a jury and it'll cost you."

Baxter nodded a couple of times as he looked down at the desk. "I know, I know. I don't want people to think that I didn't love Susan. Even though we had plenty of trouble, even though it didn't look like the marriage was going to work, I . . . I still loved her. I suppose I always would have . . . always will."

A few seconds of silence went by in the office before Sam said, "So your wife was alive when you left her office."

"Of course she was."

"And she was the only one there."

"That's right. Everybody else had gone to lunch, but Susan stayed to work right through. She did that a lot."

Sam thought for a second and then asked, "Did you see anybody as you were leavin'? Somebody in the parkin' lot, maybe?"

Baxter shook his head and said, "There were a few cars there, as I recall, but they were all empty. I suppose they belonged to people who were in some of the other offices in the complex."

There were some questions Sam wanted to ask about the crime scene, but not while Baxter was there, he decided. He wasn't going to start talking about gruesome details in front of the dead woman's husband.

So he changed tacks by asking, "Was that the only real problem between you and Mrs. Baxter? The way she felt about you bein' a vet?"

Baxter sighed again and said, "That was just a flash point, something that set us off. We weren't really compatible in a lot of other ways. And there were times when . . . well, when Susan wasn't faithful to me."

D'Angelo leaned forward in his chair and said, "You don't need to be saying things like that, either. You don't know that for a fact, Hank. You told me she always denied cheating on you, and you never caught her in the act."

"I just know, okay?" Baxter bit out a curse. "You think a husband doesn't just know?"

"Not to be too cynical or anything," D'Angelo said with a faint smile, "but it's always been my experience that husbands and wives don't know nearly as much as they think they do, good *or* bad."

"Maybe not," Baxter muttered, "but I *know*."

"How about you?" Sam asked.

"I just told you—"

"No, I mean did you ever fool around on your wife?"

Baxter started to come up out of his chair as he said, "Damn it—"

D'Angelo held up both hands to stop him. The lawyer's voice was sharp as he said, "You think the district attorney won't ask you the same question, and worse?"

Baxter settled back, but his face had an angry glare on it as he said, "No. I never cheated on my wife. Not once. And I had opportunities, too."

"Probably better not to say that, as well," D'Angelo said.

"I'm sorry," Sam said. "I'm not tryin' to upset you, Hank. But one thing I've learned from helpin' Phyllis is that if you believe somebody's innocent, the best way to prove it is to find out who's really guilty."

D'Angelo said, "That's irrelevant. My only concern is convincing a jury that Hank didn't kill his wife."

"Yeah, but if you can point to somebody else and show how all the evidence proves they did it, that's pretty convincin'."

"You've got a point, I suppose," D'Angelo said as he inclined his head. "You think if Hank had a girlfriend, she might have a motive for killing his wife."

"I didn't have a girlfriend," Baxter said.

"Under the circumstances, that might be a shame."

"There's somebody else I'm interested in," Sam said. "Kyle Woods."

Baxter looked genuinely surprised. He said, "Woods? What does he have to do with this? I'm not sure he and Susan ever even met."

"You and Woods had some sort of disagreement. What was that about?"

"I don't know what you're talking about," Baxter said, but Sam saw the way his eyes darted toward D'Angelo. Baxter was worried about saying something in front of the lawyer, which made Sam think that Woods had indeed been mixed up in something illegal. Baxter had either been involved in it, too, or at least Woods had tried to get him involved in it.

"You used to be Woods's vet and you took care of all those prizewinnin' dogs of his, didn't you?"

"Yeah. He was one of my customers, but so are a lot of other people. I don't see what that has to do with Susan's murder."

"Then you shouldn't mind sayin' why you dropped him. Or did he drop you?"

Baxter's jaw tightened. He said, "I told Woods to find another vet. I just didn't like the guy. He's smug and arrogant and just a big jerk. If you'd ever spent even five minutes around him, you'd know that."

Sam did indeed know that, but he didn't explain how he did. He wasn't the one accused of murder here.

"I guess you didn't know Woods offered your assistant Tommy a job," Sam said.

Baxter leaned forward sharply. "He what?"

"From what Holly said, Woods wants Tommy to help him out with his dog-breedin' business."

Baxter shook his head and said, "No. Absolutely not. That would be the worst thing for Tommy to do. I'll have a talk with the kid."

"He'll need a job if this place closes down."

"Who said the practice is going to close down?"

"People are takin' their pets elsewhere now. I didn't want to, but I even made an appointment with another vet to check Buck's leg in a few days."

Baxter subsided and muttered, "That's probably a good idea. I don't have my mind on work these days, and it's best not to take a chance with pets. But that doesn't mean it'll always be this way."

"Maybe not. I hope not. I'd rather bring Buck here when he needs his cast taken off."

Baxter looked at his watch and said, "That's all. I've got to go home and get ready for the funeral. You don't mind giving me a ride, Jimmy?"

"Of course not," the lawyer said. "I brought you by here so you could check on things, didn't I?"

"You don't have to keep babysitting me. I'm not going to do anything crazy."

"Hey, nobody said you were, pal." D'Angelo turned to Sam and said, "You'll tell your friend Mrs. Newsom everything we talked about here?"

Sam nodded and said, "I sure will. She started out tryin' to stay out of this case, you know. I did, too."

"Well, I'm glad you both changed your minds. Like I said, I'm not proud. I'll take all the help I can get."

"You sort of tricked me the other day in your office, though. You were talkin' to me under false pretenses, as they say."

"I think you were doing a pretty good job of that yourself, buddy boy."

Sam chuckled. Despite the vast difference in their backgrounds, he found that he was starting to like Jimmy D'Angelo.

He just hoped that the lawyer was as canny as he seemed, and that between D'Angelo, Phyllis, and him, they could find the evidence they needed to prove Hank Baxter was no murderer.

Chapter 18

Since the deadline was approaching rapidly to submit recipes to the contest being sponsored by *A Taste of Texas*, Phyllis spent the morning polishing hers. She had tried a couple of different versions of the white chili casserole and was satisfied she wasn't going to be able to improve it, so after looking over everything one last time, she used the form on the magazine's website to submit the recipe and enter the contest online.

That felt odd to her, even a little wrong. To someone of her generation, recipes were supposed to be written down, preferably on a three-by-five index card, and kept in a plastic box made for cards that size. Phyllis had spent literally decades keeping track of her recipes like that. In fact, she still had her recipe box tucked away on a shelf in one of the cabinets, but she hadn't used it in a good while.

"Pixels," she muttered as she turned off the computer monitor.

"What did you say, dear?" Eve asked without looking up from her needlework.

"Oh, nothing important," Phyllis said. "Just lamenting the passage of time and the changes in modern life, I suppose."

Eve shook her head and said, "There's no point in that. Life is going to change whether we want it to or not. It always has and always will."

"That doesn't mean we have to like it," Phyllis said as she got up from the computer.

"No, but I try not to dwell on it, myself. What's that old saying? 'Life is what happens when you're making other plans.' I find that it saves time to just leave yourself open to new experiences."

Eve was a fine one to say that, sitting there and doing needlework like an old woman, Phyllis thought.

But the thing of it was, after all the trials and tribulations and downright tragedies Eve had experienced in her life, sitting calmly and doing something just to pass the time really was a new experience for her. As Phyllis realized that, she smiled and said, "You're right, of course, Eve," and then went out to the kitchen to prepare lunch. She didn't know exactly what time Sam was going to be back, but she was just going to fix hero sandwiches. They were better if made the night before, but it didn't really matter that much. Susan Baxter's funeral was at two o'clock, she reminded herself, and Sam had expressed his intention of attending. She thought he would probably come in soon, so he'd have time to get ready after he'd eaten. As for herself, Phyllis still hadn't decided whether she was going to attend, although she was leaning in that direction.

Sam came in just as she was finishing up the sandwiches. He grinned and said, "Looks like good timin' on my part."

"You usually have good timing when it comes to food," she said. "Did you find out anything?"

"Maybe," Sam said.

"Let me tell Carolyn and Eve that lunch is ready and then you can tell me all about it."

When the four of them were sitting around the kitchen table with their sandwiches, chips, and iced tea, Sam explained how he had discovered the link between Tommy Sanders and Kyle Woods, then encountered Hank Baxter and Jimmy D'Angelo at the vet clinic.

"Under the circumstances, I sort of had to come clean with them," Sam said with a slightly sheepish look on his face. He recounted the conversation he'd had with the two men in Baxter's office.

"Wait a minute," Phyllis said. "This lawyer, Mr. D'Angelo, he spoke to you the other day because he wanted to get me involved in the case?"

"That's what he said."

A frown creased Phyllis's forehead. "I'm not sure I like that sort of manipulation."

Carolyn said, "It seems to me that he's paying you a compliment. He thinks you can solve the murder. Clearly he's been reading up on you, like he told Sam."

"Maybe so, but he lied to Sam."

"I was lyin' to him," Sam pointed out, "or at least not tellin' him the whole truth. I think I sort of like the fella, even if he is a Yankee."

"Do you think we should . . . ? What was it he said? Go to work for him as consultants?"

Eve asked, "Is he going to pay you?"

"Well, we didn't exactly talk about gettin' paid," Sam admitted. "I think it was more like we'd be volunteers, but if the cops got their noses out of joint because we were pokin' around in the case, we could tell them we were workin' for D'Angelo and they wouldn't be able to say anything."

"You'd be like Paul Drake," Eve said.

"Except Paul Drake never solved anything himself," Carolyn added. "Perry Mason always did that. The Drake Detective Agency just gathered information for him. Does this man D'Angelo strike you as another Perry Mason, Sam?"

That question made Sam laugh. He shook his head and said, "Not hardly. He may be a good lawyer—I don't really know about that—but he's not gonna go out and solve this murder himself."

"Then it's up to us, I suppose," Phyllis said. "If you want to work with him, Sam, I can go along with that. This has always been more of your case than it has mine."

"All right," Sam said. "We'll play along with D'Angelo, at least for the time bein'. Right now, though, I guess we'd better get ready if we're goin' to that funeral."

You couldn't get to be his age, thought Sam, without going to way too many funerals. Friends, relatives, loved ones . . . As time passed, the circle shrank more and more. One of these days, it would be his turn to leave the circle. A few years earlier, after watching his wife, Victoria, die a slow, agonizing death, he would have said that the day couldn't come too soon to suit him. He was through with this world and ready to move on to whatever lay beyond it.

Now . . . not so much. Phyllis had changed that, and so had having friends like Carolyn and Eve. And now he had

Buck to think about, too. The Dalmatian was a relatively young dog with a lot of good years left in him. Buck was going to need Sam around to take care of him. Sam took that responsibility seriously. Any thoughts of being ready to shuffle off this mortal coil were long gone.

Sometimes, though, you didn't have a choice.

Susan Baxter's funeral was a vivid reminder of that.

As Sam had expected, the funeral was so well attended that nobody paid much attention to him and Phyllis as they made their way from the church parking lot to the sanctuary. They were just two more mourners among hundreds who filed into the church. A lot of people from the hospital and the rest of the medical community were there. Susan had been active in society and civic affairs, too, and her friends from those parts of her life had come to pay their respects.

Sam and Phyllis took seats in one of the pews toward the back of the church, on the right side. Mournful hymns played over the speakers. Sam thought, not for the first time, how the whole thing gave him the creeps. He and Phyllis were practical people and trusted each other to see that their wishes were respected, so they had discussed what they wanted to happen after they were gone. Sam wanted to be cremated. No funeral, no memorial service. But if the weather permitted, he wanted his friends to get together somewhere outside, at a park, maybe. They could grill hamburgers and hot dogs, have a big tub full of ice and soft drinks, bring chips and pies and cookies . . . just have themselves a good time, basically, and if they felt like it, maybe say a few kind words about ol' Sam. He hoped that he would be there in spirit. If he was, it would be just about the best send-off a fella could ever hope for.

The pews up front were empty, reserved for family. As the

time neared for the funeral to begin, a number of people emerged from a door to one side and filed into those pews. Sam spotted Meredith and Jack Carlyle. He nudged Phyllis and whispered, "That's Susan's sister and her husband."

"I know," she whispered back. "I saw her at Susan's office. This is the first time I've seen Jack Carlyle except in pictures, though."

Carlyle had an arm around his wife's shoulders as they walked past the flower arrangements, which formed veritable floral mountains on both sides of the closed coffin on its gurney in front of the altar. Meredith already had a handkerchief in her hand. She used it to dab at her eyes. As they passed the coffin, Meredith shrugged her husband's hand off her shoulder, which struck Sam as a little odd. Carlyle looked like he wanted to say something to her, but as far as Sam could tell, he didn't.

The two of them went on and took their seats in the first pew in the center section, all the way at the left end of the pew. Other family members settled down beside them.

Sam knew from reading Susan Baxter's obituary that she and Hank hadn't had any children. From the looks of it, neither did Meredith and Jack. That was the way of it these days, Sam reflected. When he was young, most families had had three or four children. In the generation before his, seven or eight or even more children in a family wasn't uncommon. Now it was more like one or two . . . or none. People just didn't have time for kids the way they used to. If they were successful, they were likely to be busy with their own lives and interests. If they weren't, they were working all the time, struggling to make ends meet in an economy that seemed to be stuck permanently in quicksand.

The music was still playing, but Sam heard a commotion over it. He turned his head to look toward the doors at the back of the church.

"What is it?" Phyllis whispered.

"Looks like Hank showed up like he said he was going to," Sam told her.

Hank Baxter stood in the vestibule wearing a darker, even more somber suit than the one he'd had on earlier. Several men clustered around him, and Sam knew from the flowers they wore pinned to their lapels that they were either pallbearers or worked for the funeral home that was in charge of the service. When Hank tried to move from the vestibule into the sanctuary, a couple of the men got in his way and blocked his path. Sam had been involved in enough fights in his life to know that Baxter was ready to take a swing, and so were the men confronting him. All of them wore belligerent expressions on their faces.

"Stay here," Sam told Phyllis as he stood up. He thought for a second she was going to argue and try to come with him, but then she nodded and stayed where she was.

More people were turning to look at the confrontation now. Sam thought it might have been smarter for Baxter to stay away, but he could understand why the man wanted to be here, especially if he was innocent, as he claimed.

Of course, a clever prosecutor might claim that Baxter was just trying to make himself look innocent by coming to the funeral.

As Sam approached the vestibule, one of the funeral home men tried to stop him. The man put out a hand and said, "Please, sir, if you'll return to your seat—"

"I know Dr. Baxter," Sam said. "Maybe I can help."

The man looked pretty distressed. The voices coming from the vestibule were getting louder and angrier. Sam heard Hank Baxter say, "I have a right, damn it—"

"You don't have any rights," one of the other men interrupted. "You forfeited all those when you bashed my cousin's head in!"

So, he was a relative of Susan Baxter's and a pallbearer, Sam thought.

Baxter had gone pale under the lashing words. He stepped forward and said through gritted teeth, "If you don't get out of my way—"

"Hank," Sam said firmly as he moved closer. "Hank, you don't want to do this."

Baxter's eyes darted toward him. Sam wasn't sure Baxter even recognized him. That was how upset he was.

But then he said, "Stay out of this, Fletcher. I have a right to mourn my own wife." A little vein jumped in his forehead from the strain he was under. "I loved her. That's what nobody seems to understand. I still loved her—"

Again someone interrupted Baxter. This time it was Meredith Carlyle, who charged into the vestibule like a linebacker and screamed, "Shut up! Shut your lying mouth! You . . . you come here and ruin the last thing . . . the last thing anybody can do for my poor sister . . ."

She ran out of steam, both physically and verbally, which might have been a good thing because the men had stepped aside and left her a clear path to Hank Baxter. But instead of attacking him, she stopped and put her hands over her face as sobs racked her body.

Her husband caught up to her, put his hands on her shoulders, and said, "Meredith—"

She wrenched away from him. Turning to one of the men from the funeral home, she asked in a grief-choked voice, "Is there a private room here where . . . where this man can wait . . . until after the service?"

"Certainly," the man answered.

Meredith turned back to Hank Baxter and said coldly and with an obvious effort at self-control, "If you'll go with this gentleman and not do anything else to disrupt the service, you can have a moment or two alone with . . . with Susan . . . when the funeral is over."

"I'm her husband," Baxter argued. "I ought to—"

"It's the best deal you're going to get, Hank," Meredith said, "and it's more than I'm really inclined to give you. But if you keep making trouble, I'll call the police. Under the circumstances, which one of us do you think they'll try to accommodate?"

Baxter stared at her for a couple of long seconds, then said, "You always were a cold-blooded bitch, Meredith."

"Hey!" Jack Carlyle exclaimed. He clenched his fists and moved toward Baxter. "You can't—"

Some of the other men started to get between them to prevent a fight. Sam was close enough that he was able to put a hand on Carlyle's arm and stop him.

"Take it easy," Sam said. "Emotions are runnin' pretty high here. Folks say things they don't mean."

Carlyle's head jerked toward Sam and he looked at him as if sizing him up for a punch. Then the realization that Sam was probably thirty years older than he was seemed to sink in. He relaxed his hands.

"You're lucky, old man," he muttered.

"Don't posture, Jack," Meredith said. "It's unbecoming."

She looked at Baxter again. "You're wrong about me being cold-blooded, Hank. Very wrong. I'd like nothing more than to claw your eyes out right now. But out of respect for poor Susan, I'm not going to. Instead I'm going to give you ten seconds to accept my offer, or else I'll call the police and have you arrested for disturbing the peace." She paused. "And I'm sure the district attorney will do his best to find some way to make sure the jury at your trial knows about that."

"All right. Fine," Baxter snapped. "But don't expect me to thank you."

"I don't expect you to do anything except go to prison for the rest of your life."

Meredith turned and walked back up the aisle toward the front of the church with her husband following her. One of the funeral home men put a hand on Baxter's arm and gently urged him toward a door at the side of the vestibule. Baxter shrugged off the man's hand, but he didn't put up any argument as he was ushered into the side room.

Sam went back to the pew where Phyllis was sitting and slid in beside her.

"I knew it would cause trouble if Dr. Baxter came to the funeral," she whispered.

"Yeah," Sam agreed. "D'Angelo probably tried to talk him out of it, but Baxter's the stubborn sort. And if he's innocent, you can't blame him for wantin' to say good-bye to his wife."

"No, of course not."

It was a few minutes past the time the funeral was supposed to start, but the canned music continued to play. Several people were huddled around the front pew. Sam figured they were trying to comfort Meredith Carlyle after her brother-in-law's presence had disturbed her so much. After several minutes, everyone sat down, and the funeral got under way.

It lasted less than an hour, but it seemed a lot longer than that to Sam.

Chapter 19

It took watching a couple of John Waynes and a Randolph Scott that evening to lift the mood of black depression that Susan Baxter's funeral had caused to settle down over Sam like a cloak. Having Buck lying on the floor next to the recliner in Sam's room, so that Sam could reach down and scratch behind his ears from time to time, helped a lot, too. By the time the Western marathon was over, it was late and Sam was tired but more clearheaded.

He had carried Buck up the stairs rather than make the dog climb them with the cast on his healing leg. Now he picked up Buck to take him back down to the utility room, but instead he looked at the bed and muttered, "What the heck."

He lowered Buck onto the mattress, atop the bedspread. Buck squirmed around and quickly made himself comfortable. Sam chuckled at the sight of the Dalmatian curled up on the spread.

"We may both get our tails whipped in the mornin'," he told Buck. "But at least we'll get a good night's sleep out of it first."

Phyllis never said a word about it, though. She was an early riser and was up before Sam and Buck. She would have looked in the utility room and in the yard for the dog, and not finding him, it wouldn't have taken much deductive ability to figure out that Buck was in Sam's room. Phyllis had that much deductive ability and a whole heap more.

When Sam came into the kitchen with Buck and let the dog out into the yard, Phyllis poured a cup of coffee and set it on the table at Sam's usual place. A mixture of delicious aromas filled the room.

"Some sort of muffin bakin'?" Sam asked.

"Oatmeal berry streusel muffins," Phyllis replied. "They'll be ready in a little while."

Sam sat down and took a grateful sip of the coffee.

Phyllis went on. "How did you sleep? I know that scene at Susan Baxter's funeral bothered you. You were very quiet at supper last night."

"I'm fine," Sam told her. "Did a lot of thinkin'. I'm more convinced than ever now that Hank Baxter didn't kill his wife."

"Because he came to her funeral?"

"Because he gave in and agreed to what Meredith Carlyle offered him: a chance to say good-bye. He wasn't there to put on any kind of show. He wasn't thinkin' about how it would look for his trial. He was just hurtin'."

"Or maybe he was acting," Phyllis suggested.

"Nobody's that good an actor."

"You might be wrong about that. Some people are capable of showing remorse when there's nothing real inside them."

"Maybe, but I don't believe Hank Baxter's like that. Animals respond to him. You've seen that with your own eyes. And nobody can see through a phony faster'n a dog."

Phyllis smiled and said, "I don't think Buck's wagging tail would be admissible as evidence."

"No, but there's got to be something else out there that would be, something that'll prove Hank Baxter's innocent."

Carolyn and Eve came into the kitchen a short time later, and the four friends enjoyed a pleasant breakfast. By the time they were finished, Buck was whining at the back door. November was settling in now, and most mornings were rather chilly.

Sam let Buck in and gave him his breakfast in the utility room, then went upstairs to get dressed for the day. When he came back down, he found Phyllis dressed to go out, too.

"What's the next move in our investigation?" he asked her.

"Don't you mean your investigation?"

"Nope," Sam said. "Jimmy D'Angelo wanted you in on this and you agreed to the deal, so you're in charge again." Sam blew out a breath in an obviously mock sigh of relief and went on. "Which is mighty fine with me. All that thinkin' just wears out my brain."

"Don't sell yourself short," Phyllis told him. "You've found out quite a bit about Kyle Woods."

"Yeah, but nothin' that really points the finger of guilt at him." Sam paused and frowned in thought. "Now, if we could put him on the scene after Hank Baxter left his wife's office . . ."

"You see," Phyllis said. "There's our next move. We need to go back out there and ask some more questions . . ."

It was likely the police had already questioned everyone in the doctors' offices in the same complex where Susan Baxter had had her office. If nothing else, Warren Latimer was a competent detective. But he hadn't known everything that Phyllis and Sam did, so before they left the house, Phyllis printed a copy of one of the pictures from Kyle Woods's website so they could take it with them and ask if anyone remembered seeing Woods around Susan's office on the day of her murder.

Enough time had passed since then that the odds would be against them, Phyllis knew. People led busy lives and were concerned mostly with their own affairs. They couldn't be expected to remember everything they had seen several days earlier.

On the other hand, the news must have spread rapidly that something terrible had happened at Susan Baxter's office. That might make potential witnesses more likely to recall the details of that day, including whether or not they had noticed Kyle Woods.

This sort of legwork was tiring and frustrating. Phyllis and Sam went into the other offices in the complex and started out by asking each of the receptionists if they had seen the man in the picture around there recently. Then Sam would show them the printout of Kyle Woods's photo. Most of the time the receptionists would allow them to show the picture to billing clerks, bookkeepers, sometimes a nurse or two, anyone who was handy to the office at the moment.

But one after another, they all shook their heads and claimed not to know a thing. Phyllis saw the way they looked at Woods's picture with blank stares and was inclined to believe them.

The doctors were all busy with patients, of course, so Phyllis and Sam weren't able to ask them about Woods. As the lack of results built up, Phyllis began to get discouraged.

When she said as much to Sam, he pointed at the row of medical offices across the street and said, "We haven't asked any of those folks over there yet. Maybe one of them saw something. We don't want to give up yet."

"No, I wasn't suggesting that," Phyllis said. "It's starting to look like it's possible Kyle Woods wasn't anywhere around here that day, though."

Sam shook his head. Phyllis could see that he didn't want to believe that. He had set his sights on the dog breeder as the most likely suspect to replace Hank Baxter as Susan's murderer, and he didn't want to give up on that theory. Phyllis understood that sort of dogged determination. She had exhibited it herself on other cases in the past.

They had come over to this part of town in Sam's pickup. They got back into it now and crossed the street, which was a bigger challenge than it sounded like because Santa Fe Drive, especially this area around the hospital, had gotten so much busier in recent years, like the rest of Weatherford. Traffic was so heavy that unless you crossed at a light, you might have to wait for several minutes before a gap big enough to cross safely came along.

Sam negotiated the crossing without much difficulty, however, and pulled into a parking lot that served several different large brick buildings housing a number of medical offices.

They parked and started at one end, and even though Phyllis no longer held out much hope that they would accomplish their goal, she tried not to show that. She believed the situation was turning out as she had expected, though: People were too busy these days to remember details.

Or else they were on the wrong track entirely and Kyle Woods hadn't been anywhere around here on the day of Susan Baxter's murder, a possibility that was equally frustrating.

At first it looked like nothing was going to change, as they drew blank looks and head shakes from the first several people they showed Woods's picture. They went into the offices of a group ophthalmology practice and began asking questions of the receptionist, who surprised them by giving a little start of recognition when Sam placed Woods's picture in front of her. The woman said, "Oh, yes. I know this man."

"You do?" Sam said.

"Yes, of course. He's one of our—" The woman stopped short and looked worried. She lowered her voice and said, "Please, forget that I said anything. I shouldn't have. You know, with all the patient privacy laws."

Phyllis said, "You realize you just told us that he's a patient here, don't you?"

The receptionist put a hand to her mouth and said past it, "Oh, shoot." She was young, no more than about twenty-two, and Phyllis had a feeling she wasn't destined for a long career in the medical profession.

"Don't worry," Phyllis told her. "You didn't do anything wrong. We don't care where he's a patient. Our interest in him doesn't have anything to do with his medical situation. We're investigating a crime."

"You are?" the receptionist said. She gave them a dubious look, and Phyllis knew why. She and Sam didn't look like police detectives or even private investigators. They looked exactly like what they were: a couple of elderly, retired schoolteachers.

"We're workin' with an attorney," Sam said. "And all we really need to know is whether you've seen this fella around here in the past few days."

"You mean here in the office?" the young woman asked.

"We were thinking more of just in the area," Phyllis said. "Maybe across the street . . ."

"This has something to do with Dr. Baxter's murder, doesn't it?" The receptionist looked and sounded avidly interested now.

Phyllis said, "We're not really at liberty to go into details—"

"But you want me to," the young woman interrupted her. "That doesn't seem fair."

She had a point, Phyllis thought, but if Hank Baxter ever went to trial for the murder and this young woman needed to testify, they couldn't risk an accusation that they had influenced her testimony. District Attorney Sullivan would have that thrown out in a hurry.

"If you could just tell us what you saw—" Phyllis began.

"Jessica." Another woman had come up behind the reception counter, this one wearing a doctor's white coat. She went on. "What's this about?"

The receptionist looked back at her and said, "These people were asking me some questions, Dr. Hampton. They're investigating the murder that happened across the street."

"Really?" The doctor gave Phyllis and Sam an amused,

superior glance that rubbed Phyllis the wrong way. She went on. "I've got a few minutes before my next appointment. Come on back and ask me your questions."

Phyllis and Sam glanced at each other. This was the first chance they'd had to talk to one of the doctors in the area. They shouldn't waste it, Phyllis thought, no matter how condescending the woman in the white coat might be.

They followed the doctor to her private office, and as she led them in, she said, "I'm Kathleen Hampton, by the way."

"Phyllis Newsom," Phyllis introduced herself when they had all sat down, Dr. Hampton behind the desk and she and Sam in front of it. "And this is Sam Fletcher."

"And you're . . . detectives? With the police?"

Dr. Hampton had that smirk on her face again. Phyllis controlled her temper and said, "We're investigating Susan Baxter's murder. We're working with an attorney on the case."

"The attorney for Susan's husband?"

Sam said, "You know Hank Baxter?"

"We've met," Dr. Hampton replied with a slight shrug. "I can't say I know the man well at all. Susan and I were friends, though."

"Then I'm sure you want to see her killer brought to justice," Phyllis said.

"The police have already made an arrest, haven't they? Susan's husband killed her. I can't say as I'm surprised."

"What do you mean by that?"

"I know they'd been having trouble in their marriage," Dr. Hampton said. "Susan and I weren't as close as sisters or anything. She didn't confide her deepest, darkest secrets to me. But she said some things now and then, and it didn't take much to read between the lines. That marriage was definitely headed for divorce court." She paused. "Now I suppose a different kind of court will have the final say."

"Dr. Baxter never told you that her husband had harmed her or even threatened her in any way, though, did she?"

"Well . . . no. I don't think their problems ever descended to that level. Just a lot of shouting matches and hurt feelings. But those things can get out of hand."

Sam put the picture of Kyle Woods on the desk in front of Dr. Hampton and asked, "Have you seen this fella around here?"

"I can't answer that. You're asking me to violate doctor/patient confidentiality. That can get a person in a lot of trouble these days."

"Not hardly," Sam said. "We're not askin' you to tell us his name or even whether you know him. All we're really interested in is whether or not you saw him across the street, around Dr. Baxter's office, the day she was killed."

Dr. Hampton pushed the picture back toward Sam. "In that case I can tell you, the answer is no," she said. "A flat no. I haven't seen this man—who I'm *not* identifying as a patient of mine—for more than a month."

"Then who did you see going in and out of Dr. Baxter's office that day?" Phyllis asked.

"I didn't see anyone. Do you think I don't have anything better to do than look through my office door and watch who goes in and out of the building across the street?" Dr. Hampton made a scornful sound. "I have patients of my own to see, you know. In fact, one of them is due anytime now, so if that's all . . ."

Dr. Hampton put her hands on her desk. Phyllis knew she was about to stand up and usher them out of the office. The woman probably wouldn't agree to talk to them again, so this might be the only chance they would have to get any information out of her.

Phyllis knew it was a shot in the dark, but she asked quickly, "Did you see anyone you know over at Dr. Baxter's office the day she was murdered?"

Dr. Hampton was on her feet now. With a distracted, impatient expression on her face, she said, "Oh, good grief. Only Jack. I did see him, but there's nothing unusual about that. Now, I really have to ask you—"

"Jack Carlyle?" Sam said.

"That's right."

"Susan Baxter's brother-in-law?"

"Well, there's nothing wrong with that, is there? They got along all right." Dr. Hampton rolled her eyes. "Better than Susan and her husband, if you ask me." She crossed her arms over her chest and fixed Phyllis and Sam with a steely glare. "Now, I really do have to insist that you let me get to my patients."

They stood up, and Phyllis said, "Thank you for talking to us. Just one more thing . . . Do you remember what time Jack Carlyle was over at Susan's office?"

For a second Phyllis thought the doctor was going to be stubborn and refuse to answer, but then she said, "No, not really. Sometime during the middle of the day."

"And it wasn't unusual to see Jack Carlyle over there?"

"That's two more questions," Dr. Hampton snapped. "But no, it wasn't. Like I said, there's nothing wrong with that."

"No, of course not. Thank you again."

They left the office and went back out to Sam's pickup. Neither of them said anything until they were inside the vehicle. Then, as Sam gazed through the windshield across Santa Fe Drive, he said, "Jack Carlyle."

"We never even thought about him," Phyllis said.

"Why would we?" Sam asked. "As far as we knew, his only connection to Susan Baxter was bein' married to her sister."

"We're jumping to conclusions, you know. There could be a perfectly innocent explanation for Jack Carlyle visiting his sister-in-law's office."

"Sure there could. But Hank was convinced his wife was seein' somebody else. If he was right, and if it was Jack Carlyle, that puts him right smack-dab in the middle of the case."

"It goes even deeper than that," Phyllis said. "We need to establish exactly when Carlyle was here. If it was after Hank was, and Susan was still alive . . ."

"That means Hank couldn't have killed her."

Phyllis thought about it and said, "Well, not exactly. The police could always claim that Hank left, Jack made his visit to the office, and then Hank came back and killed Susan. Actually, it might even strengthen their case. They could say that Hank saw Jack going into the office as he drove off, and his suspicion that Susan was cheating on him was the reason he doubled back and waited for Jack to leave."

Sam grimaced.

"Yeah, I can see the cops doin' that," he said. "As long as they think they've got the killer, they'll keep their jaws clamped on him no matter what."

"It's rather suspicious, though, that Jack hasn't spoken up and told anybody he was here that day."

"Naw, not really. Why would he want to get himself all tangled up in a murder investigation, especially if he really was foolin' around with his wife's sister? There's a good chance that would come out if he did, and then he'd really be up the creek. He's been married to Meredith for a while. I imagine he's in the habit of keepin' a low profile and not doin' anything that'd get her mad at him."

"Not letting her know he's doing anything that would get her mad, you mean," Phyllis said.

"Yeah, that's right." Sam gripped the steering wheel. "No matter how much we hash it out, one thing seems pretty clear."

"What's that?"

"We're gonna have to pay a visit to Jack Carlyle," he said.

Chapter 20

*P*hyllis recalled from her Internet research that Jack Carlyle was an executive with an insurance company, but she and Sam headed back to the house to dig a little deeper before they set out again.

Sam went to the backyard to check on Buck while Phyllis settled down in front of the computer. Carolyn came into the room behind her and said, "Well, I sent in my recipe to *A Taste of Texas.*"

"That's good," Phyllis said, somewhat distracted by what she was doing. "Good luck on the contest."

"Did you see the update on their website? I noticed it while I was submitting my recipe."

That surprised Phyllis enough that she paused in typing Jack Carlyle's name into the search engine and turned her head to look over her shoulder at her friend.

"You submitted your recipe online?" she asked Carolyn.

"Yes, I did. I thought they might prefer that, even though

the announcement of the contest in the magazine said it was all right to submit through the mail. Everybody's going to these computer things these days."

"That's right; they are," Phyllis said. "You normally don't do things on the computer unless you have to, though."

Carolyn shrugged and said, "I don't want the world to pass me by completely. It's getting to where there are more and more things you *have* to do on the computer, so I thought I might as well start getting in the habit of it."

"That's probably smart," Phyllis said with a nod. "Eve and I were talking just the other day about how the world doesn't stand still for anybody."

"It certainly doesn't. What are you doing there?"

Phyllis finished typing Jack Carlyle's name and hit ENTER. As the screen changed and the results began to come up, she said, "Sam and I found out that Susan Baxter's brother-in-law was at her office on the day she was killed. We just don't know what time he was there. Evidently, he was a regular visitor, though."

"Oh, ho!" Carolyn said. "Hanky-panky with her own sister's husband."

"We don't know that's what was going on," Phyllis pointed out.

"Maybe not, but I'll bet it was the first thing you thought of, wasn't it?"

"Well, I suppose it was," Phyllis admitted.

"And surely a lover is just as likely to have committed a murder as a spouse, I would think. I'll bet somewhere they keep statistics on things like that."

"Probably."

Sam came in and asked, "What did you find out?"

"I'm just now getting to the pages I need," Phyllis said as she moved the mouse over one of the links and clicked it. She studied the website that came up and saw that the insurance company Jack Carlyle worked for had its district offices on the west side of Fort Worth. Carlyle, as a vice president, had his own page. His office was listed as being in the same location.

Sam had been reading over Phyllis's shoulder. He said, "We'll need to do some thinkin' about this. We can't just show up at his office and ask him if he's been havin' an affair with his sister-in-law, let alone ask him if he killed her."

"I think maybe some surveillance might be in order first," Phyllis said.

"You mean we should keep an eye on him, see where he goes and what he does?"

"Exactly."

Sam nodded and said, "I can do that. There's no reason for you to waste your time sittin' in a car watchin' a building."

Phyllis thought about the suggestion and agreed, not because she wanted to stick Sam with a tedious task but because she thought they might be able to accomplish more by splitting up.

"I'm going back to Susan Baxter's office," she said. "I have a hunch that young receptionist who works there might be willing to talk more if she's approached in the right way."

"Sounds like a good idea," Sam said. "I'll head for Fort Worth as soon as we've had lunch."

"Speaking of which, let's go see about that," Phyllis said to Carolyn as she got up. Sam took her place in the chair in front of the computer and started writing down the information about the insurance company where Jack Carlyle worked.

Carolyn and Phyllis decided to make lunch simple but hearty for Sam's stakeout: spaghetti with jar sauce and salad. Carolyn started browning the ground meat as Phyllis put the water on to boil.

While they worked in the kitchen, Phyllis asked Carolyn, "What was that you were saying about some update on the magazine's website? I got sidetracked by that business about Jack Carlyle."

"They've decided there's going to be a special prize for one of the winners," Carolyn said. "The person who submits the recipe they pick as the best overall entry is going to be asked to write a guest column for the magazine."

"That would be exciting," Phyllis said, "but a little intimidating, too, I would think. I know I'd hate to have to write something that people all over Texas would read."

"All over the country, you mean. *A Taste of Texas* has a nationwide circulation."

"Well, that would be even scarier."

"One of us might have to do it, you know," Carolyn said. "If one of our recipes is picked as the best."

Phyllis laughed and shook her head. She said, "Well, now I don't know what to hope for."

"If one of us wins, Eve can help us."

"That's true, I suppose." Eve had been a high school English teacher before her retirement and still knew everything there was to know about grammar and writing rules and such. Even with Eve's help, though, Phyllis would be nervous about writing something for publication. She didn't like the idea of all those readers out there judging her work.

On the other hand, she'd had a number of recipes published in the newspaper and in locally produced cookbooks, and that didn't bother her at all, even though she knew some people might try them and not like the results. Somehow that was different. As a cook she was used to having both successes and failures. That was just part of the process.

She put that worry out of her mind for the moment. She had more pressing concerns. Lunch, for one thing.

And finding out who had murdered Susan Baxter.

After lunch, Phyllis and Sam split up as planned, Phyllis heading for the hospital district in her Lincoln while Sam started toward Fort Worth in his pickup. This might be a futile errand, Phyllis thought as she drove. Susan Baxter's office might be closed and locked.

When she reached the medical complex, she saw quite a few cars in the parking lot. That didn't mean anything, she reminded herself, because there were several offices in the complex besides Susan's. She found a parking place and walked to the door, passing a car where a woman was sitting and talking on a cell phone.

It was unlocked, but when she went inside no one was in the waiting room. The glass window at the counter was closed. Phyllis looked around and debated whether she should sit down and wait, but before she reached a decision, the young woman who had been there before walked into the reception area from somewhere in the rear of the office. She saw Phyllis, came over to the window, and slid back the glass.

"Hello," she said. "I'm afraid we're not seeing any patients right—" She was obviously saying the sentence by rote, and she stopped short as she recognized Phyllis. "Oh, hi. You're back." A puzzled frown creased her forehead. "But I told you the other day about poor Dr. Baxter."

"Yes, I know you did," Phyllis said as she cast back in her memory for the receptionist's name. "Raylene, isn't it?"

The young woman smiled and said, "That's right. What can I do for you?"

Phyllis decided her best chance might be to come clean. She put a rueful smile on her face and said, "Raylene, I'm afraid I was here the other day under somewhat false pretenses."

That confused the young woman again. She said, "You don't need somebody to take out your gallstones?"

"Somebody already did, several years ago."

"But you're having trouble in that area again?"

"No. That's not it."

"Then why did you come here?" Raylene asked.

"I'm trying to find out who killed Dr. Baxter," Phyllis said.

Raylene's eyes widened. She said, "But . . . you can't be doing that. You're not a police detective . . . are you?"

"No. I don't work for the police."

"Anyway, they've arrested the killer. The other Dr. Baxter . . . the veterinarian . . . killed her. The police arrested him."

"And I'm sure that's the end of it as far as most people are concerned," Phyllis said, "but I'm not convinced of it."

"So you, what, just set out to prove that Dr. Baxter's innocent? The vet, I mean." Raylene shook her head. "That doesn't make sense. People just don't do that."

"I'm working with Dr. Baxter's defense attorney. You can call him if you'd like."

"Does that mean I have to talk to you? Is it like a rule or something?"

Phyllis hesitated. She didn't want to misrepresent the situation. That might get her in trouble, and perhaps more important, it might come back to damage Hank Baxter's defense and make it easier for the real killer to get away with murder.

"No, there's no rule that says you have to talk to me," Phyllis told the young woman. "But I would think you might want to, since I'm sure you'd like to see Susan Baxter's killer brought to justice."

"Well, of course I do," Raylene said. "But the police already arrested the other Dr. Baxter."

So they were back to that again, Phyllis thought as she tried to control her frustration.

"I just want to ask you a few questions," she said. "I won't take up much of your time. Would that be all right?" She smiled. Nobody could say no to a smiling grandma, could they?

Raylene sighed, nodded, and said, "All right. But I really don't have much time. I'm updating all the records so that when patients ask me to transfer them electronically to another doctor, they'll be ready to send."

"I imagine that's a big job," Phyllis said sympathetically.

"Yeah, it is." Raylene's eyes rolled slightly. "Not everybody seems to understand that, though."

Phyllis lowered her voice to a conspiratorial tone, even though she and Raylene seemed to be alone in the office, as she said, "Mrs. Carlyle?"

Raylene nodded and said, "I don't suppose you can blame her for wanting everything done right. She's had a lot dumped on her without any warning."

"Yes, of course." Phyllis opened her purse. She had come prepared. She had printed out another copy of Kyle Woods's picture, along with one of Jack Carlyle she had gotten off the insurance company website. She didn't think she would need the one of Carlyle, but since she was here, she might as well ask Raylene about Woods, since she and Sam hadn't come into this office earlier that morning. She handed it through the open window to Raylene and asked, "Do you know that man?"

"Oh, sure," Raylene answered without hesitation. "That's Mr. Woods. He's a friend of the other Dr. Baxter."

That wasn't true anymore, but evidently Raylene didn't know that. Phyllis said, "He's been here before with Hank Baxter?"

"That's right. And he stopped by once without him."

"When was that?"

Raylene thought about that, and again her eyes grew wide. She said, "It was the morning that Dr. Baxter was killed."

Phyllis's pulse jumped. She tried not to let her face or voice reveal what she was feeling as she said, "Are you certain about that?"

"I remember everything about that morning," Raylene said. She sighed. "It's burned into my memory."

"Did Mr. Woods have an appointment?"

The young woman shook her head and said, "No, he just stopped by and asked if he could talk to Dr. Baxter for a minute. She wasn't busy right then, so she said yes and told me to show him in. You have to understand, since Dr. Baxter was a surgeon, this isn't like a regular medical practice where you have patients coming in all the time. Her patients were referred to her by other doctors, usually specialists, and she would meet with them to discuss whatever procedure they needed to have done, but there's not a steady stream of patients coming through."

"I see," Phyllis said, nodding. "Had Mr. Woods ever come by here before to see Dr. Baxter?"

A wild thought had just crowded its way into her mind. Although the idea of the sleek, glamorous Dr. Susan Baxter having an affair with the coarse, unpleasant Kyle Woods seemed ridiculous on the face of it, Phyllis supposed stranger things had happened. If it was true, that would make Woods an even stronger suspect in Susan's murder.

Raylene dashed that hope by shaking her head.

"No. I don't think he ever came here any other time except with the vet Dr. Baxter. That's why I was sort of surprised when he stopped by."

"But Susan Baxter agreed to see him."

"That's right."

"Do you know what they talked about?"

Raylene looked a little offended as she said, "I don't eavesdrop on the doctor's conversations. What, do you think I got a glass and pressed it to the door of her private office?"

"No, of course not," Phyllis said quickly. "I didn't mean anything. I just thought you might know. Dr. Baxter could have mentioned it to you."

"Well, she didn't." In a slightly sheepish tone, Raylene went on. "Anyway, I wasn't here. Dr. Baxter had told me I could take the rest of the morning off to handle some personal stuff, so I left right after I showed Mr. Woods into her office. So I don't have any idea what they talked about or even how long he was here."

Phyllis seemed to be at a dead end in this line of questioning. Since Raylene hadn't been here and Susan was dead, Kyle Woods was the only one who knew what had happened between him and the doctor. And he probably wouldn't answer any questions about it unless he was forced to, something that Phyllis couldn't do.

"All right," she said. She needed to get back to her original reason for coming here this afternoon. "Just a couple more things. You know Mrs. Carlyle's husband, of course."

"Jack? I mean, Mr. Carlyle? Sure."

"I imagine he's been around some since Dr. Baxter's death, helping his wife get everything squared away."

"Well, not really. Meredith's pretty much taken charge of everything by herself."

"What about before Susan Baxter was killed? Was Mr. Carlyle around much then?"

Raylene got a wary look in her eyes. She asked, "What would be wrong with it if he was? They were related, weren't they?"

"Only by marriage."

"Are you trying to suggest that there might have been something going on between Dr. Baxter and her brother-in-law?"

Raylene was a little quicker on the uptake than Phyllis had expected.

"That's crazy!" the young woman went on before Phyllis had a chance to say anything else. "Jack was here a few times with Meredith, but that's all."

Phyllis thought rapidly. Dr. Kathleen Hampton had indicated that Jack Carlyle was a frequent visitor to Susan Baxter's office, but Raylene was denying that. Either Dr.

Hampton was mistaken—or lying—or Raylene wasn't telling the truth.

But there was another explanation, Phyllis realized. She said, "You told me that Dr. Baxter gave you some time off the morning she was killed. Did she give you time off very often?"

"Well . . . yeah," Raylene said with a shrug. "Like I told you, this isn't like a regular doctor's office. We don't get walk-ins"—she paused, gave Phyllis a narrow-eyed look, and went on—"unless they've got ulterior motives like you did."

"But often there are times during the day when you're not in the office."

"Sometimes, yeah. Dr. Baxter was good about that. She made plenty of money, you know, so she was nice and didn't even dock my wages when I had to go run some errands."

Of course she was nice about it, Phyllis thought. By giving her receptionist the time off, she was able to have her clandestine rendezvous with her lover. Jack Carlyle? Kyle Woods?

Both?

Phyllis had a lot to think about and a lot to talk over with Sam when he got back from Fort Worth.

"All right. I suppose I should let you get back to your work," she said.

"Yeah. Meredith's not as lenient about things like that as her sister was."

"I was under the impression that they were a lot alike. Both very driven and demanding."

"Dr. Baxter could be like that, sure," Raylene said. "But she could be nice, too." She swallowed. "I really would like for whoever killed her to pay for it. If you think there's really a chance her husband didn't do it . . ."

"That's what we're trying to find out," Phyllis said.

"Then I hope I was able to help."

"I think you have," Phyllis said.

She smiled again and said good-bye, then left the office. Thoughts whirled through her brain as she walked across the parking lot to her car.

She was so distracted she almost didn't notice that the woman she had seen earlier, talking on a phone in one of the parked cars, was still there. Probably waiting for a patient in one of the other doctors' offices, Phyllis thought idly. The woman had her head turned away, but Phyllis could tell that she wore a scarf over her hair and a pair of dark glasses.

Phyllis had gotten into the Lincoln and driven several blocks before a shock of recognition hit her. The realization hadn't soaked in at the time, but there had been something familiar about the woman.

She couldn't be sure, of course, but she thought now that the woman in the car could have been Meredith Carlyle.

Chapter 21

With the speed limits on the interstate, it didn't really take long to get from Weatherford to Fort Worth. As Sam made the drive that afternoon, he was struck as he often was by how much open land still remained on both sides of the highway. If anybody had asked him twenty years earlier, he would have said that it would all be covered with strip malls and housing developments by now. Some of the old ranching families that owned vast stretches of land had been reluctant to sell it all off, so there were still areas of rolling hills that didn't look much different than they had fifty or even a hundred years earlier.

It was only a matter of time, though, Sam thought. Already, if you knew where to look among those hills, you could spot large tracts of big, ostentatious houses jammed together on tiny lots, the sort of overblown McMansions that few people could afford these days.

Yet for some reason, developers continued to build them.

There was nothing in between anymore, as far as housing was concerned. People lived either in apartments or mobile homes, or in those big, fancy places where they could barely make the mortgage payments and were always in danger of losing their home. It didn't make sense to Sam, who was glad he lived in a house that had been built back in the days when there was still a middle class and people had some dang sense.

That thought put a grin on his face.

"And stay off my lawn, you dang kids," he muttered in a self-mocking tone.

When the interstate split between I-20 and I-30, he followed I-20 toward the southwest part of Fort Worth, where his destination was located. After a few more minutes of traveling through ranchland, he found himself surrounded by those housing developments he had been decrying earlier, along with freeway merges, fast-food joints, big box stores, road construction, and traffic, traffic, and more traffic. It had been a while since he'd been in this part of Fort Worth, and with all the road construction going on—detours, concrete barriers, orange cones, gaping earthen pits where exit ramps used to be—he wondered if he would be able to get to where he needed to be. If, indeed, he could even find the place anymore.

That worry proved to be groundless. Sam's natural sense of direction asserted itself, and even though the roads weren't exactly how they used to be, he was able to drive right to his destination: an eight-story building that looked like a giant cube of bronze-colored glass.

It was ugly as could be, not surprising for a modern office building. As Sam sat there in the parking lot, looking at it, a mental voice in the back of his head said in a robotic drone, *"You will be assimilated."* The thought brought a chuckle to his lips.

He tried to put ruthless aliens out of his mind and concentrate on the case instead. Even though this building was where Jack Carlyle's office was located, Sam had no way of knowing whether Carlyle was actually in there. And even if Carlyle was there, it might be hours before he came out. He might be a workaholic who stayed at his desk until ten o'clock at night or even later. Sam frowned as he realized that in his zeal to find out more, he hadn't really thought this through.

There was one thing he could try. He had written down not only the address of Carlyle's office but also the phone number. Now he took the piece of paper from the pocket of his denim jacket, slipped his cell phone from the other pocket, and thumbed in the number.

His name might show up on the caller ID on the other end of the call, he thought as it began to ring. He should have gotten one of those burner phones like the spies and drug lords used on TV shows. But it was too late to worry about that now.

A woman answered the call with the company name and added, "Jack Carlyle's office."

"I'd like to talk to Mr. Carlyle, please," Sam said.

"May I ask who's calling?"

Sam hesitated for a couple of seconds, then said, "Wait a minute. Did you say Jack Carlyle?"

"Yes, sir," the woman replied with only the slightest trace of impatience.

"I'm sorry. I'm callin' from the wrong list. I was actually lookin' for somebody else."

"Not a problem, sir."

The connection broke with a click.

Sam closed the phone and put it back in his pocket. The way the woman had asked who was calling was indication enough that Carlyle was there.

But the question of how long it would be before he came out still remained.

Sam told himself that he would just have to be patient, but less than ten minutes later, none other than Jack Carlyle emerged from the building's main entrance and walked quickly into the parking lot. Sam's pickup was toward the back of the big lot. He slouched a little more in the seat and pulled down the bill of his feed store cap to partially obscure his face without interfering with his view of Carlyle.

The man seemed to be in a hurry, and he didn't have a briefcase or anything else with him, as if he had dropped whatever he was doing and left his office for some reason. He got into an expensive European sedan and drove out of the parking lot.

Sam was a couple hundred yards behind him.

With the traffic over here in this part of Fort Worth, he worried that was too much distance, that he risked losing Carlyle just when he had caught a break by the man leaving work early.

Carlyle headed straight for the interstate, though, and got on I-20 headed west toward Weatherford. Maybe he was headed home, Sam thought. He didn't know where that was, but he would do his best not to let Carlyle lose him.

Carlyle had a heavy foot on the gas. Sam had to drive faster than he normally did to keep up with his quarry. He hoped they wouldn't pass a state trooper working radar. If they did, there was a good chance he'd be stopped, and then he would lose sight of Carlyle.

The shoulders and median stayed clear of Highway Patrol cars, much to Sam's relief. And some twenty minutes later Carlyle left the highway at the Santa Fe Drive exit and turned right on that road.

Traffic here wasn't as bad as it was one exit farther west at South Main, but there were enough cars on the road that Sam hoped his pickup blended in with the other vehicles as he tagged along behind Carlyle. He had no idea where the man lived. If he'd had to guess, he would have said that the Carlyle home was probably in one of the new, exclusive, gated residential developments south of the interstate, but at the moment the man was headed in the opposite direction.

It didn't take long to reach the area around the hospital. Sam frowned as he saw Carlyle turn in at the complex where Susan Baxter's office was located. Phyllis had planned to pay another visit to Susan's office this afternoon. Sam wondered if she might still be there. If she was, she might appreciate a heads-up that Jack Carlyle was in the area.

Even as he was pulling into the parking lot, Sam had his phone out. He pushed the button to call Phyllis's cell phone and heard it ringing as he steered the pickup into an empty space.

She answered quickly, saying, "Sam?"

"Where are you?" he asked.

"Why . . . I'm home," she said. She sounded a little surprised, and he knew he'd been more curt than he meant to be. "Is something wrong?"

"No," he said as he killed the pickup's engine. "I was just makin' sure you weren't still at Susan Baxter's office."

"No. I left there a little while ago. More than half an hour ago, actually. Would it be a problem if I was still there?"

"I don't know," Sam said. "Looks like Jack Carlyle is payin' the office a visit. Was his wife there when you left?"

"No, just the receptionist. Are you sure that's where Carlyle went?"

"I just saw him go inside."

"Are you where you can keep an eye on the place?"

"I am."

"Let's stay on the phone while you do," Phyllis suggested. "I learned something while I was there earlier. Kyle Woods went to see Susan Baxter just a little while before she was killed."

Sam sat up straighter behind the wheel and asked, "How'd you find out about that?"

"Raylene told me. The girl who works in the office."

"Dang. That puts Woods right back in the picture, doesn't it?"

"He was on the scene," Phyllis said. "That has to be important."

"I wonder if Hank Baxter knows about that. He might be more willing to open up about the trouble between him and Woods if he did. At the very least we need to tell his lawyer about this."

"We certainly do." Phyllis paused. "I guess we're turning out to be pretty good consultants after all."

"I guess so," Sam agreed with a chuckle. "Paul Drake better watch his back."

"Any sign of Carlyle?" Phyllis asked.

"Nope. He hasn't come back out."

"I wonder what he's doing there . . . Can you look around the parking lot from where you are?"

"Some. What do you want to know?"

"Is there a car parked there with a woman waiting inside it? A woman wearing a scarf and dark glasses?"

"Somebody incognito, eh? I've always liked that word. *Incognito.*" Sam looked around while he was talking. He reported, "I don't see anybody who looks like that. Who's she supposed to be?"

"I don't know for sure. She was there when I visited the office earlier, and after I left I got to thinking that she might have been Meredith Carlyle."

"That doesn't make any sense," Sam said. "Why would she spy on her own sister's office?"

"I don't know. But once I left she could have gone inside. She could have called her husband and asked him to meet her there."

"Told him instead of asked him, more than likely," Sam said. "You know, I was just settlin' down for a long wait outside the buildin' where Carlyle's office is, when he came out in a hurry and lit a shuck for Weatherford. When you think about how long it takes to get from where we were to where we are now, that would've been pretty soon after you left out of Susan Baxter's office."

"Then it really *was* Meredith," Phyllis said.

"Maybe. We don't have any real proof, though," Sam cautioned. "You want me to go see if I can sneak a look inside the office?"

"It's tempting . . . but I don't want you to get in trouble. Besides, there's this new development about Kyle Woods to deal with. One of us needs to talk to Mr. D'Angelo before it gets any later in the day. He may be leaving his office soon."

Sam thought about it and said, "Why don't I do that? I'll give him a call, and in the meantime I'll keep an eye on Carlyle's car and watch for his wife, too."

"All right. And then you'll be coming home?"

"Don't know," Sam said. "I reckon that depends on what happens. You never know where the trail will lead us private eyes."

"I don't know whether to laugh or tell you to be careful."

"We'll just say you did both," Sam suggested.

While he had Phyllis on the phone, he had her look up Jimmy D'Angelo's number, then said good-bye and called the lawyer. There was a chance D'Angelo might be in court, but the secretary who answered the phone put Sam right through to him.

"Mr. Fletcher." D'Angelo greeted him in a booming voice. Sam thought the lawyer had him on speakerphone. "Sam. What can I do for you?"

"We've located a witness who can put Kyle Woods in Susan Baxter's office not long before she was murdered."

There was a click, and the quality of D'Angelo's voice changed, telling Sam that D'Angelo had picked up the phone to continue the conversation.

"What witness?" he asked.

"The girl who runs the office," Sam said. "I think Phyllis said her name is Raylene."

"Raylene Bagley, that's right. I've read her deposition. She was the one who found Susan Baxter's body when she came back from lunch."

"What she doesn't seem to have mentioned to anybody is that she left for lunch early, and when she left, Woods was there with Susan. Has Hank Baxter ever told you what caused his fallin' out with Woods?"

"If he had, it would be privileged communication," D'Angelo said. "But no, as a matter of fact, he's been as tight-lipped about that with me as he has been with you, even though I've tried to convince him that it would be better for him if he were completely honest with me." The lawyer paused, then said, "I'm confident he will be once we get closer to trial. There's nothing like the thought of facing a judge and jury to make somebody willing to do whatever it takes to get them off."

"Maybe you should tell him that Woods was there on the day of the murder," Sam suggested.

"Actually, why don't you tell him? Maybe the four of us could have a meeting here at my office tomorrow morning. You, Mrs. Newsom, Hank, and me."

Sam thought about it. His appointment with the other vet to have Buck's leg checked was the next day, but not until the afternoon. He told D'Angelo, "As far as I know right now, we can do that, but I'll have to check with Phyllis."

"All right. Let me know. I'll give you my cell phone number."

He did so, and Sam wrote it down in a little notebook he took from the pickup's glove compartment. He tore the page out and tucked it away in his shirt pocket.

He had been watching the door of Susan's office while he talked to D'Angelo, but so far Jack Carlyle hadn't put in a return appearance. He was still inside, although Sam couldn't rule out the possibility that Carlyle had left the building through a back door. Carlyle's car was still where he had left it, however, so Sam thought that was unlikely.

Since he had D'Angelo on the phone anyway, he asked, "Did you ever find out anything about the murder weapon?"

"Yeah. The cops found blood traces on a paperweight in Susan Baxter's office. It's a brass dog, believe it or not. Not so hard to believe, I guess, when you consider that her husband the veterinarian gave it to her. About six inches tall and nice and heavy. Evidently, it matched the indentation in Susan's skull."

"Were there any fingerprints on it?"

"Wiped clean," D'Angelo said. "The killer tried to get the blood off, too, and it looked clean to the eye, but the blood traces showed up in forensic tests. From the way Latimer told it to me—which he didn't want to do, by the way, but he didn't have any choice; the defense has as much right to the evidence as the prosecution does—it looks like Susan and the killer were standing in front of her desk, probably arguing. The killer grabbed up the dog, walloped Susan with it, and then realized she was dead. He cleaned the blood and his prints off the dog and took whatever he used to do that with him. Then he got the idea of busting open the cabinet where the drug samples were kept to make it look like a burglary."

"And Hank Baxter's prints were on that cabinet," Sam said.

"Yeah. That's why the cops zeroed in on him."

"But he explained why they were there."

"The cops are saying that's just another attempt to mislead the authorities. That's the way they're going to tell the story."

Sam was thinking so hard he figured his brain was about to start hurting. He said, "Who's the witness that put Hank on the scene?"

"Actually, they've turned up three," D'Angelo said. "All of them work there in the same complex of doctors' offices. They say Hank got there a few minutes after noon."

Sam bit back a groan and said, "That lets Woods out, because he was there before lunch, accordin' to Raylene. If he killed Susan then, Hank would've found her body and called the cops."

"Yeah, but Woods could have come back after Hank left."

Sam remembered Phyllis saying the same thing. It was a viable theory, he decided, and knowing what had caused the trouble between Hank and Woods might go a long way toward supporting or disproving that theory.

Sam instinctively sat up a little straighter as Jack Carlyle emerged from the building. Then he remembered he was trying not to be noticed and slumped lower again.

"I've got to go," he told D'Angelo, "but Phyllis and I will be at your office in the mornin'. If we can't be, I'll let you know."

"All right," the lawyer said. "It sounds like you and Mrs. Newsom are doing a good job, Sam. Keep it up."

"We'll try," Sam said. He broke the connection as he watched Carlyle get back into his car.

Sam was torn then. He didn't know whether to follow Carlyle or wait and see if Meredith came out of the building next. After a few seconds he decided to follow Carlyle.

The man drove back down Santa Fe toward the highway. With Sam about a hundred yards behind him, he got onto the interstate and headed east, toward Fort Worth. Sam wondered if Carlyle was going back to his office.

Carlyle got off the highway after only a couple of miles, though, and turned south into one of those exclusive housing developments. It looked like Sam's guess about where Carlyle lived might be right after all. Sam couldn't follow him into the gated community, so he couldn't confirm that hunch, but he felt fairly confident about it.

There was nothing left for him to do now except head back to Phyllis's house and make sure it was all right with her for them to go to D'Angelo's office the next morning and confront Hank Baxter with what they had found out.

Sam hoped D'Angelo was right and that Hank would co-operate. The trial, if there was going to be one, was still a long way off, but one fact was undeniable:

Hank Baxter was getting one step closer to the possibility of prison with every day that passed.

Chapter 22

Phyllis was glad to see Sam when he came in late that afternoon. Not only was she eager to talk over the case with him, but she was relieved that he was all right. Whenever you were tailing someone, there was always the possibility they could realize it and get angry because they were being followed. Sam's background as a coach had left him very physically fit, especially for his age, but there was no denying that he was getting on in years and didn't need to be scuffling with anyone, especially not someone who was thirty years younger than he was.

Sam was fine, though, despite her worries. He sat down at the kitchen table and told Phyllis everything he had seen and found out while she cleaned the refrigerator. Buck sat on the floor beside him, and Sam scratched the Dalmatian's ears as he talked.

The information about the murder weapon was new to Phyllis. She winced a little as she imagined the heavy brass paperweight slamming against Susan Baxter's skull. The bowl of moldy leftovers she'd just pulled out from the back of the refrigerator didn't help with the image in her mind.

"That's an indication the killing was a spur-of-the-moment thing," she said as she emptied the bowl into the trash can. "The murderer grabbed whatever was handy and lashed out with it. A crime of passion."

Sam nodded and said, "That's the way it sounds to me, too, but if the killer had been there before, he might've known about the dog paperweight and planned on usin' it. That's not as likely, but I don't think we can rule it out."

"You're right about that." Phyllis paused in thought, then said, "What if it really was just someone who came in there looking for drugs to steal?"

"Some junkie without any other connection to the case, you mean?"

"That's right. Most crimes are just that simple and brutal and ugly."

"Maybe so, but I hope for Hank Baxter's sake that's not the way it is here. If we can't prove somebody else did it by nailin' the real killer, there's a really good chance he's gonna be convicted and sent to prison."

"Well, we're certainly not going to give up hope," Phyllis said.

"Is there any reason we can't go to D'Angelo's office in the mornin'?"

"Not as far as I'm concerned."

As it turned out, though, Jimmy D'Angelo called Sam that evening and changed the plan himself.

"Hank wants us to meet him at his clinic in the morning,"

the lawyer explained. "He said he needed to be there to check on some things anyway, and whatever we wanted to talk about, we could do it there."

"You didn't tell him about Woods?" Sam said.

"Not yet. I want to see his reaction in person."

That made sense to Sam, and when he told Phyllis about it, she agreed. Meeting at the clinic was just as easy as going to D'Angelo's office. Easier in some ways, in fact, because of the traffic and parking situation down on the square.

"I'm gonna take Buck with us," Sam said to Phyllis after promising D'Angelo they would be there. "Maybe Hank will go ahead and check his leg."

"You have an appointment with another vet to do that," Phyllis pointed out.

"Yeah, but if Hank does it, I'll just call 'em and cancel and pay for the missed appointment. I'm hopin' things will work out so Hank is Buck's vet from now on, so I'd just as soon he take care of it if he will."

"Well, if he says no, I suppose you can still take Buck to the other vet."

"That's what I was thinkin'."

The next morning there was a light mantle of frost on the grass in the backyard when Sam let Buck out, and the Dalmatian's breath fogged as he roamed around the yard. Winter was on its way. It was less than two months until Christmas.

After breakfast, Phyllis and Sam got into Sam's pickup, with Buck riding between them on the seat. He wore a harness designed for walks and car rides with a leash today and seemed to be looking forward to wherever they were going. His tongue hung out of his mouth and he looked around excitedly. Sam ran the seat belt through the halter and fastened it, and he put his arm around the dog for added security while Phyllis drove.

The meeting was set for nine-thirty. They got there a little early and went inside, taking Buck with them. Holly was the only one in the office, and she seemed to be surprised to see them.

"Mr. Fletcher," she said, "I thought you were taking Buck to the other vet to have his cast removed."

"I may still do that," Sam said, "but I thought since we had to be here anyway and Dr. Baxter is gonna be here, too, he might be willin' to go ahead and look at him."

Holly's eyes widened. She said, "Dr. Baxter is going to be here?"

"That's right," Phyllis said. "You didn't know?"

"He hasn't been here since before the funeral," the redhead said. "I haven't even talked to him since then."

"Maybe he feels like he needs to start doing something to stay busy," Sam suggested. "Anyway, he's supposed to be here in a few minutes, and so is his lawyer."

"Oh. Okay." Holly looked distracted now. "Why don't you have a seat and wait for him? I . . . I have to take care of a couple of things."

She slipped off her stool and hurried down the short hall behind the counter, disappearing around a corner into one of the other corridors. Phyllis and Sam looked at each other, and Sam's shoulders rose and fell in a silent but eloquent shrug. They went over to the bench along the front wall of the waiting room and sat down. Sam held Buck's leash.

Jimmy D'Angelo came in next, just a couple of minutes later. Sam switched the leash to his other hand, stood up, and shook hands with the lawyer.

"Hank's not here yet?" D'Angelo asked.

"Haven't seen him."

"I hope he shows up. I shouldn't say this about my own client, but the guy's a little flaky, you know?"

Phyllis said, "He's just lost his wife, and he's under a lot of pressure."

"I know. Believe me, I know. In my business, I see people in trouble all the time. Nobody needs a lawyer when they're at their best. I remember one time—" D'Angelo stopped and waved a hand. "Nah. We don't need to get into that. But while I've got you here, maybe you wouldn't mind signing something for me."

"What'd you have in mind?" Sam asked. "Sometimes when a lawyer wants you to sign something, it doesn't always turn out too good."

"In this case, it's just a document saying that you're working for me in return for good and valuable consideration." D'Angelo grinned. "I've got a check for each of you. One whole dollar, just to make things legal. Don't spend it all in one place."

Phyllis and Sam looked at each other and shrugged. They signed the documents D'Angelo produced and took the checks. They were official investigators now.

Just as they finished that bit of business, D'Angelo glanced through the door and said, "Here's Hank now."

A few moments later, Hank Baxter pushed the door open and came in wearing jeans and a thick flannel shirt. He looked like he hadn't shaved in several days. Phyllis saw D'Angelo purse his lips in disapproval for a second, and she figured he was thinking that he couldn't allow Baxter to go into court looking like that.

"All right. I'm here," Baxter said by way of greeting. "What's this all about?"

"It's about your case, Hank," D'Angelo said. "I told you that. Some new information has come to light—"

Baxter held up a hand to stop the lawyer and said, "Hold on a minute." He came over to Phyllis, Sam, and Buck, and his demeanor changed completely. He hunkered down in front of Buck and began to pet him. The dog leaned forward and licked Baxter's cheek. Grinning, Baxter asked, "How's he doing?"

"Mighty good," Sam said. "He's due to get that checkup, and I was hopin' you'd take care of it, Doc—I mean, Hank."

"Well . . . I guess I can do that. We can talk while I'm working. Bring him on back."

Baxter stood up and led the way behind the counter and around the corner into the big room that included a lab setup and a surgical table. He pointed at the table to indicate that Sam should put Buck on it.

Holly was back there with a cell phone at her ear, but she wasn't talking on it. With a frustrated sigh, she closed the phone and slipped it into her pocket. Baxter said, "Give Mr. Fletcher a hand with Buck, would you, Holly?"

"Sure," she said. She helped Sam lift Buck onto the metal table.

"Where's Tommy this morning?"

"Running late, I guess. I just tried to call him, but it kept going straight to voice mail. He probably let the battery on his phone go dead again. He's really bad about that."

Baxter washed his hands at a stainless-steel sink, then came over to the table and said, "All right. Let's take a look at that leg."

He unwrapped the elastic wrap around the cast, then examined the shaven skin near the cast front and back and pressed around on the area.

"Looks good, and he's walking well with the cast. What's this new information you say you've got, Jimmy?"

"I'll let Mrs. Newsom and Mr. Fletcher tell you about that, since they're the ones who turned it up," D'Angelo said.

Sam nodded to Phyllis to indicate that she should pick up the story.

"Dr. Baxter, is the young woman who works in your wife's office reliable?" she asked.

"Which young woman? There are several, you know." To Sam, Baxter added, "You might want to hang on to him, just in case he doesn't like the thermometer."

Sam took hold of Buck as Baxter took the dog's temperature.

"I'm talking about Raylene," Phyllis said.

"Oh." Baxter nodded. "Yeah, I suppose she's reliable enough. I don't remember Susan ever complaining about her very much. And it was always just minor stuff, the sort of boss/employee friction that comes up from time to time but doesn't really mean anything."

He checked the thermometer and nodded.

"Raylene told me that Kyle Woods was at your wife's office on the morning of the day she was . . ."

"The day she was killed," Baxter finished. "You can say it."

"All right. Woods was there. In fact, he was with Susan when Raylene left early to go to lunch."

D'Angelo said, "Did you know that, Hank?"

"Did I know that Woods was there that day?" Baxter shook his head. "No. I didn't have any idea. And I'm surprised that he was. Susan barely knew Woods. He was with me once when I stopped by there."

"Maybe Woods had a medical reason for seeing her," D'Angelo suggested. "Can you think of anything like that?"

"I don't keep up with Kyle Woods's health. As far as I know, though, he's not sick and wouldn't need a surgeon."

Sam asked, "Your wife didn't mention that he'd been there when you saw her later that day?"

"She never said a word about it. Hold on a minute. Let me get this."

Baxter peeled the plastic off a fresh roll of bandage and rewrapped Buck's leg.

"All right," he said with a smile. "I think he's going to be fine, Mr. Fletcher. The leg is healing nicely, and the cast should come off in three weeks."

Sam returned the smile and said, "Might as well call me Sam. I reckon Buck and I will be comin' here from now on whenever he needs anything."

"I'd like to think that's true," Baxter said. "But it's not really up to you or me, is it?"

"It's up to the court," D'Angelo said, "and we've got proof that a guy with a grudge against you was at your wife's office not long before she was killed."

"But I was there after that, and she was alive then."

"Woods could've come back. Maybe he threatened her, and she told him he'd better get out because you were coming by there. So he left, waited until you were gone, and then went back in to continue the argument."

"Argument about what?" Baxter asked.

"You tell us, Hank." D'Angelo pointed a blunt finger at his client. "It's time for you to come clean about what was going on between you and Woods."

Baxter's beard-stubbled jaw tightened. He said, "You don't know what you're asking, Jimmy. You want me to incriminate myself."

"Whatever you're talking about, it can't be as bad as murder, now, can it?"

For a long moment, Baxter didn't reply. Then he sighed and said, "I suppose you're right. Anyway, I didn't really do anything. As soon as I found out what Woods was up to, I told him I wanted no part of it. All I did was run some tests for him, perfectly legal tests."

Sam drew in a sharp breath as if he'd realized something. He said, "You ran tests on Texas Maximus's . . . well, to see if he could sire pups."

"That's right," Baxter said with a surprised frown. "How did you know?"

"He'd been gettin' complaints from people who had their dogs bred with Texas Maximus. The pups had little defects that kept 'em from bein' top show dogs, but Woods wouldn't return any of the money people paid him for the stud service. The pups were turnin' out like they did because Texas Maximus wasn't really their daddy."

Baxter nodded and said, "That's right. Woods was artificially inseminating the bitches while he had them at his place, using sperm from some of his other dogs. Several of the dogs that had been bred with Texas Maximus didn't turn up pregnant after the first try, and he started worrying enough he had me run the tests."

Phyllis said, "But surely Texas Maximus had sired pups in the past."

"He had," Baxter agreed. "But about a year ago he came down with an infection and ran a high fever for several days. I got him through the illness all right, and he was perfectly fine again, except for the low sperm count and extremely limited motility. It's not impossible for him to sire pups, but the odds against it are very, very high."

"And Woods was afraid it was gonna ruin his business," Sam said. "So he started goin' the turkey baster route."

Phyllis was no prude, but this discussion was getting awfully indelicate for her sensibilities. To move it away from the biological aspects of what had been going on, she said to Baxter, "Woods wanted you to help him with this scheme, didn't he?"

"Yeah, but like I said, I told him to forget it. I wasn't going to open myself up to being sued for fraud just because Woods is a greedy, underhanded son of a—"

Baxter glanced at Phyllis and stopped short.

"But I didn't turn Woods in, either," he resumed with a shrug. "Does that make me guilty of anything, Jimmy?"

"Concealing evidence of a crime is considered obstruction of justice," D'Angelo answered. "In a case like this, I doubt if the cops would have pressed charges, but it might open you up to civil liability. You were right to worry about getting sued."

Sam said, "That's why you were upset when you heard about how Tommy might be workin' with Woods. You didn't want him gettin' in trouble, either."

"He's a good kid," Baxter said, "but he can be talked into things. I told him he needed to steer clear of Woods, without going into any details, and I think he got the message. I hope he did, anyway."

Phyllis said, "There's still the matter of Woods showing up at your wife's office. I can't see any way she could be involved in his dog-breeding scheme, though."

"Neither do I," Baxter said. "That just doesn't make any sense."

"I don't want to upset you, but is there any chance that Susan and Woods were . . . romantically involved?"

Baxter looked flabbergasted by the suggestion, then angry, and finally adamant, all in short order, as he said, "That's the craziest thing I've ever heard. Woods is a slob."

"Hey, there's no accounting for taste," D'Angelo said. "I'm not exactly Brad Pitt, but I do all right with the ladies, if I do say so myself."

Baxter shook his head and said, "No. That's just impossible. I know I said I was convinced Susan was cheating on me, but not with Woods. Not in a million years."

"How about with Jack Carlyle?" Sam said.

That question seemed to catch Baxter off-balance. He frowned, gave a little shake of his head, and said, "Meredith's husband? That's not as crazy as thinking she was fooling around with Woods, I guess. Jack's a lot more her type—rich and successful—but I still don't think so. What makes you ask about Jack?"

"A witness told us that he went to Susan's office fairly often," Phyllis said. "Can you think of any reason he'd do that?"

"Well . . . they got along all right, I guess. I never heard Susan complain about him."

"What about some sort of medical condition that would give him a reason to go there? Could he have been planning some surgery?"

"You'd have to ask Jack," Baxter said. "We've always been friendly enough, too, I suppose, but we're not close or anything." His forehead creased in thought. "What you're saying is that you think Woods and Jack should both be considered suspects."

"That's what you need," D'Angelo said. "If there were other people with a good reason for wanting your wife dead, especially if they were around on the day she was killed, that helps us create reasonable doubt."

"I guess."

"Did Jack ever boast to you about romantic conquests?" Phyllis asked. "Did he give you any reason to think that he might pursue other men's wives?"

"No, not that I recall. But if he was going to pursue my wife, it would've been a pretty stupid thing for him to brag about it, wouldn't it?"

He didn't sound quite as convinced now that an affair between Susan and Jack Carlyle was as impossible as he had indicated a few minutes earlier, Phyllis thought. But they were still a long way from having any proof of that, and even if it turned out to be true, an affair didn't necessarily give Carlyle a motive for murder.

But the crime likely had been one of passion, she recalled as she thought about the murder weapon. Maybe Susan had told Carlyle she was ending their relationship, and he had taken it badly. Maybe Carlyle was the one who wanted to break up, and Susan had threatened to tell her sister about it. Those possibilities seemed feasible.

"Is there anything else?" Baxter said. "While I'm here, I'd like to check on a few other things and talk to Holly about the business."

D'Angelo looked at Phyllis and Sam, who shook their heads. They had wanted to find out the truth about Kyle Woods, and they had.

Now it was time to start digging deeper into Jack Carlyle's activities.

"I guess that's it for now," D'Angelo told Baxter. "Thanks for coming clean with us, Hank. It could turn out to be important."

"Maybe so," Baxter said.

"And thanks for takin' care of Buck," Sam added.

That prompted a smile from Baxter. "He's a good dog, very tolerant and well-behaved. And he's looking good, Sam. You can barely tell that he's the same scared, injured, starving dog you brought in here."

Sam scratched the top of Buck's head and said, "He's been a mighty good friend already."

"Let's get him down off the table."

Sam and Baxter set Buck on the floor again. Baxter told Sam there was no charge. It was part of the original fee, he said.

They all went back to the waiting room, where Holly sat behind the counter again. Phyllis thought the redhead looked nervous, but Holly managed to smile and ask, "How's Buck doing?"

"Just fine," Baxter told her. "Perfect, in fact."

"Good."

Baxter and D'Angelo followed them out of the vet clinic.

"Call me anytime if you have new information," the lawyer said to Phyllis and Sam.

"We will," Sam promised. He looked up the clinic's long driveway toward the street. "Who's that comin'?"

Baxter said, "It looks like—" He stopped, and his voice hardened as he went on. "That's Woods's pickup."

So it was. The pickup came into the parking lot and stopped. Kyle Woods got out from behind the wheel and glared toward the little group standing beside Sam's pickup. Tommy Sanders emerged from the vehicle's passenger side and looked surprised and scared at the same time.

Baxter didn't hesitate. He stalked angrily toward the newcomers and said, "Woods! What the hell are you doing here?"

Chapter 23

Woods's attitude was just as belligerent as Baxter's. He clenched his fists, stuck his jaw out, and said, "I've got a right to be here."

"The hell you do," Baxter snapped. "This is private property. My property. You're a criminal, and I want you off of it."

"Ah, you don't know what you're talking about. I haven't done anything wrong."

"Yeah, you have, and now you're trying to drag this boy into it." Baxter waved a hand toward Tommy.

Tommy still looked scared, but he said, "Wait a minute, Dr. Baxter. I'm not a boy, and you don't have to look out for me. I know what I'm doing."

"If you get mixed up with Woods and his fraud, you're a fool," Baxter said. "What are you doing, helping him pass those defective pups off as Texas Maximus's?"

"You shut your mouth," Woods warned Baxter as his mouth twisted in a snarl. "You're just making up crap now."

"We all know it's true. And I think I ought to tell the authorities about it, or at least the AKC."

American Kennel Club, Phyllis thought, her brain quickly figuring out what the initials stood for.

Woods didn't take kindly to the threat. His face went pale at first, then flushed brick red. He took a step forward just as Sam tried to move in between the two men and keep them separated.

"You fellas just take it easy—" Sam began.

It was too late. Woods was already throwing a punch. The blow was aimed at Baxter, but Sam had gotten in the way. Phyllis cried out in alarm as Woods's fist crashed into Sam's jaw and knocked him back against Baxter. The vet caught hold of Sam and stopped him from falling.

Before anybody else could react, Buck darted forward like a black-and-white-spotted flash. His leg didn't slow him down now. His teeth sank into Woods's calf. Woods yelled in pain as he reeled back against the side of his pickup and tried to shake Buck loose. He started to kick at Buck with his other foot.

The first kick never landed. As Sam caught his balance, Baxter stepped around him and hooked a punch into Woods's ample midsection. Woods's eyes bugged out as Baxter's fist plowed into his belly. He started to double over, which put him in position for Baxter to hit him in the face. Woods's head jerked back from the force of the blow and bounced off the glass of the driver's-side window.

Sam grabbed hold of Buck and pulled him away from Woods. Jimmy D'Angelo threw his arms around Baxter and hauled him back. Woods sagged against the pickup's door, wheezing and looking like he was going to pass out. He shook his head, and his expression cleared a little. He hunched his shoulders and looked like he was going to come after Baxter again.

Tommy got in his way and said, "Mr. Woods, no. You've got to stop."

"Get outta my way, kid," Woods said.

"No. I don't work for you. I still work for Hank."

"Not for much longer," Woods said with a sneer. "I don't think he can pay you from prison."

"He won't be going to prison," Jimmy D'Angelo said, "once the cops hear about how you were at Susan Baxter's office not long before she was killed."

Woods looked like those words hit him almost as hard as Baxter had, Phyllis thought. He put a hand against the pickup to support himself and said, "What? What? I wasn't . . . I didn't . . . What the hell are you accusing me of?"

"We know you were there," D'Angelo went on. "We have a witness and can prove it. So you'd better be expecting a visit from the cops. I'd say that defrauding some dog owners is the least of your worries now."

Woods still tried to put up a defiant front, but Phyllis thought she saw fear lurking in his eyes as he said, "I didn't do anything wrong. There's nothing illegal about going to a doctor's office. People do it all the time."

"What was your business with my wife?" Baxter demanded.

Woods smirked at him and said, "Maybe I had a little stud service of my own going."

"You—"

D'Angelo had let go of Baxter as they talked, but he put a

hand on the vet's arm to keep him from lunging at Woods again.

"Don't let him get to you, Hank," D'Angelo advised. "He's got it coming, but if you give him what he deserves, it might just look bad for you later."

Sam was holding on to Buck's halter. He said, "There's no reason I can't give the varmint a good thrashin'."

"Yeah, I'd like to see you try it, Gramps," Woods said. Then he pointed at Sam and went on. "Hey, I know you! You came out to my place and said you were looking for a dog. That was a lie, wasn't it? You're part of this bunch that's trying to railroad me!"

"We're just trying to get to the truth," D'Angelo said. "Why don't you tell us what you were doing at Susan Baxter's office the day she was murdered?"

"Why don't you go and . . . Ah, forget it! My time's too valuable to waste it standing around and listening to this crap." Woods looked at Tommy. "Why don't you get that stuff we came here for, and then we'll get back to what we were doing."

"I told you," Tommy said. "I don't work for you, Mr. Woods. And I think it was a mistake to say that I might. I don't want to get mixed up in anything crooked."

"It's not crooked," Woods insisted. "We're just . . . increasing the odds a little, know what I mean? The puppies that result could still be Texas Maximus's."

"You know better than that," Baxter said. "What you're doing is fraud, plain and simple, and I hope you wind up paying for it."

D'Angelo urged his client toward the door as he said, "Why don't we just go on back inside, Hank? I'll have a talk with that detective, Latimer, and tell him what we've found out. We'll let the cops handle this."

Baxter looked like he wanted to be stubborn and argue about it, but then he jerked his head in a curt nod and said, "All right. But you'd better stay away from here from now on, Woods. If I see your face around here—"

"No threats. No threats," D'Angelo broke in. "That doesn't help anybody."

"Yeah, you're already going to prison for murder," Woods said. "You don't want to add a sentence for assaulting an innocent man on top of it."

"There's nothing innocent about you," Baxter said.

He allowed D'Angelo to prod him back inside the clinic. When they were gone, Woods pointed at Buck and said to Sam, "That dog bit me. He's a menace, and I'm going to file a complaint. Animal Control's gonna put him down; you mark my words."

"Any man who'd threaten a dog ought to be put down himself," Sam said.

"You hear that?" Woods looked back and forth between Phyllis and Tommy. "I've got witnesses! This old geezer threatened to kill me. You heard him!"

"I didn't hear anything," Tommy said. "And the way I saw it, you assaulted this gentleman and his dog tried to protect him. If you file a complaint with Animal Control, I'll be happy to back up Mr. Fletcher when he files an assault complaint with the police. You should leave now, Mr. Woods."

Woods glared around at all of them and said, "You're gonna be sorry. You're all gonna be sorry." He winced and limped as he turned to open the door and get into the pickup.

"That vicious dog injured me. They're gonna have to kill him and take his brain out and check it for rabies."

Phyllis already had a hand on Sam's arm. She tightened her grip as she felt Sam stiffen with rage.

All Sam did, though, was say coldly, "I reckon there's only one diseased brain around here, and we're lookin' at the fella who has it."

Woods snarled and slammed the pickup door. He started the truck, backed around, and pulled away with a spurt of gravel.

Tommy said, "What a—" He stopped, glanced at Phyllis, and finished, "Unpleasant fellow."

"Whatever you were about to say, Tommy," Phyllis told him, "you were right the first time."

Phyllis and Sam went inside to make sure Baxter was all right, taking Buck with them. Tommy followed them.

Baxter and D'Angelo weren't in sight, but Holly stood behind the counter. She came around the end of it and punched Tommy on the chest in irritation.

"Why don't you keep your phone charged up?" she asked him. "I tried to call you."

"I'm sorry. I just forget," Tommy said.

"I wanted to warn you about Dr. Baxter being here, so you wouldn't bring that awful Kyle Woods with you."

"He's not awful," Tommy protested. "He's just . . ." His voice trailed off and he sighed. "All right, yeah, he's awful. You were right to tell me I shouldn't get involved with him."

"I was just afraid he'd get you in trouble."

Tommy put his hands on Holly's shoulders as he said, "Well, you don't have to worry about that anymore. From here on out, I'm not gonna have anything to do with the guy."

Holly summoned up a smile. "I'm glad," she said. "He hasn't already had you doing anything illegal, has he?"

"No. I just gave some perfectly legal injections to some of his dogs."

Holly put her arms around his waist and leaned against him, resting her head against his chest. "I'm glad," she said. "Now we can get back to all the plans we had without having to worry about that."

"Yeah, but we still have to worry about Dr. Baxter," Tommy pointed out. "If he goes to prison, the clinic will have to close down and we'll be out of our jobs. Then we can't save up to go to vet school."

Phyllis didn't want to interrupt the two young people, but she said, "We're going to do our best to see that Dr. Baxter isn't convicted. Where did he and Mr. D'Angelo go?"

"They're in the doctor's office," Holly said.

Sam had a worried frown on his face as he said, "I hope they won't mind us bargin' in. I've got to talk to Mr. D'Angelo about something."

Phyllis had a pretty good idea what that something was. They went over to the door of Baxter's office, and Sam knocked on it.

Baxter called in a weary voice, "Come in." Sam opened the door, and he and Phyllis went in to find Baxter sitting slumped behind his desk while D'Angelo stood in front of it.

"We wanted to make sure you were all right, Dr. Baxter," Phyllis said.

"As all right as I'm going to be until all this is over." Baxter sat up straighter as a look of concern appeared on his face. "But what about you, Sam? Woods hit you pretty hard. I appreciate you getting in the way of that punch, but you really shouldn't have."

"That wasn't exactly what I was intendin' to do," Sam said with a wry chuckle. He took hold of his chin and moved his jaw back and forth. "Everything still seems to be workin'. That's not the first punch I've taken. Luckily, I've got a pretty hard head."

D'Angelo said, "I'm going to report this incident to the police and have Woods arrested for assault. One way or another, the man needs to go away. He didn't try anything else after Hank and I came inside, did he?"

"He threatened Buck because of that bite. Said he'd have him declared a vicious dog and a menace, and that Animal Control'd put him down."

"He was very nasty about it," Phyllis added.

D'Angelo let out a contemptuous snort. "Let him try," the lawyer said. "He won't get away with that as long as Buck is my client. And if he does try, we can use the assault charge as leverage against him. Don't worry about Buck, Sam. We won't let anything happen to him."

"That makes me feel a little better," Sam said. "But I agree with Hank. I'm ready for this to all be over."

"I think we all are," Phyllis said. "Mr. D'Angelo, are you going to tell Warren Latimer what we found out about Woods being at Susan's office?"

"That's where I'm headed from here," D'Angelo said with a nod. "Latimer won't like it. He's like any other cop. Once he's made an arrest, he doesn't want to acknowledge anything that might weaken the case. But he won't have any choice because he knows that if he doesn't follow up on this new information, I'll use it against him and the prosecution at the trial. Nothing creates reasonable doubt in a juror's mind faster than hearing that the cops had a good lead they refused to follow up on."

"If you find out anything . . ."

"I'll let you know," D'Angelo promised.

Phyllis and Sam said their good-byes and left the vet clinic, taking Buck with them. As Phyllis drove, Sam scratched the Dalmatian on the head and said, "You jumped right in there to help me, didn't you, fella? You're pretty smart when it comes to knowin' who needs to be bitten, aren't you?"

"He was defending you," Phyllis said. "I'd say you have a friend for life, Sam."

Sam looked across the seat at her, smiled, and said, "More than one."

When they got Buck home, Eve patted him on the head and told him what a good dog he was and that he looked awfully handsome. Carolyn just said, "Hmph," but she followed the others out onto the back porch to watch Buck run around the backyard. The leaves had started to fall from the trees, creating a crackly carpet on which Buck romped. The yard was dappled with sun and shade as the Dalmatian played, and Phyllis thought it was a lovely scene.

Carolyn brought them all back to reality by asking, "What are you going to do now?"

"There's still Jack Carlyle," Sam said. "We haven't proved

that he was carryin' on with Susan Baxter, or even if he was, that there was any reason for him to kill her."

"We can't exactly march into his office and ask him about it, either," Phyllis said. "Maybe what we need to do is concentrate our efforts on Raylene."

Sam frowned and said, "The girl who works in Susan's office?"

"I think she's hiding something. She's bound to know more than she's been letting on. Even if Susan let her off work a lot so Carlyle could meet her there, Raylene must have seen or heard *something* that would help us. I'm wondering if Carlyle went to the office yesterday to warn her to keep her mouth shut."

"I reckon we could go see her again," Sam suggested. "Maybe ask her some more questions."

Phyllis nodded slowly. "That's about all we have left," she said.

There was no need for them to divide their forces anymore, so after lunch they got into Sam's pickup and headed for the hospital district and Susan Baxter's office. Sam drove, and as they pulled into the parking lot, Phyllis was able to take a look around for the mysterious woman she had seen there the day before.

All the cars in the lot were empty, though, and Phyllis didn't have a good enough eye for vehicles to know if the car she had seen the woman in was there or not.

Anyway, she had decided there was a good chance she'd been mistaken about the woman being Meredith Carlyle. She couldn't think of a good reason for Meredith to have been spying on her own sister's office, especially now that Susan was dead.

Sam's cell phone rang before they could get out of the pickup. He looked at the display, said, "It's D'Angelo," and opened the phone. "Hello?"

Sam listened for the next few minutes as the lawyer talked, saying "Yep" or "Uh-huh" every so often. A frown creased his forehead, and Phyllis couldn't help but wonder what Jimmy D'Angelo was telling him. Finally, Sam said, "Well, I appreciate you lettin' me know . . . Yeah, I'll tell her."

He said good-bye and ended the call. As he slipped the phone back in his jacket pocket, he told Phyllis, "That was D'Angelo."

"Yes, I know," she said, trying not to sound impatient. "Did he have new information?"

"Yeah. He told Latimer what we found out about Woods bein' at Susan's office . . . bein' right here . . . on the day she was murdered. Latimer didn't want to, but he had Woods brought in for questionin'."

"Was he as obstinate about talking to Detective Latimer as he was with us?"

"I don't really know. D'Angelo didn't say. But whether it was sooner or later, he gave up the story to Latimer. He came to see Susan for medical reasons."

Phyllis frowned and said, "Woods doesn't look like he's in very good shape, but he's a big, strapping man. What did he claim was wrong with him?"

"Not with him," Sam said, shaking his head slightly. "His daughter."

"Wait a minute," Phyllis said. "Woods has a daughter?"

Of course, there was no reason why he shouldn't, she thought. They didn't really know anything about Woods except what they learned about his dog-breeding business from the Internet, Sam's visit to the place, and their subsequent encounters with Woods. His personal life was a blank slate to them.

"Yeah, he does. She's seventeen. She doesn't live with him because she and her mom, Woods' ex-wife, moved out several years ago when the mom filed for divorce. But I guess Woods didn't stop carin' for the girl. I've got to give him credit for that. She's got some problem with the bones in her legs that makes it hard for her to walk. She'll probably wind up in a wheelchair by the time she's thirty if it's not corrected. And evidently Susan Baxter was one of the best orthopedic surgeons in these parts. Woods bein' here didn't have anything to do with his shady dog-breedin' business or his connection with Hank Baxter. Woods has even got an alibi for the time Susan was murdered. After he left here, he met his ex-wife for lunch to tell her about the meetin' with Susan. Their divorce wasn't what you'd call amicable, so she doesn't have any reason to lie for him."

"Was Mr. D'Angelo sure about all this?" Phyllis asked.

"He got it straight from Latimer, who claims to have checked it all out after talkin' to Woods. I got the feelin' that Latimer was sort of rubbin' it in D'Angelo's face, lettin' him know that the so-called suspect we'd come up with hadn't panned out after all."

"Why didn't Woods just explain about his daughter when we confronted him at the vet clinic this morning?"

Sam shrugged and said, "I don't know, unless he's just a stubborn, obnoxious varmint. Maybe he's got a few good qualities, but he's still a crook and a jerk. But he's off the hook for Susan's murder. That leaves the bull's-eye still square on Hank."

"So we're back to having Jack Carlyle as our only other real suspect," Phyllis said.

Sam's eyes narrowed as he looked across the parking lot. He said, "Maybe so, but here's somethin' odd." He pointed. "That's Carlyle's car right over there. I just recognized it from tailin' him before. He's here now."

Chapter 24

"Are you sure you're not mistaken?" Phyllis asked. "There could be more than one car like that in Weatherford."

"Maybe so, but I memorized the license plate when I was tailin' him the other day. That's Carlyle's car, all right."

Phyllis reached for the door handle. "We're going to confront him."

"We don't have any concrete evidence against him," Sam pointed out. "We don't even have much circumstantial evidence."

"He doesn't know that," Phyllis said.

A grin spread slowly across Sam's face. He said, "No, he doesn't, does he? Let's go."

They opened their doors and got out. Sam went into the office first, and Phyllis knew it was because if any trouble lurked inside, he didn't want her walking into it. Normally, he would have held the door for her and let her go first, having been raised at a time when such courtesy was commonplace.

The waiting room was quiet and empty when they stepped into it, however. Phyllis looked through the window above the counter into the office area where Raylene could be found most of the time. It was deserted as well. Phyllis looked at Sam and silently shook her head.

Sam pointed to the door leading into the hallway where the exam rooms and the other parts of the office were located. Phyllis shrugged. Sam grasped the knob, turned it as quietly as possible, and eased the door open.

As they stepped into the corridor, Phyllis heard something, quiet sounds that she recognized after a second as gasping and little moans. Sam heard them, too, and his eyes grew wide with surprise as he realized what they were.

With a determined stride, Phyllis went down the hall toward an open door on the left. Sam was right behind her. They stopped outside the door and looked into the room, where Jack Carlyle had Raylene bent backward over the paper-covered exam table as they embraced and kissed. Her blouse had pulled free of her skirt's waistband, exposing some of the skin of her belly.

Neither of them had noticed Phyllis and Sam standing there. When it seemed that they weren't going to notice anytime soon, Phyllis cleared her throat and said, "Mr. Carlyle."

Jack Carlyle let go of Raylene, yelled, and seemed to go straight up in the air half a foot. As he came down, he twisted toward the door so suddenly that he almost lost his balance and fell. Raylene cringed back against the exam table and hastily started stuffing her blouse back into her skirt.

"I thought you locked the front door!" Carlyle said.

"I thought you did!" she wailed.

Carlyle still looked startled and scared, but he seemed to regain some of his composure as he said to Phyllis and Sam, "You two don't have any right to be here. You'd better get out before I call the police."

"Go ahead and call them," Phyllis said. "Ask for Detective Latimer. I'm sure he'd be interested to hear about how you and Raylene have been having an affair. Susan Baxter found out what was going on and threatened to tell her sister. That's why you killed her, isn't it, Mr. Carlyle?"

"No!" Raylene cried. "That's crazy! It didn't happen that way at all."

"Then you killed your boss," Sam said. "You came back here after she thought you'd left for lunch, took her by surprise, and walloped her with that dog paperweight."

Raylene shook her head as tears started to roll down her cheeks. "No, I didn't. I didn't," she moaned. "I swear. Dr. Baxter didn't know anything about . . . about what's been going on with Jack and me. We didn't have any reason to hurt her. We didn't!"

"It's the truth," Carlyle said.

"But you don't deny you were having an affair," Phyllis said.

A hollow laugh came from Carlyle. He said, "It'd be sort of foolish to try to deny it now, wouldn't it? But we were very careful to keep it from Susan. I never came here unless she was in surgery or out of the office for some other reason. You can check on that if you—" He stopped short and frowned. "Wait a minute. Who are you people? It seems like I should know you, but . . ."

Raylene said, "They're helping Hank Baxter's lawyer. They don't think he killed Susan."

"Who else could have?"

"You, for one," Sam said. "Either of you."

"No, we couldn't have," Carlyle insisted. "We were nowhere near here when Susan was killed."

"Can you prove that?" Phyllis asked.

"Yeah." Carlyle looked at Raylene and swallowed hard. "We were together. At a motel. Miles from here."

"So you both have a possible motive for murdering Susan Baxter, and you're each other's alibis." Phyllis shook her head. "I don't think that's going to be good enough."

"The motel's probably got security cameras," Carlyle said with a note of desperation in his voice. "And there'll be a record of me using my credit card to pay for the room. It's a card that I only use for . . . for us, but it's in my name. The records will back me up."

"That might clear you," Phyllis said.

Sam looked at Raylene and added, "But it sounds to me like he's tryin' to throw you under the bus."

"No," Raylene said stubbornly. "You can't prove anything against me because I wasn't here when Dr. Baxter was killed. I just wasn't."

"Did anyone see the two of you together at the motel?" Phyllis asked.

"I . . . I don't know," Carlyle said. "We didn't get there at the same time. I was there first, and I texted the room number to Raylene so she wouldn't have to come through the lobby."

"Hear that sound?" Sam said to Raylene. "That's the bus comin' closer and closer."

"Wait a minute," Raylene said. "There was a maid. She

saw me there. Remember? I went to get ice and the machine wouldn't work. She helped me. She might remember that."

"That's right," Carlyle said. "You told me about it when it happened. I remember now."

Phyllis said, "You could be making that up. It's not very likely that the maid would remember you."

"But she might," Raylene insisted. "The police can find her and ask her. Let them check our alibi all they want to. They'll find out that we're telling the truth. They said Dr. Baxter had been dead for nearly an hour when I found her, and I was nowhere near the place then!"

The determined defiance that Phyllis heard in the young woman's voice was a little troubling. Would Raylene be this adamant about the situation if she was bluffing? Phyllis didn't really think so, but it was impossible to say for sure.

"Wait just a minute," Carlyle said. "Raylene's right. If the cops check all this out, they'll see that neither of us could have killed Susan. But if we're brought into the investigation, my wife is bound to find out about . . . well, about what we've been doing."

"The affair, you mean."

Carlyle shrugged and said, "Yeah. I don't want Meredith to find out. She'd just be hurt. Isn't there any way we can convince the two of you to leave us out of this?"

"Hank Baxter didn't kill his wife," Sam said. "But the only way to prove that may be to find out who really did."

"I understand, but it wasn't us. Ruining our lives isn't going to get Hank off the hook for the murder, because our alibis will hold up, I tell you. It won't do you a bit of good to blow my marriage to hell."

Raylene frowned as she looked at Carlyle and said, "But you were going to divorce Meredith and marry me anyway, Jack. I guess when you get right down to it, this just speeds things up a little."

"Yeah, but . . . I'm not really ready . . ."

And Jack Carlyle never would be ready to divorce his wife and marry this young woman, Phyllis thought. He had just been stringing Raylene along, enjoying their affair, but sooner or later he would have broken it off with her. Phyllis thought that what they'd been doing was shameful, but she blamed Carlyle for it more than she did Raylene. She was just another woman who had been taken in by a man's lies.

Evidently Raylene was starting to realize that, too, because she stared at Carlyle with growing anger.

"Jack, did you ever intend to marry me?" she demanded.

"Of course I did. The timing's just . . . just not right yet."

"Would it have ever been right?"

Phyllis caught Sam's eye and inclined her head toward the door. When he asked quietly, "Are you sure?" she nodded.

As they eased out of the room, Carlyle and Raylene were still talking, their voices slowly rising in anger. When Sam and Phyllis reached the waiting room, Sam said, "I've got a hunch those two are about to break up."

"If the circumstances were different, I'd say that's a good thing because they'd be more likely to testify against each other, but I think they're telling the truth."

Sam opened the office's front door and held it for Phyllis. As they started toward the pickup, he said, "They didn't really sound like they were bluffin'. But if neither of them killed Susan, where does that leave us?"

"Back where we started," Phyllis said. "Why don't we go over the whole thing? Start at the beginning and go over everything we know about the case, everything we heard anyone say or saw them do."

"You think there's something we've missed?"

"There has to be . . . unless Hank really killed his wife."

Sam shook his head as he opened the pickup's passenger door for Phyllis.

"I'm not gonna believe that until there's just no other choice. We'll sit right here and hash the whole thing out again."

They sat in the pickup and cast their memories all the way back to the beginning of the case: their visit to the animal shelter and their "adoption" of Buck. Phyllis went over everything she remembered about that day, and Sam filled in any gaps with the things he recalled. They proceeded through Phyllis and Carolyn's visit to the clinic to ask about bringing doggie treats for the Halloween party, then the party itself, where the police had shown up with the tragic news of Susan's death and arrested Hank Baxter for her murder.

"We didn't even know Jack Carlyle then," Phyllis said. "We'd only seen Susan a couple of times and never really talked to her."

"And yet we've spent all this time tryin' to find out who killed her," Sam said.

"Only because we want to help Hank. Although the idea of anyone getting away with murder doesn't sit well with me, no matter who the victim was."

Sam chuckled and said, "We've seen plenty of proof of that the past few years, I reckon."

"This was a brutal crime, and whoever committed it deserves to be brought to justice. I thought for sure it would turn out to be Kyle Woods or Jack Carlyle." Phyllis sighed. "But I've been wrong before. Let's get back to the case. What happened next?"

"I went out to the vet clinic the next day. That was when Meredith and Jack were there givin' Holly and Tommy a hard time, the first time I met those two. Meredith was all worked up about her sister bein' dead, of course, but those two kids didn't have anything to do with it and she didn't have to light into 'em the way she did, threatenin' to take over the clinic and sell it. Tommy tried to tell her she couldn't do that, but she just bulldozed over him and said that Hank tryin' to frame some junkie for the murder wasn't gonna work and he was gonna be found guilty. And sure enough, that's what happened, the part about the cops not buyin' the frame, anyway. The bein' found guilty part is still up in the air, I guess."

"I suppose so." Phyllis frowned for a moment, then said, "Wait a minute. When did you go see Mr. D'Angelo?"

"The first time, you mean?"

"Yes."

Sam scratched his jaw, thought for a few seconds, and said, "It was later that same day. That was when he told me about the cops' case against Hank."

"Including the broken drug cabinet with Hank's finger-prints on it."

"Yeah." Sam's hands had been gripping the steering wheel loosely. Now they tightened on it as he turned his head to stare at Phyllis.

In unison, they said, "I know who killed Susan Baxter."

At that moment, the squeal of tires on pavement made

both of them look around sharply. Jack Carlyle had emerged from the building and was stalking angrily across the parking lot toward his car. One of the other cars in the lot had roared out of its space, and now it shot straight toward Carlyle.

For a second he didn't seem to notice the vehicle barreling toward him. Sam threw the pickup door open and lunged out as he yelled, "Look out!"

Carlyle realized his danger at the last moment and tried to throw himself out of the way. He was a little too late. The car's fender clipped him and sent him spinning through the air. He crashed to the pavement and rolled over in a limp heap, stunned or worse.

The car's driver slammed on the brakes. Phyllis saw the backup lights flare as Sam ran toward Carlyle. She leaped out of the pickup as well.

"Sam, look out!" she cried.

The driver gunned the gas and sent the car squealing in reverse toward Sam and Carlyle. Sam got his hands under the injured man's arms and heaved him up. He fell backward, taking Carlyle with him, and the car barely missed them.

Phyllis had her phone out and called 911. They were less than half a mile from the police station, so she hoped help would arrive in moments.

They might not have moments, though. Meredith Carlyle had already brought her car to a stop and slid out from behind the wheel. She stalked toward her husband and Sam with a gun held out in front of her in both hands.

"Get away from him!" she yelled at Sam. "He's the only one who deserves to die!"

"Mrs. Carlyle," Phyllis said as she approached carefully

from the side. "Meredith. Please. You don't want to do this. There's already been enough tragedy." With an effort, she kept her voice pitched in a steady, calming tone.

Meredith's face was streaked with tears. The gun in her hands didn't waver as she said, "He has to die. He has to pay for what happened to Susan."

"Your husband didn't kill your sister, Mrs. Carlyle," Phyllis said. Her hand was in her purse, which she had brought with her from the pickup. "You know that. You know he didn't kill her, because you did."

Fresh tears rolled down Meredith's cheeks. She said, "I didn't mean to. I never meant to."

"I know," Phyllis said. "That's why you have to put the gun down."

The pistol wavered a little in Meredith's grip.

Jack Carlyle seemed to have regained his senses. His leg was bent at a slightly unnatural angle, and he was in obvious pain as he and Sam sat there on the parking lot, unable to move because of the gun menacing them. Carlyle could talk, though, and he said in a strained voice, "Please, Meredith. I never wanted to hurt—"

That was a mistake, Phyllis saw instantly. Meredith wanted no part of his apologies. She stiffened and the gun's barrel, which had drooped slightly, came up again and she cried, "But it's still all your fault!"

That was when Phyllis shot the woman with the taser she had just slipped out of her purse.

Phyllis hadn't shot a gun in years and had never fired a taser except for one nonfunctioning practice round. But her aim was good and the twin probes went through the sleeve of

Meredith's coat and buried themselves in her right arm. That arm jerked toward the sky and the gun went off with a little pop as electrical current surged through Meredith and knocked her off her feet. The gun flew out of her fingers as she continued to spasm.

Sam was on his feet quickly and scooped up the weapon. He backed away and kept the gun pointed at the ground until he was well out of reach; then he set it down. Meredith wasn't a threat anymore, so Phyllis set the taser on the pavement and backed off, too.

Jack Carlyle started to whimper about his leg. Sam gave him a cold look and said, "You'd better just shut up, mister. I don't reckon anybody's in the mood to listen to it."

A moment later, nobody could hear Carlyle anyway, since the wailing of the sirens on the police cars that came skidding into the parking lot drowned out everything else.

Chapter 25

"I guess it's moot now, since Meredith Carlyle has confessed," Jimmy D'Angelo said, "but I'm not sure I understand how you knew she was guilty."

He was sitting in one of the armchairs in Phyllis's living room with a cup of coffee on the little table next to him. The room was crowded because Phyllis, Sam, Carolyn, and Eve were there, too, along with Holly Cunningham and Tommy Sanders. Hank Baxter stood in front of the picture window, looking out at the autumn dusk settling down.

"It was really just one little slip of the tongue," Phyllis said from the sofa where she sat with Sam. Buck was curled up on the floor at Sam's feet, snoozing contentedly despite the crowd in the room. He had been plenty excited earlier, though, greeting everyone as they came in.

Phyllis went on. "When Sam first met Meredith and Jack Carlyle out at the vet clinic, Meredith said something about Hank trying to frame some druggie for Susan's murder. But when she said that, the police and the district attorney hadn't released the information about the broken drug cabinet with Hank's fingerprints on it. They didn't do that until later in the day. Meredith couldn't have known anything about an attempted frame-up unless she was the one who had done it."

"That's it?" D'Angelo said. "That's what convinced you she was guilty?"

Sam said, "Yeah, and if I'd had enough sense to say something to Phyllis about it right away, we could've solved this days ago. But when I told her what happened at the clinic, I left out that part without even thinkin' about it."

"In all fairness, we had no reason to suspect Meredith or Jack at that time," Phyllis said. "It was only in the past couple of days we realized that Jack might have a motive. But in reality he didn't, because Susan didn't know about the affair between Jack and Raylene."

Carolyn said, "I'm trying to follow this. Mrs. Carlyle knew her husband was having an affair . . . but she thought it was with Susan Baxter? Her own sister?"

"That's right. She was suspicious of Jack and had been following him, and when she saw him sneaking around Susan's office, she assumed Susan was the one Jack was cheating with. It didn't occur to her that Jack was carrying on with one of the women who worked in the office." Phyllis shook her head. "It seems the two of them had always been natural rivals. Meredith was quick to think the worst. Then, when she confronted Susan with her accusations and Susan denied knowing what she was talking about, they argued . . . and Meredith lashed out without thinking about what she was doing."

"She'll get off with manslaughter," D'Angelo predicted.

"Murder in the second degree, maybe. But probably manslaughter because some clever defense attorney will make it sound like Susan attacked Meredith first. He'll try for self-defense. The jury won't buy that, though. They'll go for manslaughter."

Tommy said, "Maybe you should take her case."

D'Angelo shook his head and said, "Nah. That wouldn't really be a conflict of interest, but I'd rather steer clear of it anyway."

Holly said, "She must have felt awful once she realized what she'd done. And then it had to be even worse once she figured out Mr. Carlyle was still cheating on her. She'd killed her own sister for no good reason. I almost feel sorry for her."

"No matter how awful she felt, she was cunning enough to try to set up that frame," Phyllis said. "It almost worked even better than she expected. She didn't know that Hank had been there just a short time earlier and had taken some medication out of that cabinet. Instead of some anonymous junkie, which was what Meredith was hoping for, her own brother-in-law got the blame."

"And then she rode that bit of luck for all it was worth," Carolyn said. "Causing a fuss with Hank at the funeral made it look even more like she thought he was guilty."

"She couldn't stop being suspicious of her husband, though. She started following Jack again when she decided he was still involved with someone else. That was her I saw in the parking lot, spying on him. Then today she was lurking nearby in her car, and when she saw him show up and go inside, she lost control again. She waited for him to come out and tried to run over him. When that didn't work, she was going to shoot him."

"She would have, too," Sam said, "if Phyllis hadn't tasered her." He grinned. "That was pretty good shootin'. I didn't know you even had a taser."

"I've been carrying it for a while," Phyllis admitted. "I hate to say it, but it's a more dangerous world than it used to be."

"Especially with people like Meredith Carlyle in it," Carolyn said. "What a terrible, terrible woman."

Hank Baxter finally turned away from the window and shook his head. He said, "No, Meredith's not terrible. Just angry and very, very sad. I can almost understand how she felt. I was convinced that Susan was cheating on me. It made me so crazy sometimes I might have tried to bash my own brother's head in if I believed he was the one she was with."

"I don't think you'd have ever done that," Sam said. "Not as good as you are with animals."

Baxter smiled faintly and said, "It's easy to be gentle with animals. They have much purer souls than we humans do."

No one in the room could argue with that.

After a moment, Baxter went on. "There's no evidence that Susan was having an affair, is there?"

"None that we turned up," Phyllis told him.

"So I was just paranoid."

"You had troubles in your marriage. Those things can grow into unfounded suspicions."

"And craziness," Baxter said.

"I reckon there's some of that in every marriage," Sam said.

D'Angelo drank the last of the coffee in his cup and set it back on its saucer. He said, "The important thing is that

Hank's name is clear and he can go back to doing what he does best: taking care of animals."

"Amen to that," Sam said.

Buck's tail thumping lightly against the floor punctuated that sentiment.

A month had passed, and Sam was sitting on the back porch on a lazy, sunny afternoon with his long legs stretched out in front of him, crossed at the ankle, while he read an old Western paperback. Buck dozed beside him, curled in a ball now that he had the cast off. The weather was unseasonably warm, but Sam knew that wouldn't last.

The Dalmatian lifted his head as the back door opened and Phyllis came onto the porch. She reached down to scratch his ears, making his tail wag.

"He likes that," she said.

"Of course he does," Sam said. "It must feel good."

"What'll you do if I scratch your ears?"

Sam grinned and said, "You can find out."

"Maybe later," Phyllis said as she propped a hip on the porch railing. "I just got an e-mail. I won my part of the contest at that magazine."

"Whoa." Sam put a bookmark in his paperback and set it aside. "That's great news. Have you told Carolyn?"

"Not yet. There's a little more to it than that. You remember how the grand prize winner was supposed to write a guest column for the magazine?"

"I heard you and Carolyn sayin' something about it one day." Sam stood up. "Are you sayin' you're the grand prize winner?"

"I'm afraid so."

"What do you mean, afraid?" Sam said. "That's even better news!"

"Not necessarily. They've decided they don't want me to write a guest column."

"Oh." Sam nodded and shrugged. "Well, that's a shame, I guess—"

"They want me to write a regular column. Every month. Starting right away."

"Well, what do you know about that?" Sam slid an arm around her shoulders and she leaned against him. "You're gonna be famous."

"But I never *wanted* to be famous. I just wanted to live a nice, quiet, peaceful life."

Buck suddenly shot off the porch and raced across the yard, barking. The squirrel that had dared to come down out of a tree onto the ground darted back up the trunk. It paused on a branch and chattered down angrily at Buck.

Sam squeezed Phyllis's shoulder and laughed. He said, "I've got a feelin' peace and quiet stand about as much of a chance around here as Buck does of catchin' that squirrel!"

Recipes

Hearty White Chili Casserole

For the chili mix:

Ingredients

1 whole medium onion, diced

4 cloves garlic, minced

2 whole cans green chilies, chopped

1 pound dried great northern beans, rinsed

8 cups chicken broth

2 whole jalapeños, sliced and half the seeds removed

1½ tablespoons ground cumin

½ teaspoon paprika

½ teaspoon cayenne pepper

½ teaspoon white pepper

3 cups cooked diced chicken

salt, to taste

1 cup milk

2 tablespoons cornmeal

Directions

In a large pot over medium-high heat, sauté onions and garlic for 2 minutes. Add chopped green chilies, then rinsed beans. Pour chicken broth into the pan. Add sliced jalapeños. Season with cumin, paprika, and cayenne and white peppers. Place lid on pot and reduce heat to low.

Cook for 1 hour, and then add chicken. Cook for another hour.

When beans are tender, salt to taste, mix milk with cornmeal and pour into the chili. Cook for an additional 10 minutes to thicken. Check seasoning and adjust.

Pour chili into large casserole dish.

For the cornbread crust:

Ingredients
½ cup butter, melted

¼ cup white sugar

2 eggs

1 cup buttermilk

½ teaspoon baking soda

1 cup cornmeal

1 cup all-purpose flour

½ teaspoon salt

1 cup Monterey Jack cheese, grated

⅔ cup fresh or frozen yellow corn, thawed

Directions
Preheat oven to 375 degrees F.

Mix butter and sugar, add eggs and beat until well blended. Stir buttermilk and baking soda into mixture. Stir in cornmeal, flour, and salt until blended but with a few lumps, then fold in cheese and corn. Pour batter onto the white chili mix.

Bake in the preheated oven for 30 to 35 minutes, or until a toothpick inserted in the center comes out clean.

Serves 8–10.

Hearty Breakfast Casserole

Ingredients

3 cups water

1 cup uncooked grits

¼ cup butter, divided

1½ cups shredded cheddar cheese, divided

6 eggs

¼ cup milk

12 slices cooked bacon, crumbled

Salt and pepper to taste

Directions

Preheat oven to 350 degrees F. Lightly grease a large baking dish.

Bring water to a boil in a large saucepan and stir in grits. Reduce heat, cover, and simmer about 5 minutes, until liquid has been absorbed. Mix in half of the butter and 1 cup cheese until melted.

Beat together the eggs and milk in a bowl and pour into a greased skillet. Lightly scramble, then mix into the grits.

Add crumbled bacon to the grits.

Pour the grits mixture into the prepared baking dish. Dot with remaining butter and top with remaining cheese. Season with salt and pepper.

Bake 30 minutes in the preheated oven, until lightly browned.

Serves 8.

Peanut Butter Sweet Potato Dog Biscuits

Ingredients

1 sweet potato, boiled or baked

¼ cup peanut butter

1 egg

2 cups wheat or all-purpose flour

1 tablespoon coconut oil

1 teaspoon cinnamon, ground

1½ cups old-fashioned oats

Directions

Boil or bake or microwave sweet potato. Allow to cool before removing the peel if baked or microwaved.

Preheat oven to 350 degrees F and line cookie sheets with parchment paper or aluminum foil. [If using foil paper, you need to spray it with cooking spray.]

With a mixer, blend all your ingredients together except oatmeal. When ingredients are combined, fold in oats with a spoon. If dough is too wet, add more flour. Roll out cookie dough to ¼-inch-thick cutout with any shape cookie cutter. Fill your cookie sheets. Bake for 35 to 40 minutes, until biscuits are hard to the touch. Let them cool and place in airtight container.

Makes 36 biscuits.

Pumpkin Dog Biscuits

Ingredients
1½ cups whole wheat flour
1 cup oat flour*
2 eggs
½ cup canned pumpkin
Water

Directions
Preheat oven to 350 degrees F.

Mix together the flours, eggs, and pumpkin in a bowl. Add water as needed to help make the dough workable like you would pie crust. The dough should be dry and stiff. Roll the dough into a ½-inch-thick disc. Cut with cookie cutter.

Bake in preheated oven until hard, about 40 minutes, turning after 20 minutes.

Makes 2 dozen biscuits.

*Oat flour can be cheaply made. Place rolled or old-fashioned oats into the bowl of your food processor or in a blender. Pulse the oats until they are finely ground, about a minute. One mounded cup of rolled oats will yield approximately 1 cup of oat flour.

Coconut Cream Pie Cookies

For the crust:

Ingredients

5 cups all-purpose flour, plus extra for rolling

2 teaspoons sugar

2 teaspoons salt

2 cups (4 sticks) unsalted butter, very cold, cut into cubes

¾ cup ice water + more if needed

Directions

In a large bowl, combine the flour, sugar, and salt and mix well. Cut the butter up in ¼-inch pieces and scatter over the dry ingredients. Toss to mix. Using your fingers, two knives, pastry blender, or food processor, rub or cut the butter into the flour until it is broken into small pea-size pieces. Sprinkle half of the water. Toss with a fork to dampen the mixture. Add the remaining water in two stages. Continue tossing the mixture until it seems packable. If it's still too dry, add 1 teaspoon of cold water at a time until the dough is the desired consistency, working in the water with your fingertips. Using your hands, pack the dough into 4 balls, then flatten into disks, wrap with plastic wrap, and refrigerate for 30 minutes to 1 hour before rolling. Try not to handle dough too much.

For the filling:

❧

Ingredients
¾ cup half-and-half

¾ cup canned coconut milk

1 egg

⅓ cup white sugar

3 tablespoons cornstarch

⅛ teaspoon salt

½ teaspoon vanilla extract

⅓ cup sweetened shredded coconut

3 egg whites

3 tablespoons white sugar

Topping
2 tablespoons white sugar, for sprinkling

Directions

In a medium saucepan, combine the half-and-half, coconut milk, egg, sugar, cornstarch, salt, vanilla extract, and shredded coconut and mix well. Heat on low, stirring constantly for about 20 minutes, until mixture has thickened.

Transfer to a medium bowl and chill in the refrigerator for 2 hours.

Preheat oven to 400 degrees F. Line cookie sheet with parchment paper.

Roll out one disk of crust at a time. Using a 3-inch round cookie cutter, cut 10 rounds from the pie crust.

To make each cookie, top half of the rounds with 2 to 3 teaspoons of the coconut cream. Top each with second crust round. With fork, firmly press edges to seal. Place on cookie sheet.

Bake 6 to 8 minutes, until set.

Meanwhile, in a small bowl, beat egg whites with electric mixer on high speed until fluffy. Gradually add 3 tablespoons white sugar until a smooth meringue forms.

Remove partially baked cookies from oven. Spread a small amount of meringue over the top of each cookie. Sprinkle sugar over tops.

Bake 4 to 6 minutes longer, until edges and meringue tops are golden brown. Transfer cookies to cooling rack. Cool about 10 minutes before serving.

Store in airtight container in refrigerator.

Makes 20 cookies.

Pumpkin Vanilla Chip Cookies

Ingredients

3 cups all-purpose flour

2 teaspoons baking soda

1 teaspoon ground cinnamon

½ teaspoon ground ginger

¼ teaspoon ground nutmeg

¼ teaspoon ground cloves

1 cup (2 sticks) salted butter, softened

1 cup white sugar

1 cup light brown sugar

2 large eggs

2 teaspoons vanilla extract

1 cup canned pumpkin puree

2 cups (12-ounce bag) Hershey's Premier white chips

Nonstick cooking spray or parchment paper

Directions

Preheat the oven to 350 degrees F. Spray cookie sheets with nonstick spray or line them with parchment paper.

In a large bowl, whisk together the flour, baking soda, cinnamon, ginger, nutmeg, and cloves. Using a large mixer bowl, beat the butter until smooth. Beat in both sugars, a little at a time, until the mixture is light and fluffy. Beat in the eggs 1 at a time, then mix in the vanilla and pumpkin puree. Slowly beat the flour mixture into the batter in thirds. Stir in the chips. Scoop heaping tablespoons of cookie dough onto the prepared cookie sheets and bake for 15 to 20 minutes, or until the cookies are lightly browned around the edges. Remove from the oven and let cookies rest for 2 minutes. Take the cookies off cookie sheets and cool them on wire racks.

Makes 5 dozen cookies.

Hero Sandwich

Ingredients

½ cup olive oil

1 tablespoon lemon juice

3 tablespoons red wine vinegar

1 clove garlic, minced

2 tablespoons chopped fresh parsley

2 teaspoons fresh oregano

½ teaspoon black pepper

1 4-ounce can black olives, chopped

1 small jar roasted red peppers, chopped

1 loaf French bread

½ pound sliced ham

½ pound sliced turkey

¼ pound sliced salami

½ pound sliced provolone cheese

12 leaves spinach

1 large tomato, sliced

Directions

In a medium bowl, combine olive oil, lemon juice, vinegar, and garlic. Season with parsley, oregano, and pepper. Stir in olives and peppers. Set aside.

Cut off the top half of the bread. Scoop out just a little of the bread from the top to make room for all the layers when it's put on top of the sandwich. Spoon ⅔ of the olive mixture into the bottom. Layer with ham, turkey, salami, provolone, spinach, and tomato. Pour remaining olive mixture on top, and replace the top half of the bread. Wrap securely in plastic wrap and refrigerate at least 2 hours. It's even better the next day. Cut up into serving sizes.

Serves 6.

Oatmeal Berry Streusel Muffins

For the muffins:

Ingredients

1⅓ cups all-purpose flour

1 cup oat flour

4 teaspoons baking powder

½ teaspoon salt

¼ cup butter, softened

⅓ cup sugar

1 egg

1 teaspoon vanilla extract

1 cup milk

1½ cups fresh or frozen chopped berries

For the streusel:

½ cup brown sugar

⅓ cup all-purpose flour

¼ cup cold butter

Directions

Mix the dry ingredients in one bowl with a whisk or fork to thoroughly distribute all ingredients completely.

In another bowl, cream butter and sugar. Beat in egg and vanilla; mix well.

Add liquid ingredients to dry ingredients all at once. Mix until the dry ingredients are just moistened, 15 to 20 light strokes. There should be some small lumps. Fold berries gently into the batter near the end of mixing.

Overmixing can cause muffins to be tough and to bake unevenly.

Fill 12 greased or paper-lined muffin cups two-thirds full. In a small bowl, combine the sugar and flour; cut in butter until crumbly. Sprinkle over muffins. Bake at 400 degrees F for 18 to 20 minutes or until browned. Cool for 5 minutes before removing to a wire rack.

Makes 1 dozen muffins.

Don't miss any of the Fresh-Baked Mysteries

by

Livia J. Washburn

Read on for an excerpt from

The Fatal
Funnel Cake

Available from Obsidian.

$\mathcal{S}$am Fletcher came into the living room, sat down on the sofa, looked at the television, and said, "I just don't get cookin' shows."

From the other end of the sofa, Phyllis Newsom glanced over at him. "That's because you're not a cook," she said. "I've never understood the appeal of fishing shows."

"Me neither," Sam said. "Now, I like to fish, mind you, but the idea of sittin' there and watching some other fella sit in a boat and fish—well, that's just not something I want to spend a lot of time doing."

Carolyn Wilbarger, who was sitting in one of the recliners—but not reclining—had her knitting in her lap. Without looking up from her needles and yarn, she said, "At least it's not NASCAR. Why in the world anyone would sit there and watch a bunch of cars drive around and around all day is just totally beyond me."

From the other recliner, Eve Turner added, "Anything is

better than those awful reality shows where people sit around and yell at each other all the time."

"They should make a reality show about us," Sam said.

The three women all turned their heads to look skeptically at him, even Carolyn. She said, "A reality show about a bunch of retired schoolteachers living in a house in Weatherford, Texas? I don't think that's what TV producers consider dramatic, Sam."

"We've got plenty of drama," Sam said. "Why, you could make a whole show just about Phyllis and the way she—"

He stopped in midsentence, and Phyllis was glad he had understood the warning look she was giving him.

For more than six months now, ever since the tragic events following Eve's wedding and honeymoon, there had been an unspoken agreement in this big two-story house on a shady side street in Weatherford: No one talked about murder.

Of course, it was hard to forget how that ugly subject had come up on a number of occasions in recent years. More than once, a member of this very household had fallen under suspicion, and it was thanks to Phyllis's efforts that the actual killers had been uncovered. Sam was probably right, she thought. Some sensationalistic television network probably could make a series about the murder cases in which they had all been involved. But the chances were that everything would be changed for TV and the results would be dreadful. Not only that; it would draw way more attention than any of them wanted. From what Phyllis had seen, becoming a celebrity often ruined a person's life.

So it would be just fine with her if no one ever mentioned the word *murder* around her again.

Sam, bless his heart, knew that, even though he had forgotten for a moment. So now he changed the subject by saying, "What show is this, anyway? I know I've seen that gal before."

"Of course you have," Phyllis said. "I don't see how anyone could have missed seeing her in the past few years. This is *The Joye of Cooking*, and that's Joye Jameson."

"Nice-lookin' young woman," Sam said.

Carolyn said, "Hmph. Trust a man to reduce everything to physical appearance."

Phyllis felt like she ought to come to Sam's defense, so she said, "Well, you can't deny that she *is* attractive."

That was true. Joye Jameson, who was in her midthirties, Phyllis estimated, had a wealth of thick, wavy auburn hair that framed a heart-shaped face with a dazzling smile. At the moment she wore an apron over a green silk blouse that went well with her hair and coloring and matched her eyes. The apron had a sunburst design embroidered on it.

With the camera on her, Joye stood at a counter covered with mixing bowls, spoons, a rolling pin, and the other utensils and accoutrements of the project she'd been working on during today's show. Smiling that unshakable trademark smile directly into the camera lens, she said, "That buttermilk pie we put in the oven a while ago ought to be just about ready. Let's have a look at it, shall we?"

She turned and went along the counter, and the camera angle changed to show her opening an oven. Using pot holders, she reached in and took out a glass pie plate that she placed on a cooling rack on top of the counter.

"I think it looks beautiful," Joye said as yet another camera took an overhead close-up of the pie, which did indeed look good with its lightly browned crust and filling. The shot went back to Joye as she continued. "Of course, we'll have to let it cool before we cut it, but we have another one just like it that I baked earlier today. A couple of tips about serving this heavenly pie. If you want to avoid a messy, crumbly pie, let it cool to room temperature before slicing. I know what you're thinking— you like your pie warm with ice cream. If that's the case, you can either have a messy slice, or put that slice in the microwave and warm it up a little before putting the ice cream on top. And the last but not least important tip about serving: Don't lick your fingers between each served piece."

She turned, revealing that while the camera had been pointed elsewhere, someone had placed a second pie on the counter. It was already cut into pieces. Joye took one of them out with a pie server and put it on a fine white china plate decorated with flowers around its edge. She picked up a fork, cut off a bite, put it in her mouth, chewed, and closed her eyes for a second in obvious pleasure before she said, "Oh, my, that's good."

There was a close-up of the piece of pie with a bite missing, then another shot of the whole pie that had just come out of the oven. "Now, remember, if you'd like a copy of the recipe, it's on the website," Joye went on. "And if you'd like tickets for the show here in Hollywood, you can request them through the website as well."

Applause came from the previously unseen studio audience as a camera panned over them, then went back to Joye.

"Now I have a special announcement," she said. "In two weeks the show will be going on location to Dallas, Texas, for the big State Fair of Texas. For those of you unfamiliar with it, it's a spectacular fair held every fall with cooking and arts and crafts competitions galore! We'll be showcasing some of the winners, and I'm very excited about sampling some of the best cooking in the great state of Texas."

Carolyn had lost all interest in her knitting for the moment. "Did you hear that?" she asked Phyllis.

"I heard," Phyllis replied. She couldn't stop herself from leaning forward a little on the sofa. Joye Jameson's announcement definitely had caught her attention.

Joye went on. "One thing we're going to be doing . . . Do you know what a funnel cake is? Do you know, Hank?"

The camera that had been on Joye swiveled around so that it showed another of the huge, bulky TV cameras, along with the burly, shirt-sleeved man running it. He grinned and shook his head. Phyllis couldn't tell if he really hadn't heard of funnel cakes before or if he was just playing along with Joye.

"How about you, Reed?" she asked, and the camera moved to another man, this one wearing a suit and a headset. He didn't look particularly happy about being on television, but he forced a smile and shook his head.

"A funnel cake is a delicious deep-fried treat that's poured from a funnel into hot oil," Joye continued as the shot returned to her. "I'm sure a lot of you have had them. They're a legendary snack at state and county fairs all over the country, along with corn dogs and cotton candy and lemonade. The ones at the State Fair of Texas are supposed to be some of the best, so we're going to find out. I plan to try the winning recipe from this year's funnel cake competition. Won't that be fun?"

More applause from the audience indicated that they

agreed with her. Either that or the APPLAUSE sign was flashing, Phyllis thought, then scolded herself for being a little cynical.

"So if you're in Dallas in a couple of weeks, or anywhere in the vicinity, I hope you'll drop by and see us. We'll be broadcasting live from the fair every day!" Joye's smile threatened to overwhelm the screen. "In the meantime, I'll see *you* tomorrow, and remember . . . always find the joy in life every day!"

More applause, more shots of the happy audience. One of the cameras pulled back to reveal the set with cameras, boom microphones, and crew members arrayed around it. Joye picked up her fork and resumed eating the piece of pie she had taken a bite of earlier. Credits began to scroll up the screen as a young woman with long brown hair, wearing jeans and a sweater, came out from the wings to talk with Joye. The shot switched to a graphic of the show's website address and some fine print that Phyllis didn't bother trying to read.

"Isn't there a cookbook called *The Joy of Cooking*?" Sam asked.

"Yes, there is," Phyllis said as she used the remote to mute the sound on the TV.

"But she calls her show *The Joye*—with an *e*—*of Cooking*?"

"That's right."

"And she can get away with that?"

Carolyn said, "Joye is her name. How could anyone complain about that?"

"I'm not complainin'. Just strikes me as a little strange, that's all."

"Cooking shows strike you as strange," Carolyn said with a dismissive note in her voice. "You said so yourself." She turned to Phyllis, pointed a finger, and went on. "You heard what she said."

"I did," Phyllis said.

"You know what that means. We have to go."

Sam said, "To see that show?"

"No, to the state fair," Carolyn said. "Why don't we make a week of it? We can enter some competitions, check out all the exhibits—"

"Maybe ride some of the rides on the midway," Eve suggested.

"I think we're all too old for roller coasters," Carolyn said.

Eve smiled. "Speak for yourself."

Phyllis was glad to see that. It had taken quite a while for Eve to start getting over everything that had happened, but she was beginning to get some of her usual feisty nature back. If Eve wanted to ride a roller coaster, that was just fine.

But she might have to ride it by herself. There was no way Phyllis was getting on one of those things.

She said, "I have to admit I'm intrigued by that funnel cake competition. I've never made any before. I think it would be fun to give it a try."

"I think I'll stick to the more traditional baking contests," Carolyn said. "I've got a new cookie recipe I'd like to try out."

Something occurred to Phyllis to temper her enthusiasm. She said, "There's just one problem. The fair is in Dallas. That's a pretty long drive to be making every day, and think of the traffic."

"My cousin lives in Highland Park," Carolyn said. "That's just right up the freeway. She's been asking me to come visit her. Her husband passed away last year, you know, and her children are all grown and gone, so she has that big empty house. I'm sure she wouldn't mind."

"You don't think we'd be imposing?" Phyllis asked.

"No, I don't. It certainly won't hurt to ask."

"That would make it a lot easier," Phyllis admitted.

Sam had gotten up and gone over to the computer desk in the corner, evidently having lost interest in the conversation about the state fair. Now he turned the desk chair around to face his housemates again and said, "You know what? They have other kinds of cookin' contests besides the ones for pies and cookies and funnel cakes and stuff."

"Like what?" Phyllis said.

A grin stretched across Sam's craggy face. "Like the notorious Spam cook-off."

"Why in the world would we be interested in a Spam cook-off?" Carolyn wanted to know.

"Well, I wasn't necessarily thinkin' about you ladies . . ."

Carolyn's eyes widened. "You?" she said. "You're going to enter a cooking contest?"

"I was thinkin' about it. I've fried up many a panful of Spam in my time. And you and Phyllis seem to get so much fun out of these competitions, I figured why not give it a try?"

"Why not indeed," Phyllis said. "I think it's a fine idea, Sam."

"I still think it's odd," Carolyn said, "but you can do what you want, I suppose. Then it's settled. If my cousin agrees to let us stay with her, we're going to the state fair."

Phyllis nodded and said, "We're going to the state fair."

Photo by James Reasoner

Livia J. Washburn has been a professional writer for more than twenty years. She received the Private Eye Writers of America Award and the American Mystery Award for her first mystery, *Wild Night*, written under the name L. J. Washburn, and she was nominated for a Spur Award by the Western Writers of America for a novel written with her husband, James Reasoner. Her short story "Panhandle Freight" was nominated for a Peacemaker Award by the Western Fictioneers. She lives with her husband in a small Texas town, where she is constantly experimenting with new recipes. Her two grown daughters are both teachers in her hometown, and she is very proud of them.

CONNECT ONLINE

liviajwashburn.com